CHANTEL NUNN

Whispers Of Passion

To Amanda, Queen, Mini, and Kay,
The best friends a girl could ever have.
I couldn't have done this without you.
Your love, encouragement, and unwavering belief in me carried
me through the hard days and inspired me on the good ones.
This book is as much yours as it is mine. I'm so lucky to have you.

Acknowledgments

Trigger Warning

This book contains mature and potentially distressing themes that may be triggering for some readers.

Please proceed with care.

Whispers of Passion includes content involving:

- Emotional, verbal, and physical abuse (including references to an abusive past relationship)
- Stalking
- Sexual assault
- Power dynamics, control, and BDSM elements
- Public sexual situations
- Intense emotional trauma and healing

While this is a love story filled with passion, healing, and transformation, it explores dark and difficult experiences along the way.

Your mental and emotional well-being is important. If any of these topics are triggering for you, please prioritize your care and choose what feels right for you.

One

Chapter 1

The hum of conversation and the hiss of the espresso machine filled the air as Amelia adjusted the strap of her leather bag and scanned the room for an empty seat. The downtown café was her usual escape, a brief oasis from the relentless pace of her marketing job. She exhaled, savoring the scent of freshly brewed coffee that promised a fleeting sense of normalcy.

The place was busier than usual, with professionals hunched over laptops and groups of friends laughing over lattes. She sighed and joined the line, ordering her standard black coffee, strong and straightforward much like how she'd tried to keep her life these past few years.

As she waited for her order, she couldn't help but overhear snippets of conversations around her, a couple debating weekend plans, a woman venting about a disastrous date, and a man on a call speaking in hushed but urgent tones. The café was alive with stories, each person lost in their own world.

Amelia found comfort in the anonymity, in being just another face in the crowd.

With her coffee in hand, she turned, but her thoughts, preoccupied with the presentation she had to finalize later, betrayed her. A moment of clumsiness sent the cup tilting unsteadily. Hot liquid threatened to spill over her hand when a firm grip steadied hers.

"Careful," a deep, velvety voice said.

Startled, she looked up into dark eyes that locked onto hers with an intensity that made her stomach flip. He was tall, with sharp cheekbones and a jawline that could cut glass. His tailored suit clung to his broad shoulders and the crispness of his white shirt suggesting a man who paid attention to details.

"I didn't mean to startle you," he continued, his lips curving into a faint smile that revealed just enough charm to disarm her completely. "But I couldn't let a good coffee go to waste."

Words failed her. Her mind tripped over itself trying to catch up.

"Thanks, but I had it under control," she said finally, her tone sharper than she intended, a defense mechanism she'd long ago perfected.

"Of course you did," he replied, the amusement in his voice unmistakable.

His hand lingered on hers for a fraction of a second before he stepped back.

"Sometimes even the most capable need a little help, though."

She stepped aside, heat rising to her cheeks. "Well, thanks again," she muttered, brushing past him toward the only empty table by the window.

As she sat, she caught a glimpse of him from the corner

of her eye. He was still standing near the counter, his gaze following her momentarily before he turned to place his order. Her pulse quickened against her will.

Who was this man?

Amelia shook her head and pulled out her laptop, determined to refocus. Her inbox was overflowing, and she had a pitch to perfect before her afternoon meeting. The world didn't stop for brief, unsettling encounters with strangers who looked like they belonged in the pages of a fashion magazine.

Still, as her fingers hovered over the keyboard, she replayed the moment his hand had touched her, the firmness of his grip, the knowing look in his eyes, and the way his smile hinted at secrets he wasn't ready to share.

She'd built walls around herself over the years, but something about him had slipped through a crack.

Her phone buzzed snapping her out of her thoughts. A quick glance at the notification reminded her of the day's tasks. She pushed the encounter to the back of her mind chalking it up to nothing more than a fleeting distraction.

Amelia was finally starting her work when the scent of cologne drifted toward her. It was subtle but distinct, an intoxicating mix of cedarwood and something she couldn't quite place. She looked up to find him standing beside her table, holding a cup in one hand and a business card in the other.

"I'm sorry to interrupt," he said smoothly, "but I realized I never introduced myself. I'm Lucas."

She hesitated, unsure whether to be annoyed or intrigued.

"Amelia," she replied cautiously.

"Amelia," he repeated, as though testing how her name felt on his tongue. "Nice to meet you. I'll let you get back to your work, but if you ever feel like your coffee might need rescuing again…"

He placed the business card on the table, the corners of his mouth lifting in that same infuriatingly confident smile.

Before she could respond, he turned and walked away, leaving her staring at the card.

Lucas Cross. CEO.

Beneath his name was a phone number and an email address, along with the logo of a high-profile tech firm she'd heard of.

She leaned back in her chair, card in hand, and allowed herself a small, wry smile. Whatever just happened, it was going to be impossible to forget.

She tucked the card into her bag and tried to refocus on her work, but her thoughts betrayed her. His voice wrapped around her name like a caress and his effortless confidence was maddening.

Men like Lucas Cross didn't just appear out of nowhere. They had a purpose and she couldn't help but wonder what his was.

The thought pulled at a tightly locked part of her heart, one she'd worked tirelessly to fortify. The truth was that Amelia didn't trust easily anymore. Not after everything she'd been through. Betrayal clung to her like a shadow, a quiet reminder of how trust had cost her before.

Friends she'd confided in. A partner she'd loved. All of them had left scars she couldn't entirely hide, no matter how much time had passed.

She clenched her fists under the table. Charm was a lie , she'd learned that lesson the hard way and Lucas Cross wore it like a weapon. People weren't always what they seemed, and letting them in only gave them the power to hurt her.

Amelia's gaze drifted back to her laptop, her fingers flying over the keyboard as she poured her focus into her work. Logic and productivity were safe. Predictable.

Unlike the man who'd left his card and disrupted her carefully curated sense of control.

Two

Chapter 2

Lucas Cross sat tucked in the corner of the café, hands wrapped around a cup of black coffee that had long since gone cold. Conversations buzzed around him, the clink of mugs, the soft chatter blending into a steady hum but he wasn't really tuned in.

His eyes had found Amelia.

Helping her wasn't part of the plan. Talking to her? Even less so. But when he saw her fumble with her laptop bag and coffee cup, his body just moved. No second thoughts. No plan. Just… instinct.

Now, she sat across the room, tucked into a booth by the window, typing away on her laptop. The sunlight streaming in through the glass cast a soft glow around her, highlighting the slight crease in her brow as she focused. She would pause occasionally, biting her lip as if lost in thought, then type something with sudden, determined energy,like she had just cracked some unspoken code.

Lucas shouldn't be watching her.

But he was.

And the worst part? He wasn't even sure why.

Amelia had walked into his world without warning, and now she was in his head. He hated that because he didn't get curious about people. He didn't let himself notice things like how she tucked a strand of hair behind her ear when she was thinking or how she bit her lip in concentration while working away at her laptop.

He didn't let himself wonder what she was working on. Or what her voice would sound like if she said his name.

But here he was, sitting in a damn coffee shop, his untouched coffee growing cold in his hands, watching a woman who should mean nothing to him.

He should've walked away the second their hands brushed before that unfamiliar spark settled in his chest.

But he hadn't and that was dangerous because Lucas hated distractions. Distractions made you weak. He had been weak once and he had paid for it.

The steady drip of rain from the ceiling was the only sound in the tiny apartment. The air was thick with the stale scent of cigarettes and cheap vodka.

Lucas sat against the peeling wallpaper, knees drawn up, fingers curled into the fabric of his worn jeans.

He had learned to be still. To be quiet because reacting only made things worse.

His mother sat at the kitchen table, shoulders slumped, fingers wrapped around a half-empty bottle. She wasn't asleep but she wasn't here either.

The front door slammed open. Lucas didn't flinch, he had learned not to.

Gerald stumbled inside, his boots tracking mud across the already ruined carpet. The stink of whiskey clung to him like a second skin. His bloodshot eyes flicked toward Lucas's mother, his lip curling in disgust.

"Spent all my money again, didn't you?"

She didn't answer.

Lucas held his breath, willing her to say nothing. *Just let it pass.*

But she let out a bitter, slurred laugh.

"What money?"

The slap came fast, snapping her head to the side. The bottle crashed to the floor, shattering into jagged shards.

Lucas moved before he could stop himself.

Before he could think about what would happen next.

Before he could remember that mistakes cost you every-thing.

"Leave her alone," he said, his voice firm despite how his stomach twisted.

The room went silent.

Gerald turned toward him slowly, his expression shifting from amusement to something far worse.

Given how much whiskey he'd swallowed, he moved faster than he should have.

A fist slammed into Lucas's ribs,sharp, breath-stealing pain.

But he didn't fall. He *never* fell. Because that would show weakness and weakness invited more.

Gerald grabbed him by the collar, yanking him up until they were eye to eye. His breath reeked of alcohol, his grip tight enough to bruise.

"You think you're gonna be something?" he hissed. "You're nothing. No one gives a damn about you."

Lucas knew that was true. No one was coming to save him. No one cared what happened to him and if the world didn't care about him, then he wouldn't care about the world.

That night, Lucas made a choice. He would never be weak again. He would never let anyone have control over him and one day, he would be the one with the power.

Lucas inhaled deeply, pulling himself back to the present and forcing the ghosts of his past back into their cages. He had spent years making sure he never let himself feel like that again. He had built walls, walls that no one, *no one*, could break through.

So why the hell was Amelia in his head?

Why had one simple, fleeting interaction managed to rattle him?

His gaze flicked back to her. She was still typing, lost in her own world, unaware she had disrupted his.

Lucas clenched his jaw.

Caring was dangerous.

Caring made you vulnerable.

Caring gives people power over you.

And power was something Lucas would never let go of again.

Three

Chapter 3

The rhythmic clicking of keyboards filled the open-plan office as Amelia stared blankly at her computer screen, her fingers hovering over the keyboard. The latest ad campaign she was working on should have had her full attention, but her mind kept drifting.

Lucas Cross.

The name shouldn't mean anything to her. He was just a stranger, a man she had met in a coffee shop earlier that morning. A man who had helped steady her coffee, who had barely said a word, yet whose presence had lingered in her mind long after he had walked away.

She sighed, shaking her head, forcing herself to focus on the campaign.

"Amelia!"

She jumped slightly as Sophia plopped into the chair next to her desk, her best friend's grin wide and mischievous.

"What?" Amelia asked, arching a brow.

Sophia leaned in, lowering her voice conspiratorially. "We are going out tonight."

Amelia groaned. "Sophia, no. I have work, I have deadlines,"

Sophia rolled her eyes. "You always have work. But guess what? Work will still be here tomorrow, and you need a night out."

Amelia hesitated. She hadn't been to a club in ages, and the thought of dancing, drinking, and being surrounded by sweaty bodies didn't sound appealing. But then again, she felt off all day. Like something was unsettled inside her. Maybe going out wouldn't be the worst idea.

She sighed. "Fine. But just for a little while."

Sophia grinned in victory. "That's my girl."

The day dragged on, the glow of Amelia's computer screen blurring before her eyes as she forced herself to finish the last of her tasks. Emails were sent, reports were finalized, she let out a deep sigh of relief by the time five o'clock rolled around.

"Come on, let's go," Sophia chirped, appearing beside her desk, already gathering her things.

Amelia groaned, rubbing her temples. "Are you sure about this?"

Sophia rolled her eyes. "Oh, now you're backing out?"

"No, no," Amelia said, standing and stretching her arms above her head. "I just need a minute to remember why I agreed to this."

Sophia smirked. "Because you, my dear, need to loosen up. And I'm not letting you go home and curl up with Netflix like you always do."

Amelia sighed dramatically, grabbing her bag. "Fine. But if I regret this, I'm holding you personally responsible."

"I'll take full credit when you end up having the time of your life."

They walked out of the office, stepping into the cool evening air. The streets bustled with after-work traffic, people hurrying toward their plans for the night. Amelia inhaled deeply, letting the crisp air wake her up from the exhaustion of the workday.

"Your place or mine?" Sophia asked as they headed toward the subway.

"Mine," Amelia decided. " I'll actually feel decent if I don't have to borrow something from your closet of barely-there outfits."

Sophia gasped in mock offense. "Excuse me, my closet is legendary."

"Your closet is dangerous," Amelia countered, laughing.

They took the train across the city, chatting about everything and nothing as the evening glow dimmed into the night. When they arrived at Amelia's apartment, she felt slightly more excited about going out.

As soon as they stepped inside, Sophia beelined for the speakers, putting on an upbeat playlist. "Now, let's get hot and irresistible," she declared.

Amelia gave a little shake of her head but couldn't stop the smile. Fine she was in. She slid off her blazer, already feeling the day start to fall away.

Time to loosen up.

She exhaled, fingers raking through her hair as she shifted gears from meetings and deadlines to music, laughter, and maybe a drink or two. Just for tonight, she could let go.

Sophia, of course, was already rifling through Amelia's small but well-organized closet. "No, no, no," she muttered, pushing aside a few modest dresses before grinning and pulling out a sleek black number. "This. This is the one."

Amelia eyed the dress warily. "I don't know…"

Sophia rolled her eyes, holding it up against Amelia's frame. "It's sexy, but not too sexy. It hugs your curves in all the right places. And paired with heels? You're gonna have every man in that club begging for your attention."

Amelia sighed, knowing she wouldn't win this battle. "Fine," she relented, snatching the dress from Sophia's hands. "But if it's too much, I'm changing."

"Deal."

"You're enjoying this way too much," Amelia muttered, clutching the dress like a reluctant sacrifice.

Sophia just grinned. "You'll thank me later."

Amelia grabbed her makeup bag and headed into the bathroom. The mirror reflected the remnants of her long workday. Tired eyes, a hint of stress still lingering in her expression. But tonight wasn't about work, tonight was about letting go.

She started with her hair, letting it down from the ponytail she had kept it in all day. Loose waves cascaded over her shoulders, giving her an effortlessly sultry look. She ran her fingers through them, tousling them slightly before moving on to her makeup.

A soft golden shimmer dusted her eyelids, enhancing her hazel eyes, followed by a subtle smoky liner. Her lashes curled upward with a few swipes of mascara, making her gaze look darker and more intense. She added just a touch of blush to warm her cheeks, finishing it off with a nude gloss that made her lips look full and inviting.

She stepped back, tilting her head and taking in the final

result. Effortless. Flirty and dangerous.

Just as she turned to leave, Sophia poked her head into the bathroom. "Damn, girl," she whistled, her eyes scanning Amelia from head to toe. "You look hot."

Amelia laughed, rolling her eyes. "It's just a dress and some makeup."

"No, it's the dress and the makeup," Sophia corrected. "And tonight, you are the woman."

Amelia shook her head but couldn't help the small smile playing on her lips. Maybe it had been too long since she had let herself feel this way. Beautiful, confident and ready to have fun.

Sophia, of course, had gone complete bombshell. Her red mini dress clung to every inch of her body, paired with sky-high heels that Amelia could never dream of walking in. Her blonde curls bounced as she did a playful spin. "Now, let's accessorize."

She handed Amelia a delicate gold necklace and matching earrings, then dug into her shoe collection before emerging with black strappy heels.

Amelia eyed them suspiciously. "I am not falling on my ass in these, Sophia."

Sophia grinned. "That's why we practice."

After a few test steps (and Sophia's promise to catch her if she tripped), Amelia was finally ready.

Sophia grabbed her arm, practically bouncing with excitement. "Let's go before you change your mind."

Amelia took one last look at herself in the mirror.

Tonight was what she needed.

Maybe for once, she could stop thinking, stop worrying.

She turned to Sophia, smirking. "Let's do this."

With that, they grabbed their bags and headed out into the night.

The club pulsed with energy, the bass vibrating through the floor as Amelia and Sophia stepped inside. The scent of alcohol and expensive cologne mixed with the heat of bodies moving to the music. Neon lights flashed above the dance floor, illuminating the space in flickering blues and purples.

Sophia grabbed Amelia's hand, pulling her toward the bar. "First, drinks. Then, we dance."

Amelia laughed, shaking her head. "Fine, but nothing too strong."

The bartender, a handsome man with tattoos lining his arms, smirked as they approached.

"What can I get you, ladies?"

"Two tequila shots," Sophia said without hesitation.

Amelia groaned. "I hate you."

"No, you love me. Now, drink up."

The bartender slid two shot glasses toward them. Sophia grabbed hers instantly, lifting it in the air. "To new experiences and letting loose."

Sophia leaned in, scanning the crowd. "So, what's the plan tonight? A little flirting? Maybe a cute guy to keep you company?"

Amelia rolled her eyes. "I came here for you, not for a hookup."

Sophia pouted. "You are no fun."

Amelia sighed but clinked her glass against Sophia's before tossing it back. The liquor burned down her throat, hot and sharp, but by the time it settled in her stomach, a warmth spread through her veins.

Sophia grinned. "Now, we dance."

Before Amelia could protest, Sophia grabbed her hand and pulled her onto the crowded dance floor. Bodies moved around them, heat and energy pressing in from all sides. The music thrummed through her, syncing with the beat of her heart.

She let herself feel it.

The pulsing rhythm. The rush of adrenaline. The way the alcohol softened the edges of her thoughts made her feel lighter and freer than she had in weeks.

She swayed her hips, closing her eyes momentarily, letting the music take over.

And then,

Sophia's grip on her arm tightened.

"Amelia," she breathed, her voice suddenly lower, teasing.

Amelia's eyes flicked open. "What?"

Sophia didn't answer immediately. Instead, she subtly nodded toward the far end of the club, where the VIP section sat elevated behind a black velvet rope.

"Don't be obvious," Sophia whispered, "but someone is definitely watching you."

A shiver trickled down Amelia's spine.

Slowly, she turned her head, letting her gaze drift over the sea of people, over flashing lights and flickering shadows, until her eyes landed on him.

Lucas Cross.

The man from the coffee shop.

He leaned against the VIP railing, a glass in his hand, his sharp blue eyes locked directly on her.

A spark ignited low in Amelia's stomach.

The dim lighting made his features even sharper,his strong

jawline cast in shadow, his dark hair slightly tousled, his tailored black dress shirt unbuttoned just enough to hint at the toned muscles beneath.

The very sight of him sent heat rushing through her veins.

Their eyes met.

Lucas didn't look away.

Neither did she.

The air between them crackled, thick with something heavy and unspoken.

Sophia leaned in, giddy. "Holy shit, Amelia. Who is he?"

Amelia swallowed, her throat suddenly dry. "I... I met him earlier. At the coffee shop."

Sophia's brows shot up. "Okay, is it just me, or is he mentally undressing you from across the room?"

Her breath caught in her throat because that's exactly what it looked like.

Lucas brought his glass to his lips, slowly sipping whatever dark liquor was inside. His eyes never left hers. He exuded confidence,control,and dominance.

And it did something to her.

Her pulse quickened, her body responding to him in a way that had nothing to do with logic and everything to do with desire.

Then, he did something that made her stomach flip.

He tilted his head slightly, beckoning her forward. It wasn't an invitation but more like a dare.

Amelia's heart slammed against her ribs. She should look away and just ignore him but she didn't. Instead she took a slow and deliberate step forward in his direction.

Lucas smirked, like he already knew she would. He didn't move, he just watched her.

His smirk was slow, almost lazy, but his eyes. They were anything but. The intensity behind them sent a shiver down her spine, like he already owned the moment. Like he had been waiting for her to make this choice.

"Holy shit," Sophia whispered, trailing just behind her. "You're actually going over there?"

Amelia barely heard her.

The closer she got, the more aware she became of him.

Lucas was now seated in the VIP section, one arm draped casually over the back of the leather booth, his fingers lazily tapping against his glass. His posture was relaxed like he was entirely in control of the situation, like he knew she would come to him.

Like this was already his game to win.

She stopped just outside the velvet rope separating VIPs from the rest of the club, suddenly unsure of what to say or do.

Lucas let the silence linger.

Then, slowly, he leaned forward, resting his forearms on his knees, his eyes dragging over her figure in a way that made her skin burn.

"You came," he murmured, his voice smooth, dark.

Amelia swallowed, trying to keep her expression neutral despite how her body reacted to him. "Did I have a choice?"

Lucas's smirk deepened.

"There's always a choice, Amelia."

The way he said her name sent a shiver through her, like he was testing the way it felt on his tongue, like he already knew he'd be repeating it.

Behind her, Sophia was practically vibrating with excitement, but Amelia barely registered it.

Lucas stood slowly towering over her as he reached for the velvet rope. He lifted it with a flick of his wrist, holding it open. "Join me."

Amelia hesitated.

Every rational part of her screamed that this was a bad idea. Lucas Cross was the type of man who devoured women like her and left nothing but their shadows behind.

But she wasn't feeling rational. She was feeling reckless.

And maybe just for one night, she wanted to see what it was like to burn.

Her lips parted slightly, her breath shallow as she stepped beneath the rope, stepping into his world.

Lucas's fingers brushed against her hip as she passed him, a barely-there touch, but it sent a wave of heat straight to her core.

The moment she sat down, a waiter appeared beside them as if summoned by Lucas's presence alone. "What can I get for you?"

Lucas didn't even glance at the menu. "A bourbon for me." Then, his gaze slid back to Amelia. "And for her?"

His question was simple, but something was behind it, a test.

Amelia straightened her spine. "Whiskey. Neat."

Lucas's lips twitched, his approval evident. "Good choice."

The waiter disappeared, leaving them in the intoxicating bubble of their own tension.

Lucas leaned back against the booth, watching her like a puzzle he wanted to unravel.

"So tell me, Amelia," he murmured, his voice a low hum beneath the pounding music. "Did you follow me back here because you were curious..." He paused, tilting his head slightly. "...or because you knew exactly what you were doing?"

Her breath caught in her throat.

Because the truth?

She didn't know anymore.

Amelia's heart pounded as she met Lucas's gaze, the heat thick enough to suffocate between them.

Everything about this moment about him, felt like a carefully laid trap and she had just stepped right into it.

Lucas watched her in that slow, deliberate way, his fingers tracing the rim of his glass as he waited for her answer.

She should lie. It was curiosity that she had wandered over without thinking that she hadn't noticed him watching her first.

But somehow, she knew he'd see through it.

So instead, she tilted her chin up holding his gaze. "Maybe a little of both."

Lucas's lips curled at the edges, something dark flashing behind his sharp blue eyes. "Honest. I like that."

The waiter returned, placing their drinks in front of them before quickly disappearing. Amelia picked up her glass, the weight of it cool in her hand, and took a slow sip of whiskey, letting the warmth slide down her throat.

Lucas did the same; his movements were effortless and controlled.

"Tell me something, Amelia." His voice was deep, cutting through the thick beat of the music around them. "Do you always follow strangers into VIP sections?"

She arched a brow. "Do you always watch women from across the room like you're hunting them?"

His smirk deepened. "Only the interesting ones."

A slow, unsettling shiver ran down her spine.

The weight of his attention was all-consuming, pressing into her, stripping her bare without him even touching her.

And God, she hated how much she liked it.

Lucas leaned forward, his elbow resting on the table between them. "What is it about you?" he mused, studying her like he was trying to figure her out.

Amelia let out a soft laugh, shaking her head. "What are you talking about?"

"You don't belong here." He gestured around the club, where bodies moved in drunken, rhythmic chaos. "You're overthinking. Over analyzing." His gaze flicked over her features, and then,softly, knowingly,he added, "You don't know how to let go, do you?"

Her breath caught.

Because he was right.

Amelia was always in her head, always calculating, controlling and second-guessing.

His fingers slid lazily along the side of his glass, his movements slow and deliberate. "Let me guess," he murmured. "You're here tonight because your friend dragged you out, not because you wanted to come."

Her lips parted slightly.

Lucas smirked at her silence. "And you haven't stopped thinking about this morning, have you?"

A flush crept up her neck because God help her, he wasn't wrong.

His voice dipped lower, his words curling around her like smoke. "I wonder..." He tapped his fingers against his glass, watching her carefully. "What would happen if you stopped thinking for a little while?"

Amelia swallowed.

Everything about him, his presence, his words and the way his voice dripped with temptation was pulling her under.

"And what exactly are you suggesting?" she asked, her voice softer than she intended.

Lucas's gaze darkened.

He reached for his drink, taking a slow sip, never breaking eye contact. Then he set it down, shifting slightly closer.

"I'm suggesting," he murmured, "that you let me show you how."

Lucas's gaze flicked to Sophia, still standing nearby, sipping her drink and not-so-discreetly watching their interaction with a knowing smirk.

"I'm going to steal her away," he said smoothly, his voice low and commanding.

Sophia arched a brow, clearly amused. "Oh? And what if she doesn't want to be stolen?"

Lucas turned his attention back to Amelia, his lips tilting into a smirk. "She does."

Amelia's stomach flipped, and she barely had time to process his words before his fingers brushed against her wrist. The contact sent a rush of heat through her, his touch firm but unhurried, like he already knew she couldn't resist.

He was right.

She didn't resist.

Lucas pulled her to her feet, his grip sliding effortlessly from her wrist to her waist as he guided her through the crowded club. People pressed in on all sides, the music vibrating through her ribs but Amelia could only focus on the solid warmth of Lucas's hand on her lower back.

He led her onto the dance floor, past shifting bodies and

flashing lights, until they were in the center of it all where the bass was deepest, where the energy in the air was thick and intoxicating.

Then he turned to her, his hands finding her waist and pulling her close.

"Dance with me," he murmured.

It wasn't a request.

Amelia swallowed hard, her fingers instinctively gripping his biceps as she felt herself melt into his heat, presence, and control.

Her heart hammered violently in her chest and every alarm bell in her head screamed to push him away.

But her body, her traitorous and starving body leaned in instead, drawn to the dark gravity of him.

Lucas danced like he did everything else with complete control.

His hands stayed just high enough on her waist to be respectful but his body pressed closer, a subtle but unbreakable cage.

Amelia tried to keep a sliver of space between them.

Tried to remind herself who she was.

What she had promised herself she would never allow again.

But then he shifted, his thigh slipping between hers the heat of him sinking into her skin and her breath caught in her throat.

She was drowning and she wasn't sure she wanted to come up for air.

Lucas's hand slid a fraction lower, his fingers grazing the curve of her hip.

His other hand brushed her bare shoulder, the lightest touch yet it left a trail of fire in its wake.

"You can pretend you don't want this," he murmured, his mouth brushing against her ear.

"But your body tells the truth."

Amelia shivered violently. It wasn't just the words, it was the way he said them like he already owned every secret she tried to hide.

She turned in his arms, trying to put distance between them but he simply adjusted, moving with her and pulling her tighter against him in the pretext of the dance.

The hard line of his body pressed along hers, making her acutely, painfully aware of just how male he was and just how badly part of her wanted to surrender to him.

No.

No.

She couldn't be that girl again.

The one who mistook danger for love.

The one who handed her heart to a man who would crush it without a second thought.

"You're dangerous," she said breathlessly, the words slipping out before she could stop them.

Lucas smiled slow, dark, devastating.

"And you," he murmured, voice threading through her like smoke, "are still standing here."

Her heart slammed against her ribs so hard it hurt.

She hated him for that smile.

For the way he saw through her so easily.

For the way her body betrayed her with every beat of the music, every shuddering breath.

The song shifted, slower, heavier.

And Lucas didn't give her a chance to escape.

He pulled her closer, their bodies pressed so tightly together there was no mistaking the heat radiating between them.

Amelia closed her eyes just for a moment, letting herself feel it, the reckless freedom and the forbidden thrill.

Then, Sophia's voice cut through the haze.

"There you are!"

Amelia blinked, reality snapping back into place as Sophia wove through the crowd, her eyes flicking between them with undisguised amusement.

"You look like you had fun," she teased, crossing her arms.

Lucas smirked, unbothered. "She did."

Amelia shot him a look but the way his smirk deepened and his fingers stayed on her waist made it very hard to argue.

Sophia grinned. "Well, Cinderella, it's almost two in the morning, and we should probably get going before you decide to run off with your handsome stranger."

Lucas's eyes flicked to Amelia. Daring her. "Would that be such a bad thing?"

Her stomach flipped but she forced a breath, regaining some control.

"As fun as that sounds," she said, voice steady, "I should probably get home."

Lucas studied her, something unreadable flashing behind his gaze. Then with a slow nod, he released her but not before dragging his fingers down her waist in a lingering caress.

It sent a shiver through her.

"I'll see you soon, Amelia," he murmured, his voice holding something that felt like a promise.

She should have questioned it.

Should have asked why he sounded so confident.

But instead, she just turned away, forcing herself to follow Sophia toward the exit, away from Lucas's pull.

The cool night air hit her like a wave when they stepped outside, the club's neon glow flickering against the pavement.

Sophia nudged her, grinning. "Oh, you are so screwed."

Amelia exhaled shakily, still feeling Lucas's hands' phantom weight and hunger in his gaze.

"I know," she murmured, voice barely above a whisper.

And the worst part?

She wasn't sure she minded.

Lucas leaned back against the leather seat of the car, staring blindly out the window as the city blurred past.

He should feel victorious.

He'd gotten what he wanted,her attention. Her reaction.

That reckless, delicious spark he hadn't felt in years.

Instead, he felt… restless. Frustrated. Raw.

He closed his eyes, dragging a hand through his hair.

He could still feel her in his hands, the soft curve of her waist and the way her body had fit against his like a missing piece he hadn't realized he'd been searching for.

Worse, he could still smell her.

Something sweet and clean, clinging to his clothes like a ghost.

He swore under his breath, sharp and low.

It wasn't supposed to be like this.

She was supposed to be another distraction. A pretty face. Nothing more.

He didn't get attached.

He didn't let anyone close enough to see the things he hid, the broken and bleeding parts of himself that even he couldn't bear to look at.

And yet when Amelia Monroe looked at him, it was like she could see right through the walls he'd spent years building.

Like she saw the storm underneath the surface… and wasn't afraid of it.

Or worse wanted to heal it.

Lucas's hands curled into fists on his lap. He didn't need saving. He certainly didn't want saving.

If he wasn't careful, she would become the one thing he couldn't control.

The thought should have made him angry.

Instead, it left him hollow. Hungry.

He opened his eyes, the city lights reflecting cold and sharp in the glass.

He would have her.

But he would do it on his terms.

And when the time came, he would be the one to walk away.

Not her.

Never her.

Four

Chapter 4

The cold night air did little to cool the heat still thrumming in Amelia's veins.

She slid into the cab's backseat, Sophia following close behind, practically vibrating excitedly. The car door had barely shut before Sophia turned to her, eyes wide and lips already forming a mischievous smirk.

"Okay," Sophia said, dragging out the word. "What the hell was that?"

Amelia exhaled, pressing her fingers against her temples. "I don't know."

"You don't know?" Sophia gaped. "Babe, you just walked straight into the gravitational pull of a man who looked at you like he was about to devour you."

Amelia shifted in her seat, arms crossing over her chest. "It was just dancing."

Sophia snorted. "That wasn't dancing. That was foreplay

set to bass-heavy music."

A slow, unwelcome shiver traced Amelia's spine and she hated how much she agreed.

Lucas had been everywhere, his hands at her waist, his breath at her ear, his voice a dangerous silken thread wrapping around her pulse. And the worst part? She had let him.

Worse than that, she had wanted it.

Sophia was still watching her, waiting, knowing. "So? Spill. Are you gonna call him?"

Amelia let out a dry laugh, shaking her head. "He's not the kind of guy you call Soph."

Sophia's brow arched. "Oh? And what kind of guy is he?"

Amelia hesitated, biting the inside of her cheek. *The kind that makes you forget logic. The kind that makes you want things you shouldn't.*

She exhaled, shaking her head. "It doesn't matter. I'm not interested."

Sophia let out a disbelieving laugh. "Bullshit."

Amelia turned toward the window, watching as the city's neon lights blurred past. She could still feel Lucas's weight on her waist and the heat of his fingers pressing into her skin.

She clenched her hands into fists, willing herself to forget.

"He's dangerous," she murmured.

Sophia paused, her teasing expression softening slightly. "Dangerous, how?"

Amelia didn't answer.

Because she wasn't sure she had the words.

Because Lucas wasn't Ethan, he hadn't hurt her, belittled her, or done anything but look at her, touch her, and make her feel like she was on the edge of something dangerous.

And maybe that was worse.

Maybe that was what she was terrified of.

The cab slowed as they reached Amelia's apartment. Sophia sighed dramatically, clearly sensing she wouldn't get anything more. "Fine. Keep your secrets, Monroe. But I know you're thinking about him."

Amelia stepped out of the cab, forcing a smile. "Goodnight, Soph."

"Goodnight, liar," Sophia shot back with a wink before the car pulled away.

Amelia pulled Lucas's business card from her bag as she climbed the stairs to her apartment.

Lucas Cross. CEO.

The card felt heavier than it should have.

She placed it on the counter, turned off her phone, and went to bed,determined not to dream about him.

Five

Chapter 5

Lucas Cross didn't chase women.

They chased him but tonight was different.

Back in his office at CrossTech, hours after leaving the club, he couldn't stop thinking about her.

Amelia.

Her name had woven itself into his thoughts like a slow-burning echo. He'd only just met her, but something about her curious yet guarded, hesitant but tempted had left a mark.

His office perched high above the city skyline, was dark except for the glow of his computer screen. A glass of whiskey rested on his desk untouched. Work had piled up from the moment he walked in, but his focus kept slipping,back to her.

Leaning back in his chair, he exhaled slowly before pulling up a file on his screen.

One of the many perks of owning a tech empire? Information was power.

And power was something Lucas wielded effortlessly.

A few keystrokes, a secure login and there it was.

Her work profile.

Amelia Monroe

Marketing Associate – Vanguard Media

Lucas's smirk deepened. Interesting.

Vanguard Media was one of the companies his firm worked with regularly, a high-profile client and one of the biggest marketing firms handling tech accounts in the city.

And it just so happened…

He had a meeting there tomorrow.

His smirk grew into something sharper.

Fate or coincidence?

He didn't believe in either.

There was only opportunity.

The next morning Lucas arrived at Vanguard Media's head-quarters just after 9 AM, dressed in a tailored charcoal suit his presence commanding the moment he stepped inside. The click of his Italian leather shoes echoed through the marble-floored lobby, his assistant following closely behind, tablet in hand.

The receptionist,young, nervous,flushed slightly as he approached.

"Mr. Cross, welcome," she stammered. "The meeting is scheduled for 9:30 but the executives are gathering now."

Lucas gave a sharp nod. "Good. I'll wait inside."

The boardroom was sleek minimalist, expensive but Lucas barely noticed. His thoughts had already zeroed in on her.

Amelia was here. Somewhere in this building.

And now that he knew it?

There was no way he was leaving without seeing her.

Leaning against the conference table, he pulled out his phone scrolling through his schedule with absent focus. The murmur of executives gathering barely registered.

Then he heard a familiar voice, soft and feminine. His gazed snapped up and there she was.

Amelia completely unaware that the man she had been dancing with last night was now standing in her workplace, watching her like a hunter who had just found his prey.

She was speaking with a colleague, a few files clutched in her hands. Dressed in a fitted blouse and pencil skirt, her hair pulled into a sleek ponytail she looked nothing like the woman he had held against him on the dance floor last night.

But Lucas saw *her.*

Saw the same hesitation, the same guarded resistance that made him want to break through her walls just to see what lay beneath.

She hadn't seen him yet.

He could change that.

He would change that.

Straightening, Lucas buttoned his suit jacket and stepped forward.

Time to see just how much of last night she had really forgotten.

Lucas moved with purpose, his steps slow, deliberate almost predatory.

Amelia was still oblivious to his presence, too caught up in her conversation with a colleague to notice him approaching. But Lucas wasn't a man who could be ignored for long.

"Amelia ." Her name left his lips in a deep, controlled murmur.

The effect was instantaneous. Amelia stiffened, her fingers tightening around the files in her hands. Slowly, so slowly, she turned toward him.

The moment her eyes met his, he saw it. The recognition and the shock.

A flicker of something else. Something she wasn't ready to name.

"Lucas?" she breathed, blinking as if trying to convince herself that he was actually standing in front of her. Here. At her work.

He let his smirk curve at the edges of his lips, enjoying her reaction far too much.

"Surprised to see me?"

Amelia straightened, smoothing her hands down her skirt, her expression quickly shifting into something neutral, professional,but he wasn't fooled.

"I… Yes," she admitted, clearing her throat. "I didn't know you had business here."

Lucas arched a brow. "Didn't you?"

She swallowed, visibly composing herself, before gesturing to the glass-walled conference room. "Are you here for the Vanguard-CrossTech meeting?"

His gaze didn't waver. "I am."

Amelia nodded, her posture perfectly polite, perfectly controlled. "Then I won't keep you. I should get back to,"

"I have time." He didn't let her escape.

Amelia hesitated. "Lucas…"

His smirk didn't fade. "You ran off last night before we could finish our conversation."

Her lips parted slightly, as if she wanted to argue, to deny but instead she exhaled sharply, shaking her head.

"That wasn't running," she muttered.

He tilted his head slightly, enjoying the way she tried so hard to keep herself steady under his scrutiny.

"I disagree."

She huffed shifting her weight as if debating her next move.

Lucas leaned in slightly, lowering his voice just for her. "Didn't think you'd see me again, did you?"

Her jaw tightened. "Honestly? No."

He grinned. A challenge.

"Then maybe," he murmured, his eyes never leaving hers, "you don't know me as well as you think."

She let out a breath that sounded dangerously close to a curse before glancing around as if making sure no one was paying attention to them.

"This is my workplace Lucas," she said quietly.

"I know."

"And you're a client."

He shrugged. "Does that change anything?"

Her eyes flashed. "It should."

Lucas smiled, slow and dangerous.

"Then why doesn't it?"

Amelia froze, her breath catching ever so slightly.

And that was all the answer he needed.

She could pretend to be unaffected. She could hide behind professionalism, behind control, behind whatever excuse made her feel safe.

But Lucas wasn't blind.

He saw the way her pulse flickered in her throat. The way her lips parted slightly as if she was trying to find the right words, words that never came.

She felt it.

That pull. That tension. That undeniable, unrelenting spark.

And now?

She had nowhere to run.

A voice from behind them broke the moment.

"Ah, Mr. Cross! We're ready for you in the boardroom."

Lucas didn't look back.

He locked eyes with Amelia for a beat longer, letting the silence linger just enough for her to feel him.

"See you inside, Amelia," he said, voice low and deliberate.

And with that, he turned and walked into the meeting.

Amelia stood frozen in place, her heartbeat pounding against her ribs as Lucas Cross walked away,completely unbothered, completely in control.

She exhaled sharply, gripping the files in her hands just to keep herself grounded.

How the hell had this happened?

Last night Lucas had been a stranger, a dangerously charming, ridiculously attractive and overly confident stranger she had danced with in a moment of reckless indulgence.

And now?

Now, he was standing in her office, speaking to her like he already owned the space around her, like he was testing her resolve just for the fun of it.

She needed a moment.

Amelia turned, walking briskly to the break room, where she placed her files down and pressed her hands against the cool counter top, inhaling deeply.

This is fine.

You're a professional.

He is a client.

A client who had just watched her dance in a club like she had no inhibitions.

A client who had held her body so close that she could still feel the heat of his hands on her waist.

A client who had just made it very, very clear that he wasn't done with her yet.

She let out a groan, rubbing her temples.

"Trouble in paradise?"

Amelia jumped, spinning around to find Sophia standing in the doorway, arms crossed, grinning like she had just walked into her favorite drama unfolding in real-time.

"Oh, don't give me that look," Sophia teased, stepping inside. "I saw the way he was looking at you."

Amelia glared. "We are not talking about this."

Sophia smirked, unfazed. "Oh, we are absolutely talking about this."

"Sophia,"

"Come on, Amelia," she interrupted, perching on the counter. "A hot, insanely powerful billionaire just walked into our office, and instead of giving his full attention to a multi-million-dollar business deal, he decided to flirt with you." She wiggled her brows. "I'd say that's worth a little conversation."

Amelia groaned, sinking into a chair. "He's impossible."

"And you love it."

"I do not."

"You do."

Amelia glared harder. "He's my company's client."

Sophia shrugged. "And?"

"And that means I shouldn't be thinking about last night."

Sophia grinned. "But you are."

Amelia dropped her head onto the table.

"I hate you."

"No, you hate that you like him."

Amelia stayed silent.

Because Sophia was right.

She had liked it. Every single second of it. Every touch. The worst part was….. Lucas knew it to.

By the time Amelia walked into the boardroom, she had convinced herself that she had everything under control.

She had taken a few deep breaths. Pulled herself together.

She was a professional.

She wasn't going to let him rattle her.

…At least, that had been the plan.

Then, she made the mistake of looking at Lucas.

He was sitting at the head of the long, polished table, effortlessly confident, his suit tailored to perfection, his piercing blue eyes locked onto her the second she stepped into the room.

And he smirked.

Like he knew exactly what she had been thinking about since their conversation outside.

Amelia's fingers tightened around her pen.

Don't react.

She moved to her usual seat across the table, forcing her expression into something neutral, unaffected but Lucas's presence was undeniable, filling every inch of space with silent dominance.

The executives began the meeting, discussing projections, partnership details, marketing strategies but Lucas barely said a word.

He just watched her.

Not in an obvious way.

Not in a way that anyone else in the room would notice.

But Amelia felt it.

She felt his gaze burning into her every time she shifted in her chair, every time she reached for a document, every time she spoke.

And when she finally glanced up, meeting his stare across the table, he leaned back slightly dragging his thumb slowly across his lower lip.

A casual effortless movement.

But God help her, she felt it everywhere.

Heat pooled in her stomach, her body betraying her despite every rational thought in her mind screaming that this was dangerous.

Lucas Cross wasn't just watching her.

He was toying with her.

And he was enjoying every second of it.

She exhaled slowly, tearing her gaze away, forcing herself to focus on the actual conversation.

Stay in control.

Stay professional.

But then,

"Ms. Monroe," the Vanguard CEO addressed her. "You'll be taking the lead on CrossTech's marketing campaign, correct?"

Amelia froze.

Wait.

What?

Her eyes shot up, landing on her boss, who was nodding at her like this was completely normal.

"Yes," her boss confirmed. "Ms. Monroe is one of our best. She'll be working closely with Mr. Cross and his team to ensure a seamless partnership."

Amelia's stomach dropped.

Lucas leaned forward, slowly, deliberately his smirk widening just enough to make her pulse jump.

"Perfect," he murmured, his voice smooth as silk.

This was not happening.

She could not be working with him.

Not after last night.

Not after the way he was looking at her now.

And definitely not after she had spent the entire morning trying to forget how his hands had felt on her body.

She forced a steady breath, schooling her features into something neutral, professional. Unbothered.

"Understood," she finally said, keeping her voice even. "I look forward to working with Mr. Cross and his team."

A low hum of amusement came from Lucas's direction but he didn't say a word.

He didn't need to.

Because the look in his eyes said everything.

The meeting continued, discussions about campaign timelines, branding strategies and marketing rollouts filling the space but Amelia barely heard a thing.

She was too aware of him.

The way he sat back in his chair, one hand resting against his chin, his fingers tracing his lower lip absentmindedly. The way his sharp blue eyes flicked to her every time she spoke, every time she moved.

It was infuriating.

By the time the meeting wrapped up, Amelia felt drained not because of the work but because of the sheer effort it had taken to pretend she wasn't affected by Lucas's presence.

Executives began filing out of the room, shaking hands, exchanging pleasantries. Amelia started gathering her notes desperate to escape,

Until a smooth, familiar voice cut through the air.

"Ms. Monroe. A word."

Her stomach clenched.

Slowly, she lifted her gaze to find Lucas still seated watching her. Waiting.

The other Vanguard employees trickled out, leaving them alone in the glass-walled conference room. Through the transparent walls, the office buzzed with movement,people working, talking, walking by,but inside this room?

It felt like just them.

Amelia inhaled sharply, squaring her shoulders. "Yes?"

Lucas stood slowly, adjusting the cuff of his suit jacket with practiced ease. The movement was calculated, just like everything else about him.

He took his time stepping closer, the polished floor silent beneath his steps, until he was only inches away.

Too close.

Not touching, but close enough that she could feel his heat, close enough that the air shifted between them.

Then he reached out, brushing his fingers against a loose strand of hair that had fallen near her cheek.

Amelia's breath caught.

A flicker of something dark, something possessive, flashed in Lucas's eyes.

Then, his voice dropped to a murmur,low, dangerous.

"You left too early last night."

Her pulse pounded.

She hated how easily he unsettled her, how his presence alone disrupted her entire equilibrium.

She swallowed hard, forcing herself to meet his gaze. "I don't recall there being a required departure time."

Lucas's smirk was slow, deliberate. "No, but we weren't finished."

Her lips parted slightly, her breath unsteady. "Finished with what?"

Lucas leaned in, his mouth so close to her ear she could feel the heat of his breath.

"This," he murmured, his fingers barely skimming down her arm,light, teasing, claiming. "The game we're playing."

Amelia's stomach tightened, a rush of heat curling low in her belly.

"This isn't a game, Lucas," she whispered, hating how her voice wavered.

His chuckle was dark, unchallenged.

"Isn't it?"

His fingers lingered for half a second longer before he stepped back, leaving a void of heat where he had been.

Amelia exhaled shakily, willing her heart rate to return to normal.

Lucas adjusted his cuff again as if their moment hadn't just shattered every ounce of self-control she had left.

"I'll see you soon, Ms. Monroe."

And with that, he was gone.

Amelia stood frozen, her hands curled into fists at her sides.

Damn him.

Damn him for being right.

Six

Chapter 6

Amelia had every intention of leaving by six.

By seven, she was buried in market reports.

By eight, she gave in to the reality of another late night.

And by eight-thirty, everything changed.

Lucas Cross was in her doorway.

"You're still here," he said, his voice smooth, unhurried. He leaned against the doorframe like he had nowhere else to be.

But his eyes they were sharp, probing, undressing her with nothing more than a look.

Amelia forced herself to keep typing. "Some of us actually have to work."

Lucas made a low sound in his throat, something amused and dark. He stepped into the room without invitation. His presence wrapped around her, thickening the air.

"I'd like to review the initial campaign concepts," he said smoothly, every word like velvet edged in steel.

She finally looked up, arching a brow. "Right now?"

He glanced at his watch, an expensive silver piece peeking from beneath his tailored cuff,then back at her.

"Unless you'd prefer five a.m.?"

Amelia's jaw tightened, heat pulsing beneath her skin. She wasn't naive, she knew exactly what Lucas was doing. Testing her. Poking at her walls.

"Fine," she snapped, flicking her hand toward the chair. "Sit."

Lucas didn't budge. Didn't even blink.

Instead he moved around the desk, slow and deliberate. Predatory.

Amelia's pulse stumbled. Her chair felt suddenly too small, the room too warm.

He braced one hand on the back of her chair, the other on the desk beside her laptop. Close. Too close. His scent, crisp cedarwood and something darker wrapped around her, making it impossible to think straight.

"Show me," he said, voice dipping lower, rougher.

Amelia swallowed hard and clicked open the presentation. "These are the preliminary concepts for the CrossTech campaign."

Lucas's suit brushed against her bare arm, a whisper of fabric against skin, igniting a shiver she couldn't suppress.

"Good," he murmured. "Now explain."

His words were a challenge.

Amelia fought the urge to shrink away. Fought the stronger urge to lean into him.

"The new angle modernizes your brand without losing prestige," she said, keeping her voice even. "It positions CrossTech as powerful and accessible."

Lucas tilted his head slightly, his breath brushing the side of her face.

"And the tagline?"

"Power. Redefined," she said.

Silence stretched between them, taut and heavy.

"Fitting," he murmured.

Her skin prickled, heat pooling low in her belly. Anger stirred, reckless and sharp, a defense against the way he made her feel so small, so exposed. She looked up at him, forcing a smirk she didn't quite feel.

"Must be exhausting," she said lightly, "thinking you're always the smartest one in the room."

For a moment, the air between them snapped taut.

Then Lucas's hand slammed flat against the desk.

The sound cracked through the office like a gunshot.

She jolted violently, heart lurching painfully against her ribs. The room shrank, the air sucked from her lungs.

For a split second instinct took over, an old, sharp terror slicing through her. Memories she thought she'd buried crashed into her: slammed doors, raised voices, the sick, helpless drop of her stomach when she knew she'd made a mistake she couldn't fix.

But then another instinct rose, just as fierce. Hunger. A reckless, irrational pull toward the man standing so close, his control fraying at the edges.

Amelia forced herself to look up.

Lucas's jaw was rigid, the muscle ticking violently, his chest rising and falling in sharp, uneven pulls. But it was his eyes that rooted her to her chair, dark, furious and raw.

It wasn't just anger.

It was devastation.

And God help her, for one terrifying unthinkable heartbeat,

all Amelia wanted to do was reach for him. To smooth away whatever storm raged beneath that beautiful, broken surface.

She curled her fists into the armrests, nails digging deep.

Don't be stupid. Don't reach for someone who could destroy you.

Lucas caught himself ,physically caught himself. His hand flexing once against the desk before he straightened. His movements were jerky, mechanical like a man slamming armor back over bleeding wounds.

The lazy, arrogant smirk slid back into place.

But it was too perfect. Too polished.

Amelia had seen the truth beneath it.

She had *felt* it.

"Approved," he said casually, like he hadn't just shattered the fragile peace between them.

She blinked, struggling to catch up. "What?"

"The campaign," he said, stepping back. "It's approved."

Amelia stared at him, her heart pounding. "You made me explain every detail… when you'd already decided?"

Lucas shrugged, the motion smooth, practiced. "I wanted to hear you sell it."

Her hands curled tighter around the chair. "You're impossible."

He checked his watch again, utterly unbothered. "It's late. You should head home."

"You're the one still in my office," she snapped.

Lucas smiled slowly, a dangerous devastating smile that made her stomach flip.

He leaned down one last time, his mouth brushing close to her ear, his voice a dark promise.

"Careful, Amelia," he murmured, the warmth of his breath skating down her neck. "You keep peeling back layers… and you might not like what you find."

A violent shiver tore through her.

Her fingers dug into the leather armrests as she fought the irrational urge to reach for him, to break every rule she'd built around her heart.

Lucas straightened, smoothing his cuff with casual elegance.

"I'll see you in the morning, Ms. Monroe."

With one last look slow, deliberate and far too knowing. Lucas peeled back the layers she fought to keep hidden.

Then he turned and walked away, leaving her breathless.

Furious.

And aching for more.

Seven

Chapter 7

Amelia had convinced herself that last night was a fluke.

It's a one-time thing.

Lucas Cross had loomed over her desk, invaded her space and tested her resolve but she had survived. She had held her ground. She hadn't melted.

That had to count for something.

So when she walked into the office the next morning, she told herself it was just another day.

That conviction lasted about thirty seconds.

Because the first thing she saw when she reached her desk? An email from Lucas.

LUCAS CROSS | RE: Campaign Adjustments

Amelia,

I want to go over a few revisions to the proposal. My office. 10 AM.

No question. No please. It's just a demand wrapped in

politeness, his signature crisp and bold beneath the message.

Amelia exhaled sharply, clicked out of the email and told herself it didn't mean anything. It was just business.

10:05 AM – CrossTech Headquarters

She was five minutes late on purpose.

Petty? Maybe.

Necessary? Absolutely.

Lucas's office was perched on the top floor of CrossTech's glass-and-steel fortress, an entire wall of windows framing the skyline. His desk was sleek, his shelves perfectly curated and the whole space had the same refined dominance as the man who owned it.

Lucas was seated when she entered. His suit was impeccable and his gaze immediately locked onto hers as she stepped inside.

"You're late," he said.

Amelia arched a brow. "You'll survive."

The ghost of a smirk flickered at the edge of his lips.

Without waiting for an invitation she sat across from him, crossing her legs and placing her tablet on her lap. "You wanted to discuss adjustments?"

Lucas leaned back in his chair, his fingers steepled together, assessing her like she was a puzzle he wasn't entirely done solving.

Then, finally he spoke.

"The campaign is strong," he said. "But I want to refine the messaging. Make it feel more personal."

She frowned. "More personal?"

Lucas nodded. "CrossTech isn't just about power and innovation. It's about experience. People trust what they relate to."

Amelia tapped her fingers against her tablet. "You want to humanize it."

His gaze didn't waver. "Exactly."

She nodded, considering. "Alright. We can tweak the narrative. Maybe include more behind-the-scenes content, customer testimonials,"

"I was thinking something different," Lucas interrupted smoothly.

Amelia narrowed her eyes. "Such as?"

His smirk was slow, deliberate. "I want you to experience it firsthand."

She blinked. "Excuse me?"

Lucas leaned forward slightly, his elbows resting on the desk. "You're leading the campaign. You should understand the product beyond research and numbers. I want you to spend time with me at CrossTech. See how it runs, how the innovations work and how we shape the market."

Amelia stared at him. "You want me to shadow you?"

"For a few days." His smirk deepened. "I'll be on my best behavior."

She did not believe that for a second.

"This isn't necessary," she said flatly. "I can do my job just fine without playing 'Shadow the CEO.'"

Lucas shrugged, completely unfazed. "Consider it an immersion experience. Call it whatever makes you feel better."

Her fingers curled around the tablet in her lap.

She hated that it made sense.

She hated that he knew it made sense.

And she hated how his eyes darkened ever so slightly, like he knew this was another game, another step forward.

"If I agree to this," she said slowly, "there are rules."

Lucas tilted his head slightly, amused. "Rules?"

She lifted a finger. "One: This is professional. No games."

Lucas's lips curved like he was already planning to break that rule.

"Two," she continued before he could speak, "I set the schedule. I'm not following you around like some intern."

Lucas nodded once, his expression unreadable. "Fair enough."

She exhaled. "And three,"

"Too late," he murmured, standing effortlessly. "You already agreed."

Amelia gritted her teeth, standing as well.

"This is a terrible idea," she muttered.

Lucas smiled. "For who?"

She didn't answer.

Because the truth?

She wasn't sure anymore.

She reached for her tablet, ready to remove herself from his office before he could say anything else to throw her off balance, but just as she turned, Lucas's voice stopped her.

"Stay."

One word. Low, quiet, absolute.

Amelia froze for half a second before forcing herself to turn back. She would not play his game.

"Why?" she asked, keeping her voice carefully neutral.

Lucas's gaze flicked over her, sharp and assessing, like he was deciding how much to say or hold back.

Then, he leaned against the edge of his desk, arms folding across his chest. "If we're doing this, let's start now."

Now.

Of course.

Amelia exhaled, ignoring the small, traitorous thrill that ran through her spine. "Fine," she said lifting her chin. "What exactly do you have in mind?"

Lucas's smirk deepened, slow and deliberate. "A tour. My way."

She crossed her arms. "I've been through the CrossTech office already."

His eyes glinted. "Not with me."

Something about how he said it, so confident and self-assured made her pulse flicker. *Damn him.*

Amelia let out a slow breath as if she were completely unaffected. "Alright, then," she said, gesturing for him to lead the way. "Let's get this over with."

Lucas chuckled, low and amused, before pushing off the desk.

"Try to keep up, Ms. Monroe."

And then he walked toward the door, expecting her to follow.

Amelia squared her shoulders, gripping her tablet before stepping in line beside him.

Amelia followed Lucas out of his office, determined to treat this like any other work obligation.

It wasn't personal.

It wasn't anything.

It was just business.

She repeated the thought like a mantra as they stepped into the sleek, glass-walled corridor of CrossTech's top floor. The view was breathtaking; the entire city spread below them but Amelia barely noticed.

She was too busy trying not to notice him, how he owned

the room without trying, how his cologne carried the sharp, clean scent of power and wealth.

It was distracting. Infuriating. Impossible to ignore.

Lucas walked with an easy, unhurried pace, his hands in his pockets as if he wasn't leading her through his company but rather through something far more intimate.

She refused to let it rattle her.

They stepped into the executive wing first. Lucas gestured slightly as they passed through. "You've met most of the senior team already but these are the people who ensure everything runs smoothly."

Amelia nodded, keeping it professional. "It's a well-oiled machine."

Lucas shot her a sidelong glance, his smirk lazy. "It has to be."

They continued down the hall, stopping at a large glass-walled conference room that was currently empty. Lucas opened the door, nodding for her to step inside.

Amelia hesitated, but only for a fraction of a second before following him in.

"This," Lucas said, leaning casually against the table, "is where the real work happens."

Amelia arched a brow. "As opposed to the fake work?"

His smirk deepened. "As opposed to the things that happen when the meetings are over."

Her pulse skipped. That was not business talk.

She refused to take the bait. Instead, she walked to the windows glancing out over the city. "I imagine this is where you make the big decisions. The deals that push CrossTech forward."

Lucas didn't answer immediately.

When he did, his voice was lower and thoughtful. "Not just the business decisions."

She turned back to face him, brows drawing together slightly. "Meaning?"

Lucas pushed off the table, closing the space between them with slow, deliberate steps that caught her breath.

Then ,too close but not touching he murmured, "I don't make decisions lightly, Amelia."

A shiver ran down her spine.

And she hated that he could do that to her with just a few words, a look, a calculated shift in proximity.

She exhaled, regaining control. "Good to know," she said, tilting her head slightly. "I'd hate to think you were impulsive."

Lucas chuckled a soft, knowing sound. "You'd be surprised."

His gaze dipped, just for a second, to her lips.

Amelia felt it like a brush of heat against her skin.

And then, just as quickly he stepped back, his expression shifting effortlessly into something neutral, unreadable.

"Come on," he said smoothly. "There's more to see."

Amelia let out a slow breath before following him out of the room.

The deeper they went into CrossTech, the clearer it became that Lucas had built more than just a tech empire, he had built an entire world.

Everywhere they went people straightened when they saw him. They nodded and greeted him with respect and reverence as if he weren't just their CEO but someone who owned the air in the room.

It should have been intimidating.

But Lucas moved through it with confidence that came from knowing he belonged.

He stopped in front of a sleek, reinforced door. A private lab separated from the rest of the company.

"This is where the next generation of our products are designed," he explained, pressing his palm against a biometric scanner. The lock released with a quiet hiss, and the door slid open.

Amelia hesitated.

Lucas glanced back at her, one brow arched. "Nervous?"

She squared her shoulders. "Of course not."

Liar.

She stepped inside and Lucas followed, the door sealing shut behind them with a quiet finality.

The lab was sleek and futuristic filled with cutting-edge prototypes, holographic displays and the hum of technology that had yet to be released to the market.

Lucas moved toward one of the sleek interfaces activating a touch display.

"This is what I meant when I said I wanted you to experience the product," he said. "I don't just want a marketing campaign. I want you to understand why this matters."

Amelia exhaled, pushing aside the tension from earlier, focusing instead on the tech before her. "Alright," she said, stepping up beside him. "Show me."

Lucas glanced at her before he swiped the screen, bringing up a 3D projection of the latest CrossTech device.

As he spoke, outlining the breakthroughs, the potential, the way it could shake up the entire industry, Amelia stopped bracing herself.

For the first time during the tour she wasn't focused on his stare, his nearness or the charged silence between them.

She was focused on the work.

And Lucas noticed.

Because when he turned slightly, watching her as she studied the projection, there was something different in his expression.

Something softer.

Something real.

Amelia felt it before she even turned her head. Their eyes met and for one brief, unguarded second, the game slipped.

Lucas didn't smirk. Didn't challenge. Didn't push. He just… looked at her.

And that was more dangerous than anything else.

Amelia swallowed. "What?"

Lucas's lips parted slightly like he was about to say something,but then, in a smooth motion, he locked the screen, turned away and walked toward the exit.

And just like that, the moment was gone.

Amelia exhaled sharply before following him, pretending her heartbeat wasn't unsteady.

Eight

Chapter 8

The Nightmare -

She could barely breathe.

The air felt heavy, crushing her chest, tightening around her ribs.

She stayed still, made herself small because one wrong move, one wrong word might be all it took to set him off.

Ethan stood in the doorway, half his face swallowed by shadow, the other lit by the flickering glow of the kitchen light. His jaw clenched, once, twice. His fingers curled and uncurled, like they were waiting for a signal.

It was coming.

Amelia froze. Her instincts screamed. Her back straightened, breath caught in her throat.

"I saw you with him today," Ethan said, voice low, almost casual.

Her stomach dropped. "What?"

He stepped forward slow and deliberate.

She stepped back. Just one step.

Wrong move.

His mouth twitched, not quite a smile. He noticed. He always did.

"You think I didn't see?" he said, soft but seething. His eyes burned cold and unrelenting. "You smiled at him, Amelia."

"I......I was just being polite," she stammered, too quickly. Too late.

His laugh cut through the air sharp, bitter, empty.

"Polite," he repeated, like the word tasted rotten.

Then he moved.

His hand locking around her wrist, unforgiving. Her skin throbbed beneath his grip. She gasped, stiffening, pain shooting up her arm. But she didn't fight.

Not anymore.

Fighting only made it worse.

His voice dropped to a whisper, breath brushing her cheek, grip crushing.

"I hate when you make me do this," he said, deadly quiet. "You make it so fucking hard to be good."

Her pulse pounded.

Make him think you understand. Make him believe you're sorry.

"I....I wasn't thinking," she whispered, lowering her gaze keeping her voice soft. Non-threatening.

He studied her for a long moment, his fingers squeezing once before finally letting go.

"That's the problem, Amelia," he said, his voice smooth, condescending. "You don't think."

Tears burned behind her eyes, but she refused to let them

fall. He liked it when she cried.

"You need me," he continued, tilting his head slightly. "I keep you in line. You know that, don't you?"

She nodded because it was the only answer that wouldn't end with his hands on her again.

Ethan sighed, his fingers brushing over the spot he had just gripped like he could erase the red mark blooming on her skin. "See? You're learning."

She swallowed back bile.

"I'm only hard on you because I love you," he added. "You get that, right?"

No.

She never said it. Never dared.

Instead, she whispered, "I know."

Ethan smiled, pressing a kiss to her forehead. "Good girl."

And Amelia stood there, still as a statue, waiting for him to turn away, lose interest, and let her breathe again.

Waking Up -

Amelia gasped as she bolted upright, chest heaving.

Darkness. Silence.

Her fingers curled into the sheets, her skin damp with sweat. It had been months and still, she woke up like this trapped and haunted.

She forced herself to breathe,in, out, in, out.

You're safe. He's not here. He can't hurt you anymore.

The mantra was automatic. It didn't always work.

Her phone buzzed on the nightstand, the bright screen cutting through the shadows.

She hesitated before reaching for it.

Lucas's name flashed across the screen.

Lucas Cross: *I'll see you soon.*

Amelia's stomach twisted, not with fear but with something more complicated. More dangerous.

Lucas was dominant. Intense. The kind of man who took up space, who didn't just command attention,he demanded it.

But Lucas wasn't Ethan.

Ethan made her feel small.

Lucas made her feel like she was on fire.

That terrified her.

Because power wasn't always about fists or bruises, sometimes, it was about control. About how much someone could make you feel.

And Amelia wasn't sure she could survive being powerless again.

Nine

Chapter 9

She hadn't forgotten the tour. How each step seemed to pull the space tighter around them, the silence between his words charged with something unspoken. He spoke with confidence, sure but it was the look in his eyes that had knocked the air from her lungs.

There'd been a current between them. Neither of them acknowledged it, but both of them felt it.

The way he looked at her.

The way she couldn't help but look back.

The way the air had turned heavy, electric, too much of something she didn't want to name.

This wasn't her. She didn't blur lines. Didn't play games.

Whatever Lucas Cross thought this was, she planned to shut it down.

But it didn't take long to realize Lucas had no intention of being shut down.

Which was why, at exactly 4:07 PM, her office door opened. No knock. No hesitation.

She didn't look up.

Only one man moved with that kind of quiet confidence.

Fingers still moving across the keyboard, she said dryly, "Ever heard of knocking?"

Lucas didn't answer. Instead, the door clicked shut behind him and the sound sent a flicker of irritation and something else she refused to name through her chest.

Amelia sighed, sitting back in her chair. "What do you want, Lucas?"

Lucas leaned against her desk like he belonged there, one hand slipping into the pocket of his tailored slacks. "I'll be picking you up at eight."

Amelia blinked. "I'm sorry, what?"

He smirked. "I'll give you time to process."

Her eyes narrowed. "For what, exactly?"

Lucas tilted his head slightly as if amused by her resistance. "Dinner."

Amelia scoffed, crossing her arms. "And you think I'm just going to have dinner with you?"

"Yes."

The arrogance, the absolute certainty in his voice sent a sharp jolt of irritation through her.

She shook her head, standing. "Lucas, I'm not going to dinner with you."

He studied her for a long moment and then as if he had already predicted every single one of her refusals, he spoke again.

"It's already arranged. I made the reservation this morning."

Amelia's jaw clenched. "That's not how this works."

Lucas's gaze dragged over her, slow and knowing. "That's exactly how this works."

She exhaled sharply, shaking her head. "You can't just decide things for me."

Lucas stepped closer. Too close. She could feel the faint heat of his presence, close enough that she had to fight the instinct to step back.

His voice dipped lower. "I don't decide for you, Amelia."

A slow pause.

"I decide for me."

Her breath caught, a single betraying flicker in her pulse, and Lucas saw it.

Of course, he did.

His smirk deepened just enough to unravel something hot and infuriating in her chest.

"I could make this easy for you," he continued, voice almost thoughtful. "I could ask. I could give you a choice. Let you pretend you're not interested. Let you walk away."

There was another beat of silence.

Then, a dark, knowing smirk.

"But you don't want me to."

Amelia's fingers curled into fists, frustration curling in her stomach because the worst part?

He was right.

And he damn well knew it.

She swallowed, trying to keep her voice even. "And what happens if I just don't show up?"

Lucas exhaled a quiet chuckle, his thumb dragging idly across his lower lip, a casual, effortless movement that felt anything but casual.

"You will."

Two simple words.

Not a challenge.

Not a threat.

It was just an undeniable truth. He had already mapped out every possible move she could make and knew exactly how this would play out.

Amelia hated that her stomach tightened just slightly at the certainty in his voice.

She inhaled sharply. "You're insufferable."

Lucas's smirk didn't fade. "And you're still going to meet me at eight."

She glared at him, lips pressing into a tight line.

Lucas stepped back as if allowing her the illusion of space before casually adjusting the sleeve of his jacket.

"Wear something you like," he added as if he hadn't just steamrolled through her objections.

Then without waiting for a response, without giving her another chance to refuse, he turned and walked out, leaving her breathless, frustrated and far too aware that he was right.

Because she was going to show up.

And they both knew it.

Amelia told herself she wasn't nervous.

That she was only going to prove a point, to show up, sit through this ridiculous dinner and walk away unaffected.

Amelia stood in front of the mirror, smoothing her dress for what felt like the hundredth time. The emerald silk clung perfectly, the neckline bold enough to make her pulse jump. She couldn't remember the last time she'd felt this nervous.

But Lucas wasn't just another date.

He was different. He made *her* feel different steady, seen. Like he was always paying attention. Like he *knew* her. From the way she tucked her hair behind her ear when she was anxious, to the way she held her breath when he got too close.

Her phone buzzed on the vanity. A text from Lucas.

Be ready in five. I don't like waiting, Amelia.

She swallowed, a warm pulse spreading through her chest. He always spoke like that direct, confident, like his words were meant to be obeyed. And the worst part? She liked it.

Amelia hesitantly turned to her jewelry box before reaching for the delicate gold necklace she always wore. Instead, she picked up a simple choker, black satin, understated but undeniably suggestive. She bit her lip, pulse fluttering. Would he notice?

Of course, he would.

She took one last look in the mirror smoothing her dress. Then, with a deep breath she went to meet him.

By the time she stepped outside her building, the night air was cool against her skin, a stark contrast to the heat curling low in her stomach.

And there he was.

Leaning against the sleek, black car parked at the curb. A vision of tailored perfection and effortless power.

Lucas Cross looked dangerous not in the way of knives or fists, but in the way he could unravel you without ever laying a hand.

His charcoal suit was sharp, tailored to perfection because of course it was.

And when his eyes found her, it was like he'd already

imagined the dress, the look, the entire night. Like none of it surprised him.

A slow, smug curve pulled at his lips.

"You're late."

Amelia lifted her chin, holding his gaze steady. "You're lucky I came at all."

He let out a low hum, stepping in just close enough to thicken the air between them tight, electric and impossible to ignore.

"Oh, Amelia." His voice dipped lower, smooth as silk, smug as sin. "You were always going to show up," he said, a quiet certainty in his voice.

Amelia scoffed, aiming for indifference, but the heat curling in her stomach betrayed her. He wasn't wrong and that infuriated her more than anything.

And the way his lips curved just slightly, like he could see that realization flicker across her face, made her want to wipe that look of him.

Of course he'd picked somewhere exclusive.

Private. Lavish. The kind of place where shadows clung to the walls and the silence buzzed with things no one dared say out loud.

The lighting was low and indulgent, casting everything in soft edges and blurred intentions.

It was the kind of place where secrets were spilled over aged whiskey, where power changed hands with a look.

The kind of place Lucas Cross brought a woman when he planned to take his time until she forgot where she ended and he began.

The hostess greeted him by name, voice warm, a little too

bright.

Naturally.

No need to ask about a reservation of course he had one.

She guided them through a candlelit maze to a table tucked deep in a velvet corner, hidden from the world.

Exactly where he wanted her.

Amelia sat first, gripping the edge of the menu as if it could keep her grounded.

Lucas settled into his seat across from her, completely at ease like he wasn't watching her every reaction, tracking every flicker of hesitation, every moment of defiance.

Then, without glancing at the menu, he said, "Red or white?"

Amelia blinked. "Excuse me?"

Lucas arched a brow. "Wine."

She hesitated for half a second too long, and his smirk returned.

"Red, then."

Before she could argue, he was already gesturing to the waiter, ordering a bottle of something expensive with the kind of casual confidence that made her want to throw her water in his face.

Instead, she leaned back slightly, crossing her arms. "Do you always assume you know what people want?"

Lucas took his time looking at her, his gaze dragging over her in a way that made her pulse betray her.

"Only when I'm right."

Amelia hated that her stomach tightened at that.

She hated how he made her feel like he had already won, as if he was waiting for her to realize it, too.

She forced herself to keep her expression neutral. "Well, you're wrong. I was going to order white."

Lucas exhaled a quiet chuckle. "No, you weren't."

Her eyes narrowed. "You're insufferable."

"And yet, here we are."

The waiter arrived, pouring their wine and for a few moments, silence stretched between them.

Not awkward.

Not strained.

Just… charged.

Lucas lifted his glass. "To successful business partnerships."

Amelia hesitated before lifting hers. "To strictly professional relationships."

Lucas's lips twitched, but he clinked his glass against hers anyway.

She took a sip, feeling the smooth warmth of the wine slide down her throat, feeling Lucas's eyes still on her as she placed her glass back down.

She cleared her throat, shifting slightly. "So, tell me, Lucas. Is this your strategy?"

He arched a brow. "Elaborate."

She gestured vaguely. "Cornering women in their offices, telling them when and where to meet you. Steamrolling them into doing whatever you want?"

Lucas smirked. "I prefer to call it persuasion."

Amelia let out a quiet scoff. "That's one word for it."

His gaze darkened slightly, something slow and dangerous flickering behind his amusement.

"If you didn't want to be here, Amelia," he said smoothly, "you wouldn't be."

The words hung between them.

Heavy. True. Undeniable.

Amelia swallowed. Damn him.

She could argue. Could push back. Could throw out a sharp retort.

But they both knew the truth.

She wanted to be here.

Maybe not in a way she could admit to herself.

Maybe not in a way that made sense.

But she was here.

And Lucas knew it.

His smirk softened slightly, his eyes still locked onto hers as he lifted his glass again.

"To things we can't quite explain."

Amelia hesitated.

Then, before she could stop herself, she clinked her glass against his.

Took a sip and ignored how her pulse betrayed her with every second of his presence.

Amelia should have left after the first drink.

That had been the plan. Show up. Sit through dinner. Remind Lucas this wasn't anything and walk away with her self-control intact.

But somehow, it was nearly ten, and she was still here.

Still sitting across from him in this dimly lit, dangerously intimate restaurant, sipping wine. Still locked in a battle of words and glances that neither of them was willing to lose.

And she was starting to think Lucas had never once considered losing.

"Tell me something, Amelia."

His voice was low, smooth, laced with that quiet, undeniable dominance that made her stomach tighten even though she refused to let it show.

She lifted a brow, swirling the last wine in her glass. "I

wasn't aware this was an interrogation."

Lucas smirked. "Humor me."

Amelia sighed, setting her glass down. "Fine. What?"

He leaned in slightly, resting his forearms on the table. "Why are you still here?"

Her pulse jumped, betraying her but she didn't let it show.

Instead, she tilted her head slightly, her lips curving into something dangerously close to a challenge.

"I could ask you the same thing."

Lucas chuckled, low and deep. "You could. But we both know the answer."

She arched a brow. "Do we?"

Lucas didn't blink. Didn't hesitate.

"I wanted to see how long you could pretend you don't want this."

The words sent a sharp, unwelcome thrill through her chest, curling around her spine and settling somewhere too deep, too warm.

She kept her expression neutral even as her heart kicked against her ribs.

"You're very confident, aren't you?" she murmured, lifting her glass again.

Lucas tilted his head, watching her with something dark and unreadable.

"Confidence comes from knowing the outcome before the game is played."

Amelia exhaled slowly. The stem of her glass was cool beneath her fingertips, unlike the heat that was steadily climbing through her body.

She shook her head, exasperated. "You really think you have me all figured out, don't you?"

Lucas's smirk was slow, dangerous in its ease.

"No," he said, voice lower now. "But I'm enjoying the process."

Her stomach flipped an entirely unwelcome reaction and she forced herself to set her glass down before she shattered it in her grip.

"This is business," she reminded him, her voice sharper than intended.

Lucas didn't even blink. "Is it?"

Her breath caught.

It wasn't the words.

It was the way he said it like he already knew this wasn't just business. Like he was simply waiting for her to catch up and admit it to herself.

She parted her lips, ready to fire back, to deny it, shut it down before it crossed a line she wasn't willing to blur.

But then…

Lucas moved.

It was subtle.

His arm extended slowly across the table, just a tiny, deliberate shift forward.

And then the back of his fingers brushed against the inside of her wrist.

Barely a touch.

Barely anything.

But it sent a shock wave through her body so sharp and sudden that she almost jerked away.

Almost.

Lucas saw it.

Felt it.

And he looked at her for the first time tonight like she had just confirmed something he'd been waiting to prove.

Amelia hated that her breathing had gone uneven.

Hated that her skin still tingled where his fingers had grazed her.

Hated that Lucas Cross was looking at her like he had just won.

"I should go," she murmured, her voice quieter now, barely steady.

Lucas didn't move his hand.

Didn't pull away.

Didn't let her escape that easily.

"Why?"

She swallowed. "Because this," She exhaled sharply, shaking her head. "This is a mistake."

Lucas exhaled a quiet laugh, slow and indulgent.

"I never make mistakes."

Her jaw clenched. "Then you've finally made your first."

His smirk was dangerously close to something softer, something almost amused.

"Tell me you didn't feel that," he murmured, voice barely above a whisper.

Her stomach twisted.

Because she couldn't.

Silence stretched between them, thick and suffocating, before she finally forced herself to pull her hand back.

Lucas let her.

But not before the corner of his mouth curled, making her pulse stutter.

Amelia cleared her throat, reaching for her bag. "Thank you for dinner. I'll see you at the office."

She stood quickly, pushing her chair back, desperate to put

space between them.

Lucas watched her for a long moment, then nodded once.

"Let me take you home."

Her eyes narrowed. "Absolutely not."

Another smirk, slow and knowing. "You're impossible."

She exhaled sharply. "And you,"

She stopped, shook her head, and turned on her heel, heading for the exit.

Lucas didn't follow immediately.

But she felt his gaze on her every step of the way.

She stepped into the cab, exhaling as the door shut behind her. Her pulse was still too fast, and her skin was still too warm. She pressed her fingers against her temples, eyes closing for half a second before she whispered, just for herself,

"Damn him."

Ten

Chapter 10

The dream started with music.

Low. Sultry. Bass-heavy.

That deep, familiar pulse that slipped through the air, into skin, down to the bone. The kind that loosened control, made you forget everything but the beat.

The heat.

The hands.

Amelia knew this place.

The club.

The neon lights flickered between crimson and gold, bodies moved in time with the music, and the air was thick with sweat, desire, and something dangerous.

And then,hands.

Strong. Sure. Undeniable.

Fingers pressing into the dip of her waist. A slow, deliberate pull.

She knew who it was before she even turned around.

Lucas.

His body against hers. His breath warm at her ear.

The heat of his palms sliding down, fingertips brushing the hem of her dress just enough to make her shiver.

"Amelia."

She exhaled sharply her hands gripping his forearms, but he didn't let her pull away.

Didn't let her move at all.

"You don't run from me," he murmured against her skin, his lips barely grazing the curve of her jaw. "Not here."

She hated the way her body melted into him.

Hated the way he moved against her like he had done this a thousand times before.

Like he already knew exactly how she would react.

Lucas's hand slid lower, fingers skimming the inside of her thigh, his grip tightening when she sucked in a breath.

"Tell me to stop," he murmured against her skin.

Her nails dug into his shoulders, anchoring herself to him.

She should have said the words. Should have pulled away.

But when she opened her mouth, nothing came out. Only a trembling breath.

And then heat. Lips.

A slow, consuming kiss that melted whatever defenses she had left.

His hands drew her closer, backing her into the wall, his body firm, unrelenting against hers.

Her stomach flipped. Her skin burned. Need coiled through her, sharp and overwhelming.

And then.....

She woke up.

Amelia jolted upright, heart racing, breath ragged.

The room was dark. Still. Lucas Cross was nowhere near her.

But her pulse pounded in her throat, her skin flushed, her body aching in ways she really didn't have the patience for.

She dragged a hand down her face and let out a shaky breath.

"Jesus Christ."

Just a dream.

Only a dream.

A stupid, ridiculous, completely unacceptable dream.

She flopped back against the pillows, staring at the ceiling.

She was losing her mind.

That was the only explanation.

Because this?

This was not happening.

Lucas Cross was not invading her subconscious, was not crawling into her thoughts at night.

Her phone vibrated on the nightstand.

She glared at it.

Like the universe was taunting her.

With a deep sense of dread, she reached over and grabbed it, unlocking the screen,

LUCAS CROSS 7 HOURS AGO

Did you make it home safely?

Her stomach flipped.

She hated that her first reaction wasn't annoyance.

Hated that it was something else entirely.

She stared at the message for five seconds before throwing the phone onto the bed and groaning into her pillow.

This wasn't good.

This was very, very bad.

By the time she got out of bed, she had convinced herself that the dream meant nothing.

That Lucas meant nothing.

She wasn't attracted to him.

She wasn't thinking about his hands, his mouth, his voice murmuring her name like a promise and a threat all at once.

She was fine, absolutely totally fine.

She marched into the shower, turned the water ice cold and scrubbed away every traitorous thought that had infiltrated her brain.

By the time she stepped out, wrapped in a towel, she was determined to be normal today.

To go to work and pretend like Lucas Cross hadn't just taken up real estate in her subconscious.

She pulled on a fitted pencil skirt, a white silk blouse and her best I'm unbothered attitude.

Flawless. Professional. Untouchable.

She glanced at her phone again. His message still sat there, unread. Her fingers hovered over the keyboard. The smart thing to do? Ignore it.

The next best thing? A short, unemotional response.

She typed.

Amelia Monroe: Yes.

She hit send.

Three dots appeared immediately.

Her pulse jumped.

Then,

LUCAS CROSS: Good.

Amelia stared at the screen for three seconds before tossing her phone into her purse and gritting her teeth so hard she nearly cracked a molar.

No.

She was not doing this today.

She grabbed her bag, her keys, and her last shred of dignity and walked out the door.

She had work to do.

And Lucas Cross was the last person on her mind.

(Or at least, that was what she would keep telling herself.)

Amelia was fine.

Totally fine.

Except… she wasn't.

She'd spent the entire subway ride to work trying to scrub the dream from her mind. Every spark of heat, every trace of Lucas's touch still echoing in her thoughts.

She wouldn't let it affect her.

She wouldn't even *think* about it.

And she sure as hell wouldn't let Lucas see a single crack when she walked into the office.

So when she stepped into the Vanguard Media building, her expression was perfect calm, cool and unreadable.

Until she saw the envelope on her desk.

Her stomach turned cold.

Because she knew that handwriting.

No.

Not today.

Not now.

Her fingers curled around the edge of her desk as she stared at the envelope.

No name. No return address.

But she didn't need one.

Because she already knew who had left it.

She reached for it slowly, too slowly. Her breath locking in her throat as she peeled back the flap.

The moment she saw the first words, her entire body went still.

You look beautiful when you sleep.

I wonder if he knows what you taste like when you beg.

Her stomach dropped.

Her hands went ice cold.

And suddenly, the dream, the restaurant and the entire morning all vanished.

Because this?

This was real.

Her breath came fast, too shallow. Too much. Too soon.

She hadn't seen him in months.

She had convinced herself he had finally let go.

But Ethan never let go.

And now?

He was watching.

Again.

Eleven

Chapter 11

Lucas strode into Vanguard Media's sleek, glass-walled offices like he owned them.

He didn't but that had never stopped him from acting like he did.

The receptionist sat up straighter the second she spotted him, voice a touch breathless. "Mr. Cross welcome. They're expecting you in the boardroom."

He gave a single nod, not breaking stride. His assistant followed close behind, listing off meeting notes, names, the schedule for the day.

Lucas wasn't listening because the second he stepped into the open office floor, he saw her.

Amelia.

She was at her desk, posture stiff, fingers gripping the edge of her laptop like it might keep her grounded.

And her face…. She looked like she'd just seen a ghost.

Lucas's stride didn't falter.

He didn't stop. Didn't ask. Didn't let anyone around them see what he had already clocked.

But he saw it. The tension in her shoulders. There was a slight tremor in her fingers as she reached for her coffee. One she barely lifted before setting it back down, untouched.

Her breathing was off.

Not noticeable to the average person.

But Lucas was not the average person.

He was already adjusting his entire approach because this wasn't Amelia Monroe.

Not the woman who had stood her ground in a boardroom full of executives, matched his arrogance with her own and let him push her to push back harder.

This woman? This woman looked like she had just had the air stolen from her lungs.

Something was wrong.

He didn't stop walking. Didn't change his expression. Didn't let anyone see that he had already shifted focus.

But as he passed Amelia's desk, his fingers brushed the edge of her chair.

Subtle. Barely noticeable. But enough , enough for her to startle slightly like she had been lost in her head.

Enough for her to glance up, her dark eyes flicking toward him.

And the moment they did?

Lucas saw something flicker behind them.

Something raw. Something she didn't want him to see.

She masked it quickly, her expression smoothing into neutrality, but it was too late.

He had already seen the crack.

The boardroom was ahead but his attention was still on her.

Still tracking the way she shifted in her chair, she exhaled sharply and forced herself to look anywhere but at him.

She wasn't rattled because of him. Which meant, Lucas's jaw tightened slightly , someone else had done this. Someone had gotten to her first and Lucas didn't like that.

Not one fucking bit.

Still, he didn't say a word.

He didn't let on that he had noticed.

Instead, he filed away every single detail. The tension in her shoulders and her fingers tapping against the desk like she was fighting the urge to move, to run.

And then? Then, he walked into the boardroom, sat at the head of the table and proceeded to dominate the meeting like nothing was wrong.

But Amelia had just made a very critical mistake. Because now? Lucas Cross had questions and whether she liked it or not, he was going to get his answers.

Lucas sat at the head of the boardroom table, nodding as executives droned on about projections and strategies.

But he wasn't hearing a word.

His attention was locked on the woman two seats down, Amelia. Too still. Too quiet. Nothing like the sharp, composed version of her he was used to.

She was pretending everything was fine.

But he'd already seen the crack in her armor.

And now, he was just waiting.

Because she would slip again.

She had been avoiding looking at him since he walked in.

Hadn't spoken once unless directly addressed.

Had barely touched the coffee in front of her.

And beneath the table?

Her fingers were curled into tight, white-knuckled fists.

Lucas exhaled slowly, adjusting the cuff of his suit.

The meeting continued around him, but it was background noise.

The second the meeting ended, Amelia shot to her feet too fast, too tense.

Lucas didn't flinch.

Didn't look at her.

He took his time, carefully collecting his things, every movement unhurried, controlled.

But he noticed everything.

The way her shoulders locked up the moment he shifted.

The stumble in her step as she tried to beat him to the door.

The way her fingers brushed, almost instinctively, against the envelope tucked beneath her notebook.

That was all he needed.

A crack.

An opening.

So, when she slipped out of the boardroom and started walking, not toward her office but toward the break room at the far end of the hall Lucas followed.

Not immediately.

Not fast.

Just enough to keep her in his sights.

Just enough to make sure she had nowhere to go.

Twelve

Chapter 12

Amelia let out a shaky breath, palms pressed hard against the counter like it was the only thing holding her up.

She *had* to get out of that room. Away from *him.*

Because the second she stood, she felt it. His eyes on her. Watching. Waiting.

And if she'd stayed one second longer, with Lucas Cross sitting there like he already knew every secret she was barely holding together, she might've snapped.

She squeezed her eyes shut, willing the tension to go. But it stayed. It gripped tighter, curled in her gut like it had claws.

Then....

The soft click of the door behind her.

Her breath caught.

Slowly, painfully slowly she turned.

Lucas stood there, just inside the room. Hands in his pockets. Eyes locked on her with that calm, steady stare that made her pulse skip and her thoughts unravel.

Silence stretched between them. Thick. Tense.

"Who is he?"

His voice was quiet. Measured. *Too* calm.

Amelia's jaw tightened. Her heart thudded.

"Lucas…"

His head tilted slightly. "You're not going to pretend with me, Amelia."

She exhaled sharply, forcing her spine straight. "I don't know what you're talking about."

Lucas didn't blink. Didn't move. Didn't buy a single word.

She knew it and he knew it. That was the problem.

Because this time? Lucas wasn't going to let it go.

He stepped forward slow and deliberate each move like a noose tightening.

And Amelia felt it, deep and unmistakable.

The trap closing in on her.

Lucas stopped just short of touching her.

Not close enough to invade her space, but close enough to feel the heat of him, the weight of everything he wasn't saying.

"Amelia."

He said her name like it mattered. Like she mattered.

Soft, but firm. Like the truth was already his, and he was just waiting for her to catch up to it.

She looked away. She had to because if she didn't, she'd fall apart right there.

His jaw clenched. "Tell me," he said quietly, almost a whisper. "Or I'll find out myself."

Her stomach twisted hard.

Because she didn't doubt him for a second.

Lucas had power the kind that didn't need threats. Just

intention.

And if she didn't give him the truth, he'd go and dig it out of the dark himself.

And that terrified her more than anything.

Her throat tightened, fingers curling into fists at her sides.

For a moment, all she could do was breathe.

Then finally she let it go.

A breath. A confession. A surrender.

"It's my ex," she said, voice barely above a whisper, bitter and broken around the edges.

Lucas went utterly still.

Not a flicker of emotion.

Not a shift in expression.

Just a long, sharp pause that told her he was already processing this in a way she wasn't prepared for.

Amelia swallowed. "His name is Ethan."

Lucas's fingers twitched at his sides,the only indication of movement.

Amelia pushed the words out, steadying her voice even as it trembled.

"I haven't seen him in months. I thought he was gone."

Her tone dropped to a whisper. "But today… I got a note."

That was all it took.

Lucas shifted. Barely.

Anyone else might've missed it.

But not her, she saw the quiet tension roll through his shoulders.

The way his breath slowed, like he was trying to keep something contained.

The way the air around him suddenly felt darker, heavier charged.

"What did it say?" he asked, voice low.

Too calm.

Too quiet.

Dangerous in a whole new way.

Amelia froze.

She didn't want to answer. Didn't want him to know because if she said the words out loud, they'd be real.

And she wasn't ready for Lucas Cross, the one man who saw too much to know how much of a hold Ethan still had on her.

How much fear still lived in her bones.

But that hesitation?

That was his answer.

Lucas's jaw ticked once barely but she saw it.

His voice dropped even lower, laced with something sharp. "Did he threaten you?"

She didn't answer because if she said it out loud, if she admitted it then it wouldn't just be hers to carry anymore.

And she wasn't sure she was ready to share the weight of it. Not even with him.

Lucas stepped in, closer now. Slow, controlled, deliberate.

Close enough that his presence surrounded her, warm and intense and impossible to ignore.

But when he spoke again, it was softer than before.

Low. Measured.

So much more dangerous.

"You should have told me sooner."

Amelia swallowed hard, forcing her voice not to shake.

"Lucas, this isn't your problem."

He let out a quiet, humorless laugh.

And then came the smirk slow, dark, certain.

"Amelia," he said, like her name belonged to him.
His eyes flicked down to her fists, clenched tight at her sides.
Then back up pinning her in place with nothing but a look.
"Everything about you," he said, low and unshakable,
"Is my problem."

Chapter 13

Lucas hadn't planned on taking her home.

Not tonight and definitely not like this.

But the moment she mentioned Ethan tight-lipped, hesitant and barely letting anything slip, he knew.

She wasn't okay. She was hanging on, but only just.

And instead of pushing, instead of demanding answers she wasn't ready to give, Lucas simply tilted his head and said,

"Come back to my place."

Silence.

Amelia's grip tightened around her notebook. Her first instinct was to tell him no. To push back, draw a line and remind him she didn't need anyone.

But Lucas was watching her. Waiting. Not pushing. Just waiting.

"Excuse me?"

"A drink," he clarified, smooth and even. "Nothing more.

Unless, of course, you're scared of being alone with me."

Her glare had been sharp. Too sharp.

But then,she agreed.

And now?

Now, she was in his penthouse, standing in the middle of his dimly lit, floor-to-ceiling-windowed living room, looking entirely out of place.

Lucas poured two glasses of whiskey, sliding one across the bar toward her.

She hesitated for half a second before taking it.

Didn't say thank you.

Didn't need to.

He watched her as she took a sip, her fingers wrapped around the glass too tightly, like it was grounding her.

She didn't look at him.

Didn't speak.

Lucas let the silence stretch and stretch and stretch.

Until finally she exhaled. And when she spoke?

Her voice was quieter than before.

"His name is Ethan Walker."

Lucas didn't react. He swirled the whiskey in his glass, taking a slow sip, giving her time.

Amelia kept her eyes on the city skyline, the glow of the buildings reflecting in her whiskey glass.

"We were together for two years," she said finally, voice flat, detached like she was reading a report instead of her own life.

Lucas didn't say a word.

Didn't shift.

Didn't even breathe too loud.

Because something in him knew if he did, she'd shut down.

"He used to hit me," Amelia whispered, the words so quiet

they barely existed.

And the second they left her mouth, she felt like her skin had been torn open. Exposing every scar she had tried so hard to hide.

Ugly. Raw. Unbearable.

Lucas didn't move.

Didn't speak.

Just stared at her, his face unreadable but his fists, curled tight on his thighs, said everything.

She let out a sharp breath, eyes locked on the cup in her hands, white-knuckled.

"It didn't start that way," she said, voice cracking. "It was small. Quiet. Just words at first."

A pause.

"He'd tell me I was too sensitive. That I was imagining things. That no one else would put up with me."

Lucas's jaw clenched.

She blinked fast, fighting the tears.

"Then it got worse."

Her voice broke completely.

Her eyes drifted down to her wrist, her fingers ghosting over the faint scar hidden beneath the sleeve of her sweater.

"The first time he hit me, he apologized. He said he didn't mean it; he'd had a bad day that I had pushed him too far. And I," She let out a bitter, humorless laugh. "I believed him. I actually apologized to him."

Lucas's hands gripped the edge of the couch so tightly his knuckles turned white, but he stayed quiet, letting her speak.

Amelia wrapped her arms around herself as if the memories could physically tear her apart. "The bruises were always in places no one would see. My ribs, my thighs, my arms. And if he didn't put his hands on me, he made sure his words did." She blinked rapidly, fighting the sting in her eyes. "He made me feel like I was nothing without him, that I was weak. That no one else would ever want me."

"He wasn't always like that," she continued a bitter scoff curling at the edge of her words. "At first, he was… charming. Confident. The kind of man who makes you feel like the center of the universe."

Lucas's fingers tightened around his glass.

Because that? That was the trick.

Men like Ethan don't start out as monsters.

They become them so slowly that you don't even realize it's happening until it's too late.

"The worst part wasn't that I thought he was going to kill me," she whispered. "It was… for a second, I thought maybe I deserved it."

Lucas was in front of her in an instant. Not touching, not overwhelming but close enough that she could feel his warmth.

"Look at me." His voice was rough but not demanding.

She lifted her eyes, and the moment she did, something inside her cracked.

Lucas wasn't just angry. He was wrecked. His eyes burned with fury, grief and something more profound, something raw.

"You never deserved any of it," he said fiercely. "Not one second. Not one bruise. Not one fucking breath wasted on that bastard." His voice dropped lower, dangerously soft. "I swear to you, Amelia he will never touch you again."

Her breath caught. "Lucas…"

His hand lifted, fingers brushing against her cheek, not possessive, not demanding just offering comfort.

"He made you believe you were weak," Lucas murmured. "But I've never met anyone stronger."

The dam inside her shattered. A sob tore from her throat as she collapsed against him. Lucas caught her immediately, arms tightening around her, holding her like he feared she might disappear.

"I've got you," he whispered against her hair. "You're safe now."

And for the first time in a long time,she believed him.

"Stay."

Her heart stuttered at the quiet command.

It wasn't a demand. It was a plea wrapped in steel.

Amelia blinked, eyes flicking back to him. "What?"

Lucas tilted his head slightly. "Stay. Just for tonight."

Her brows pulled together. "Lucas, I,"

"Just sleep," he clarified. Not a request. A fact. "No expectations. No pressure. … stay."

Amelia hesitated and Lucas knew she was searching for a reason to say no.

But she didn't find one.

Instead after a long moment, after a slow breath, after a decision she didn't quite understand yet. She nodded.

Lucas knew right then and there.

He wasn't going to let her go because this wasn't just about protecting her.

This wasn't just about handling Ethan.

This was about Amelia Monroe standing in his penthouse, letting him be the one thing she never let anyone be.

A place to rest.

And Lucas?
Lucas was never going to forget that.

Fourteen

Chapter 14

Amelia woke up warm.

That was the first thing she noticed.

Not the strange bed. Not the unfamiliar blankets.

Not even the miracle that she had actually slept. Like really slept for the first time in months.

Just the warmth.

Deep, steady, safe.

Like for one night, the world had paused. Like it hadn't been clawing at her door, waiting to break her open.

Her body shifted slowly. Her mind floated somewhere between sleep and waking soft, quiet, unafraid.

And then… The scent of coffee.

Her eyes opened, blinking against the soft morning light.

It took just a moment to place it.

The floor-to-ceiling windows.

The stretch of city skyline.

The charcoal-gray sheets.

The furniture sleek and expensive.

Lucas's penthouse.

Last night came back all at once.

The whiskey. The quiet conversation. The moment she had said yes when she should have said no.

Amelia exhaled, pressing a hand to her temple.

She hadn't meant to stay.

She hadn't meant to let her guard down, to accept whatever Lucas was offering.

But the second he had told her to stay, something in her had stopped fighting.

Something in her had let him.

And now?

Now, it was morning.

And Lucas was still here.

Her stomach tightened slightly as she pushed the covers back, bracing herself.

Because this?

This was uncharted territory.

This wasn't power plays, boardroom battles, or the sharp edge of attraction that neither of them had entirely given into.

This was Lucas Cross, somewhere in this penthouse, waiting for her to walk out of this room.

And she had no idea what that meant.

She made herself move, legs heavy as she swung them over the edge of the bed. Her clothes were still from the night before. Blouse wrinkled, skirt riding a little too high.

And yet…She didn't feel out of place. Didn't feel exposed. She felt oddly okay.

Like nothing had happened.

Like nothing *needed* to.

She dragged a hand through her hair, breathing out slow, grounding herself before finally rising to her feet.

Then came the smell again coffee, warm and rich.

She followed it down the quiet hallway.

And there he was.

Lucas, standing in the kitchen.

Barefoot. Sleeves rolled up. Turning something on the stove like he belonged there. Like this morning was just... normal.

Amelia stopped in the doorway, eyes on him silent, still unsure what hit her harder: the comfort or the unfamiliar ache in her chest.

Because for the first time, maybe ever. Lucas Cross didn't look like a man about to take over the world.

He just looked like a man making breakfast.

The quiet clink of a spatula against the pan, the scent of coffee filling the air, the skyline glowing in the morning light behind him.

And she?

She didn't know what to do with that.

Lucas glanced over his shoulder, catching sight of her.

And then,the slightest smirk.

"Morning."

Amelia hesitated. "You cook?"

Lucas shrugged, turning back to the stove. "I make breakfast."

She crossed her arms, leaning against the counter, watching as he flipped a pancake, like he had done this a hundred times before.

"I didn't peg you as a pancakes kind of guy," she muttered.

Lucas arched a brow, glancing at her. "And what kind of

guy did you peg me as?"

Amelia rolled her eyes, but her lips almost twitched. "Something pretentious. Black coffee. Maybe eggs. No carbs."

Lucas let out a chuckle, grabbing two plates. "Pancakes are practical."

"Practical?"

He stacked the pancakes, setting one plate in front of her like it wasn't even a question if she was eating.

Then he met her gaze, that lazy confidence never wavering.

"They keep people from leaving too soon."

Her stomach flipped.

And god help her, she didn't know if it was from the way he said it or the fact that he had just handed her breakfast like it was the most normal thing in the world.

Like he had expected her to be here.

Like he had wanted her to be.

She stared at the plate for half a second, then picked up the fork.

Lucas's smirk deepened slightly before he sat across from her, sipping coffee.

They ate in silence.

Not awkward.

Not tense.

Just… quiet.

Just comfortable.

And that was almost worse.

Because comfortable was dangerous.

Comfortable meant familiarity.

Meant trust.

Meant that somehow, Lucas Cross had gone from a problem to a presence she wasn't sure she wanted to leave.

She swallowed, setting her fork down. "I should go."

Lucas leaned back slightly, watching her. "You could."

She exhaled sharply. "Lucas."

He smirked. "Amelia."

Her jaw tightened. "Don't look at me like that."

Lucas tilted his head, completely unbothered. "Like what?"

"Like you knew I was going to stay last night," she muttered.

Lucas took another sip of coffee, slow and lazy.

"I did."

Her pulse jumped.

And Lucas, the bastard saw it.

His smirk deepened.

But when he spoke again, his voice was softer.

More real.

"I wasn't going to let you be alone last night."

Amelia's throat tightened.

Because that?

That wasn't teasing.

That wasn't arrogance.

That was Lucas Cross, sitting across from her, telling her in a way only he could that he wasn't going anywhere.

That he wasn't just going to walk away.

That for some insane, impossible reason, he cared.

And Amelia didn't know what to do with that.

So she did the only thing she could do.

She finished her coffee.

Stood up.

And left before she made another mistake.

Fifteen

Chapter 15

The elevator ride up was quiet.

Amelia kept repeating the plan: grab the scarf, get out. No lingering. No second-guessing.

Lucas had been kind. Protective in a way that made her feel something she hadn't in a long time, safe. She stepped into the penthouse. The afternoon light spilled through those towering windows, painting gold beams across the room.

Her scarf sat where she left it, draped over the back of a chair. She reached for it and froze.

A door.

Just slightly open. A room she hadn't noticed before.

Logic whispered: leave.

But curiosity leaned in closer.

Would Lucas let her go in? or would he stop her with that voice low, calm, commanding?

The thought made her shiver.

Slowly, almost against her will, she reached out and pushed the door open.

Dark wood panels lined the walls, the lighting low and intimate. A deep leather chair sat in the corner, perfectly placed beside a sleek black desk. Shelves stretched floor to ceiling, filled with books that whispered of control and quiet power.

At first, it looked like just an office.

And then she saw the desk.

A length of black silk and a leather cuff. Along with a book *The Dominant's Guide to Discipline and Control.*

Her breath caught in her throat.

She shouldn't be here.

She *definitely* shouldn't be seeing this.

But now that she had she couldn't unsee it.

A floorboard creaked behind her and her stomach dropped.

She spun around, heart in her throat, half-certain she'd see Lucas standing there watching. But the doorway was empty. Just silence and the sound of her own pulse, wild in her ears.

And then the truth hit her, hard and undeniable.

Lucas wasn't just protective.

Wasn't just in control.

He was dominant.

Not the man she thought he was instead something more. Something deeper.

Her hand flew to the scarf. She grabbed it and bolted.

Out of the room and down the hall.

She didn't look back. Didn't even stop to breathe.

Just kept her head down and ran, barely registering how she made it out of the building at all.

Amelia paced the length of her apartment, phone pressed to her ear.

"So let me get this straight," Sophia says, voice tinged with amusement. "You broke into a locked room,"

"It wasn't locked," Amelia mutters.

",and you found a stash of BDSM gear and a book on how to properly boss people around in the bedroom?"

Amelia groans. "It wasn't a stash. It was just… a few things. But it wasn't normal, Soph. And the book, it was like a manual."

"Okay, so what's the problem? Lucas is hot. If he wants to tie you up, I see no downside."

"Sophia!"

"I'm just saying," Sophia teases. "Look, you said he's been nothing but respectful, right? He let you stay over; he didn't push anything. Maybe he's just into something a little… extra."

Amelia sinks onto the couch. "But why wouldn't he tell me? Why keep it a secret?"

"Because it's personal? Because he doesn't know if you'd be into it? Or maybe because he doesn't want to scare you off."

Amelia lets out a shaky breath. "Or maybe because he knows someone like me would never be able to handle it."

There's a pause on the other end of the line. "Amelia… what does that mean?"

Her throat tightens. She presses her fingers against her temple, eyes squeezing shut.

"It means…" She swallows hard. "It means that for two years, Ethan controlled everything I did and what I wore. Who I spoke to. When I could leave the apartment. And when I didn't listen…" Her voice cracks. "He made sure I regretted it."

Sophia doesn't speak right away, but Amelia can hear her breathing. When she finally does speak, her voice is gentle. "Sweetheart, I know."

"Then you know why this terrifies me," Amelia says, clutching the phone tighter. "Lucas is… intense. He's used to being in control. He gives orders and expects people to listen. That's how Ethan was. And I promised myself I'd never give a man that kind of power again."

Sophia lets out a slow breath. "I understand. I really do. But there's a difference between control and care, Amelia. Lucas didn't try to own you. He protected you. He opened his home to you when you had nowhere to go. And he never once made you feel like you owed him for it… did he?"

Amelia shakes her head, the movement instinctive, even though Sophia can't see her. "No. He didn't."

Sophia's voice softens further. "And with Ethan did you ever feel safe?"

Amelia's stomach twists. "No."

Sophia pauses, just long enough to let the truth settle. "But with Lucas?"

Amelia hesitates. The word rises from her chest, unfiltered, painful in its honesty.

"Yes."

Sophia sighs. "Look, I'm not saying jump into anything with him. I know you're still healing. But let me ask you something… what does your heart say?"

Amelia exhales slowly. "My heart?"

"Yeah. Your head is screaming no because it's trying to protect you. But if you stop and listen… what does your heart say?"

Amelia closes her eyes. Her mind is a mess of alarms,

flashing red lights screaming *danger, danger, run.*

But beneath the panic, there's something softer.

"It's telling me…" She swallows hard. "Maybe I want to know what it's like. To give up control but with someone who makes it feel safe. Maybe… I want to try."

Sophia hums gently. "Then maybe it's worth talking to him."

Amelia opens her eyes, staring blankly at the ceiling, her voice small. "And what if I get hurt again?"

There's a pause. Then Sophia answers, calm and sure.

"Then you walk away. But Amelia?"

Another pause this one heavier, careful.

"Lucas isn't Ethan. And I think, deep down… you already know that."

Sixteen

Chapter 16

Amelia's heart thudded against her ribs as she stepped into TechCross's gleaming lobby, heels echoing across the marble floor. The receptionist offered a polite smile, but Amelia barely saw her.

Her eyes locked on the name in bold letters across the far wall:

Lucas Cross, CEO.

Her grip tightened around her bag's strap.

She hadn't even fully decided to come here, only that after the call with Sophia, sitting still had become impossible.

She needed clarity. She needed *him*.

"He's in a meeting," the receptionist said gently.

"I'll wait."

She sat down in the sleek lounge, arms crossed, breath shallow.

But the longer she waited, the tighter the knot in her

stomach pulled.

What if this was a mistake?

What if facing him only makes everything worse?

But louder than the fear was the quiet truth she didn't want to admit....

What if I want to hear what he has to say?

After what feels like forever, a door opens at the end of the hall.

Lucas steps out, a storm in a tailored black suit. Confident. Effortless. The kind of presence that shifts every room without trying. His eyes scan the lobby and land on her instantly.

His face doesn't give much away. But his eyes....

There's something there. Surprise? Amusement?

Something darker, hotter, unreadable.

"Amelia."

Her name on his lips is steady, controlled. But it hums with something just beneath the surface.

He strides toward her, and every step tightens the coil in her stomach.

"I wasn't expecting you," he says, calm but laced with quiet intensity.

"I wasn't expecting to come," she replies, her voice sounding far steadier than she feels. "But we need to talk."

His eyes search hers, lingering just a second too long. Then he nods once and gestures for her to follow.

Inside his office, the door clicks shut behind them, sealing them in silence.

The space is all sharp lines and dark wood. Clean. Powerful. Controlled. Just like him.

He doesn't move behind the desk. Instead, he leans against it, arms folded over his chest, gaze locked on her.

"Alright," he says, voice low, unreadable. "Talk."

Amelia swallows, every nerve in her body suddenly on edge under his gaze.

But she lifts her chin, refusing to look away.

"I went back to your penthouse today," she says softly. "To get my scarf."

The way his jaw tightens tells her he already knows that wasn't all she found.

"I know."

That throws her. "You do?"

"Security cameras." A ghost of a smirk touches his lips. "I saw you leave in a hurry. Care to explain why?"

Amelia's pulse stumbles, but she lifts her chin. "I went into your office. The one with the door left open."

The smirk fades. His expression sharpens, and for the first time, she sees it, the carefully restrained control in his posture, the way his fingers tighten slightly where they rest against his arms.

"I see."

"Do you?" she challenges. "Because I don't."

She takes a step closer, forcing herself to hold his gaze. "I saw the book, Lucas. I saw the cuffs, the silk, all of it. And I need to know, why do you have them?"

His silence is deafening. He watches her for a moment, unreadable. Then, slowly, he stands.

He doesn't touch her. Doesn't take a step closer.

But somehow, he's already there filling the space between them with heat, tension and gravity.

"Because that's who I am, Amelia."

His voice is low, careful, but charged.

"I'm a Dominant. It's not a game. It's not just about sex. It's about trust. About responsibility. About caring for someone who chooses to give me that trust freely."

A shiver runs through her, sharp and soft all at once.

"Taking care of someone?" she murmurs. "That sounds a lot like control."

"It is."

His eyes darken, a quiet storm rising in them.

"But it's control that's given. Never taken. There's a difference, Amelia."

Her breath falters. Her heart is loud in her chest.

Still, she doesn't back down.

"I don't know if I can do that," she admits. Her voice trembling , "I don't know if I can *ever* give someone that kind of power over me again."

"Because of Ethan."

The name slices through the air.

Her stomach knots. Her lips press together.

She nods.

"Yes."

Lucas exhales slowly, then takes another step back as if giving her space. "You should know this now, Amelia I am not him. I will never be him. And I will never take more than you're willing to give."

His words hit her harder than she expected.

"And what if I don't know what I'm willing to give?" she asks quietly.

Lucas studies her, then tilts his head slightly. "Then we figure it out. On your terms."

She hadn't expected that answer.

For a long moment, neither of them speaks. The air between them is thick with unspoken things fear, curiosity, something that might even be longing.

Finally, Lucas exhales, his expression softening just a fraction. A crack in the mask he always wore.

He shifted closer, and before Amelia could process it, her back hit the wall of his office with a soft thud.

His body caged hers in, arms braced on either side of her head close enough to feel, but not touching.

The tension between them was thick and electric.

Like it could break them open if either of them moved.

His eyes locked on hers. She felt it everywhere.

She should speak, move and even push him away before things go to far. But the words couldn't leave her tongue.

Lucas leaned in slow and deliberate. Giving her time, giving her space, giving her *the choice.*

His breath brushed her cheek, and it made her knees go weak.

Her heart slammed against her ribs, too loud, too fast and fists curled at her sides.

And then panic. Sharp. Sudden. Familiar. A rush of old memories clawed their way up.

Grabbing hands. Raised voices. Cold smiles dressed as love. *Don't do this. Don't let him have that kind of hold on you.*

Lucas didn't touch her.

His hand hovered at her jaw, close enough that she could feel the warmth of it.

Waiting.

Breathing with her.

Letting her decide.

"Amelia," he said, voice hoarse with the effort it took to hold himself back.

"I won't touch you unless you want me to."

Her vision blurred for a second.

No one had ever given her that choice before.

Not when it mattered.

Tears prickled behind her eyes.

And still her body ached for him. For his touch. For the terrible, beautiful danger he represented.

She didn't know if she wanted him because he was dangerous or because, somehow he made her feel safer than she had in years.

Amelia swallowed thickly.

Her pulse roared in her ears.

Then, without thinking without giving herself time to second-guess

she moved forward, crashing her mouth to his.

Lucas caught her with a low, broken sound like something inside him snapped.

His hands cupped her jaw with infinite care, anchoring her even as the kiss deepened into something reckless and wild.

Their bodies collided, desperate and chaotic. Like two storms crashing together.

Amelia's hands grabbed his shirt, pulling him closer.

Lucas kissed her like he was starving, like he needed her.

She kissed him back like she needed saving but she didn't know if she was being saved or destroyed.

And in that moment she didn't care.

Seventeen

Chapter 17

Lucas slammed the door behind him, the sound cracking through the silence like a warning shot. Too loud and too much. But not enough to drown out the chaos inside him.

He paced the length of the darkened penthouse, dragging a hand through his hair, his pulse thrumming like it wanted out of his skin.

He could still taste her.

Amelia Monroe.

Her kiss. The fire in it. The way she threw herself into him like she *meant* it. Like she didn't care about consequences or hesitations or walls.

She tore right through his and he let her.

He should've stopped it. Should've asked her if she was ready, *really* ready.

But the second her hands found him, every line he'd drawn, every rule, every boundary. It all snapped under her touch.

Now he was here.

Alone. Hands braced on the edge of the kitchen counter, knuckles white, muscles tight, breathing like he'd run a goddamn marathon.

What the hell was happening to him?

He had rules and control. He didn't get *attached.*

Need was dangerous.

Need was weakness.

Need made you bleed.

And yet... when Amelia kissed him it hadn't felt like a victory. It had felt like surrender.

It had felt like free-falling with no hope of stopping the crash.

He squeezed his eyes shut, breathing hard.

He could still see it. The flash of fear in her eyes right before she kissed him.

Still feel the way her hands clutched at him, shaking.

Like she needed him and hated herself for it.

And something in him, something old and wrecked and buried deep had reached back for her.

Like a man crawling through the dark, desperate for water.

Lucas clenched his jaw, fury twisting low in his gut.

He couldn't afford this.

Not with her.

She wasn't some casual fling, another name he'd forget by morning.

She was *dangerous.*

Not because of what she did but because of what she *saw.*

She looked at him and didn't flinch. She looked at him and *understood.*

And worse she made him *want.*

With a sharp curse, he slammed his fist into the counter.

The crack of impact split the silence.

His knuckles burned and his chest heaved.

He was unraveling and if he wasn't careful, if he let her any closer.

She'd be the one to ruin him.

Just like everything else he'd ever tried to hold onto.

Eighteen

Chapter 18

Amelia closed the door behind her and leaned back against it, eyes falling shut as she exhaled slow and shaky.

Her whole body was still buzzing.

It had been hours since she walked out of CrossTech, but she could still feel him.

Lucas. The echo of his touch still clung to her skin. She needed to get a grip.

With a sigh edged in frustration, she slipped off her heels and padded into the living room.

The couch welcomed her like a soft collapse.

Her laptop sat on the coffee table, waiting expecting her to pick up where she left off.

But the thought of opening another spreadsheet made her stomach knot.

Work should've grounded her but it just reminded her how off-balance she'd become.

Instead she reached for the leather-bound journal tucked inside the side table drawer. It was old, the pages slightly worn, filled with thoughts she'd never dared to say aloud.

Tonight, she needed it.

Journal Entry:

I don't know what's happening to me.

I told myself I wouldn't fall for someone like him .Someone who takes up too much space and doesn't ask permission before slipping into my thoughts, my body, and my life.

But I'm slipping.

And the worst part?

I don't know if I want to stop it anymore.

She clenched her jaw, pressing her pen harder against the page.

Lucas was dangerous in a way Ethan never was.

Ethan had controlled her through fear, manipulation, and the slow, systematic breakdown of her confidence until she was nothing but a shadow of herself.

Lucas didn't need to control her.

Because she wanted him.

And maybe that was worse.

The ringing of her phone snapped her out of her thoughts.

Sophia.

She hesitated for a second before answering.

"Hello."

"You sound weird," Sophia said immediately.

Amelia huffed, closing the journal. "I literally just said hello."

"Yeah, and you said it like you're having an existential crisis. What's wrong?"

"Nothing."

Sophia let out a dramatic gasp. "Liar! Is this about a certain brooding billionaire who looks at you like he wants to throw you on a conference table?"

Amelia groaned, rubbing her temple. "You're the worst."

"I am the best," Sophia corrected. "Now spill. What did he do this time?"

"He… exists," Amelia admitted.

Sophia snorted. "Babe, you're in deep."

Amelia bit her lip, staring down at the journal in her lap. "I don't know what to do, Soph. He gets under my skin. He makes me feel…."

She stopped herself.

Sophia's voice softened. "Makes you feel what?"

"…Like I don't have to run."

The confession sat between them, thick, fragile.

Sophia sighed. "That's not a bad thing, Amelia."

"It could be."

Sophia was silent for a beat. Then gentle and cautious ,she said, "He's not Ethan."

Amelia's throat tightened. "I know."

"Do you?"

She swallowed. "He's powerful. He likes control."

"Yeah, but does he take it? Or does he wait for you to give it?"

Amelia's pulse jumped.

Because Lucas never forced her. He pushed, tested and knew precisely how to unravel her but never took anything.

Every time he touched her, every time he came close enough to steal her breath, he gave her a choice. And she always made it.

Sophia exhaled. "Maybe the real question isn't if you should trust him, Amelia." "Maybe it's if you should trust yourself."

Amelia's grip tightened around the pen.

That was the problem.

Lucas was dangerous because he made her want to believe in something again.

And she wasn't sure if she was ready for that.

Nineteen

Chapter 19

Two days later

Amelia sat cross-legged on her bed, laptop warm against her thighs, fingers hovering over the keyboard.

What am I even looking for?

Since that conversation in Lucas's office, his words had looped through her mind on repeat.

"It's given control, not taken. There's a difference."

She knew what it felt like to be controlled. Ethan had made sure of that his love conditional, his power a weapon.

But Lucas had spoken about control like it was something sacred. Something earned.

Slowly, she began to type:

what is a dominant-submissive relationship

Dozens of links popped up, clinical studies, erotic fiction, forums, personal blogs.

One title pulled her in:

"BDSM & Trust: Why It's Not What You Think."

She clicked. Read.

A real dominant never takes control. A submissive gives it freely and consciously. True dominance isn't about obedience. It's about leadership rooted in safety. A good Dominant's first duty is not power. It's protection.

Her breath caught.

"Makes them feel safe."

Her mind flashed back to Lucas stepping back when she panicked. To his voice, low and calm.

"On your terms."

This wasn't Ethan.

This wasn't fear.

This was… something else entirely.

Amelia shut the laptop gently and pressed her fingers to her temple.

Did she want this?

She didn't have the answer yet.

But for the first time, she wasn't afraid to ask the question.

The air outside was crisp, the city alive with the usual evening bustle, cars honking, distant laughter from groups of friends and conversations spilling from restaurants. Amelia pulled her coat tighter around her as she walked down the street, her boots clicking softly against the pavement.

She needed this. Fresh air and a break from her thoughts.

She had spent most of the day lost in research, falling down an internet rabbit hole of articles and forums, trying to make sense of Lucas's world. Some of what she read intrigued her, some terrified her but more than anything, it made her realize how little she understood.

Could I ever do that?

The thought lingered as she stood in line at the tiny Thai restaurant on the corner. Could she trust someone enough to let go, even in the slightest way? Could she ever believe that submission wasn't a weakness but a choice?

She shook her head, pushing the thoughts aside as she approached the counter.

"Order for Amelia?" she asked, offering the cashier a small smile.

The girl behind the counter nodded, grabbing a brown paper bag from the shelf. "Pad Thai, green curry, and spring rolls?"

"That's me."

She paid quickly, her stomach rumbling as the scent of warm spices filled the air. It was a simple, quiet moment one that made her feel like herself again, like she was just a normal woman picking up dinner, not someone unraveling years of trauma or questioning whether she could ever give a man control again.

Her phone buzzed in her pocket. She glanced down.

Lucas: Eat something tonight. And try to get some sleep.

A slight, involuntary warmth spread through her chest.

She hadn't told him about the hours she had spent researching or that she'd spent half the day curled up on her couch, stomach too tied in knots to eat. But somehow, he knew.

She hesitated before typing back.

Amelia: *I just picked up food. Thai.*

His reply came almost instantly.

Lucas: Good.

Just that. Nothing more. No pressure.

Amelia sighed, tucking her phone back into her coat pocket. She turned onto her street, the warm glow of the streetlights guiding her path.

She had no idea what she was doing.

But for the first time, she didn't hate not knowing.

She was still figuring things out.

And maybe, just maybe she wasn't as lost as she thought.

She pulled her keys from her pocket, thoughts still drifting, the warmth of Lucas's last message lingering in her chest. The night felt calm. Almost normal.

Until she saw it.

Amelia's body went cold when she spotted the envelope on her apartment door.

Her name was scrawled across the front in familiar handwriting.

No.

Her hand trembled as she reached for it, her heart hammering so hard it made her ribs ache. She shouldn't open it. She should call someone first. But dread had already seized her, and before she could stop herself, she was tearing the envelope open.

Amelia,

I miss you. I think about you all the time. I know you've been keeping your distance, but that's unfair. We have unfinished business, and you know it. You were mine, Amelia. And you will be again.

E.

Her breath came in sharp, shallow bursts. The paper slipped from her fingers, fluttering to the floor.

No. No, no, no.

She stumbled back against the wall, pressing a hand over

her mouth. Ethan wasn't supposed to know where she lived. She had changed her number, blocked him, and disappeared.

And yet, he had found her.

Panic surged in her chest, her body reacting before her mind could catch up. She grabbed her phone, her fingers moving on instinct. Before she even registered what she was doing, she had pressed a contact she shouldn't have reached for.

Lucas.

The phone rang once. Twice.

"Amelia?"

Her breath caught. She hadn't even thought about what she would say, but the second she heard his voice, something inside her cracked.

"H-he found me," she whispered. "Lucas, he knows where I live."

There was a pause. Then his voice dropped to something dangerous.

"Where are you right now?"

"My apartment."

"Are you inside?"

"Yes, but…."

"Lock the door. Don't move. I'm on my way."

The call ended.

Amelia sucked in a breath, her pulse wild.

She should have called the police. She should have called Sophia.

But instead, she had called Lucas.

And now, he was coming for her.

Amelia hadn't moved from the spot where she stood. She couldn't.

The letter lay on the floor, stark and damning, like a ghost resurrected from a past she thought she had buried. Her breaths came too fast, too shallow. She pressed her palm against the door, trying to steady herself, but it was useless.

She had done everything right: changed her number, moved to a new apartment, took different routes home, and disappeared.

Yet, Ethan still found her at work and now at home.

A hard knock at the door made her jolt. Her pulse stuttered.

"Amelia. It's me."

Lucas.

She exhaled sharply, her shaky fingers fumbling with the lock before she swung the door open.

He was standing there in a black coat, sleeves pushed up slightly, his posture rigid and tense but his eyes were the thing that stopped her breath.

Cold. Sharp. Lethal.

His gaze swept over her like an assessment, cataloging every detail, the way she gripped the doorframe, the slight tremble in her hands, and her breath still hadn't steadied. Then his eyes flicked to the floor. He saw the letter.

His expression darkened.

Without a word, Lucas stepped inside, shutting the door behind him.

"Sit," he said, his voice low but firm.

She didn't argue. She couldn't. She just moved, sinking onto the couch as Lucas crouched down, carefully picking up the letter. His jaw tightened as he read it.

When he finally looked back at her, something dangerous burned in his eyes.

Lucas folded the letter slowly and deliberately, then slipped it into his coat pocket. "You are safe."

"Am I?" Her voice cracked. "Because it doesn't feel like it."

Lucas didn't answer right away. Instead, he did something unexpected.

He sat beside her, close but not touching, his presence solid and steady.

"You called me."

Her stomach twisted. "I…."

"Not the police. Not Sophia." His voice remained even, but something was unreadable beneath it. "Me."

She swallowed hard, her fingers twisting together in her lap. "I didn't think. I just… I just needed to feel safe."

Lucas's gaze softened just enough to be noticeable.

"And you do?"

She hesitated. Then, slowly, she nodded.

His expression didn't change, but she swore something shifted in the air between them. He leaned back slightly, resting one arm along the back of the couch.

"This is what I mean, Amelia." His voice was lower now, steady and sure. "Control is only control when it's given. When you were afraid and had no time to think, you made a choice." His eyes locked onto hers. "You gave me that control."

She hadn't thought about it like that or even realized what she had done.

"And now?" she asked quietly. "What happens now?"

Lucas exhaled slowly. "Now, you let me handle it."

"Lucas….."

"I mean it, Amelia." His tone brooked no argument. "He won't come near you again."

Something final in his voice sent a shiver down her spine, not of fear, but of certainty. She believed that when Lucas said something, he meant it.

The panic began to subside for the first time since she opened that letter.

She didn't know what Lucas was capable of. Didn't know what he was planning.

But for some reason, she trusted him.

And that terrified her more than anything.

Twenty

Chapter 20

Amelia's fingers curled around the warm mug, holding it like an anchor. The tea had long gone cold, but she didn't move. She just sat there, still, staring out the floor-to-ceiling windows of Lucas's penthouse.

The city glowed beneath the night sky. She should've felt small but instead, she felt safe.

Last night, she hadn't slept. Not really.

Her mind had spun in circles of what ifs, maybes, fears she couldn't name.

But Lucas hadn't asked her to explain.

He hadn't demanded her pain, hadn't tried to fix it.

He was just *there.* Quiet. Steady. Checking the locks. Making sure she ate. Keeping the silence from swallowing her whole.

Now Sophia was here.

The buzzer had barely finished before Lucas checked the

security feed and let her in.

She entered like a storm with purpose, coat in one hand, eyes scanning the space. Her gaze lingered on the windows, the penthouse, the man standing near the kitchen.

"Okay, I have *several* things to say," she declared, dropping her bag on the coffee table. "One: holy hell, Amelia, this place? You've been *seriously* holding out."

Amelia managed a tired smile. "It's Lucas's."

"Right. *Lucas.*" Sophia's voice shifted, sharper now. Her eyes slid toward him. He stood tall, composed, arms crossed, posture still but alert.

"Should I be thanking you for playing knight in shining armor," she asked, "or should I be suspicious?"

Lucas didn't flinch. "That depends."

Sophia arched a brow. "On?"

"Whether you think I gain something by protecting her."

Sophia looked at Amelia. "Well?"

Amelia's throat tightened. She shifted on the couch, setting her mug down with a quiet clink.

"He's helping me, Soph. That's all."

Sophia didn't speak for a moment. Then she sighed and dropped beside her, curling up with a softness that only showed when she let her guard down.

"Alright. I'll save the third-degree for later."

She turned to Amelia, eyes gentler now. "Tell me. What the hell happened?"

Amelia stared down at her hands.

Where do I even begin?

Her voice, when it came, felt like it belonged to someone else.

"He knows where I live."

Sophia stilled. Her face dropped.

"Ethan?"

Amelia didn't answer. She didn't need to.

The silence that followed said everything.

Amelia gripped her hands together in her lap. "I came home last night, and a letter was taped to my door."

Sophia sat up straighter. "What did it say?"

Amelia hesitated, then looked toward Lucas. He was still standing there, watching her. He had read the letter himself, folded it carefully, and tucked it away like evidence.

"He said he missed me and that we had unfinished business. That I was his." Her voice was quieter now. "Like nothing had changed. Like the past hadn't even happened."

Sophia inhaled sharply, then pushed off the couch, pacing the length of the room. "How the fuck did he find you? You changed everything, your number, your address. There's no way he just… guessed."

"I don't know," Amelia admitted, pressing her fingertips to her temples.

Lucas, who had been silent up until now, finally spoke.

"He didn't guess."

Both women turned to him.

"Men like him don't let go easily," Lucas continued, his voice controlled. "If he found you, it means he was looking. And it means someone helped him."

Amelia's stomach dropped.

"You think he had someone follow me?"

"Or someone fed him information," Lucas said evenly. "You might not have slipped up, but someone in your past might have."

Sophia swore under her breath. "Okay, that's it. We need

to go to the police. File a report. Get a restraining order or something."

Lucas didn't react, but Amelia felt the weight of his gaze on her.

"A restraining order won't stop him," she murmured.

Sophia's expression twisted. "Amelia…."

"You know I'm right," she whispered. "Ethan doesn't care about rules. The moment he finds out I went to the police, he'll take it as a challenge."

Sophia's lips pressed into a thin line. "So what do we do? … wait for him to make a move?"

"No," Lucas said smoothly. "We don't wait. We get ahead of him."

Sophia shot him a skeptical look. "And what exactly does that mean?"

Lucas didn't flinch.

"It means," he said, "Ethan has been hunting for Amelia. It's time we let him know he's being hunted."

Sophia narrowed her eyes. "Okay, hold on. 'Hunted'? What exactly are you suggesting, Lucas? That we fight fire with fire?"

Lucas didn't blink. "I'm suggesting we stop playing defense."

Amelia felt Sophia tense beside her. Her best friend had always been fiercely protective especially after Ethan. And right now, it was clear she wasn't sure if Lucas was here to protect or control.

"And what does that look like?" Sophia challenged. "Because last I checked, you're a tech mogul, not a hitman."

A muscle ticked in Lucas's jaw. For a split second, Amelia swore she saw something flicker in his expression, something sharp. Something ruthless.

"I have resources," he said evenly. "And I have influence. I can ensure Ethan knows he's not in control anymore."

Sophia scoffed. "That sounds like you're trying to take control instead."

Amelia braced herself, expecting Lucas to snap back, but instead, he shifted his gaze to her.

"The control is hers to give," he said. "And I won't take a step further unless she wants me to."

Something inside Amelia twisted painfully. She wasn't used to that. A man waiting for her permission and choice.

Ethan had never given her that. But Lucas was giving it to her now.

Sophia exhaled sharply, rubbing a hand down her face. "Jesus." She turned to Amelia. "Look, it's your call. But don't let him decide for you just because you're scared."

"I'm not." The words came out before she could stop them. "I'm letting him because I trust him."

Sophia blinked. Lucas's expression remained unreadable.

"Okay," Sophia murmured. "Okay." She turned back to Lucas, her gaze sharp. "Then you better be sure you don't break that trust."

Lucas didn't hesitate. "I won't."

Amelia believed him.

Twenty-One

Chapter 21

After Sophia left, Amelia stood by the window, arms wrapped around her torso like armor, eyes fixed on the skyline. The city pulsed below her, alive and loud but inside her head, everything felt numb.

Ethan had found her but Lucas had come for her.

She didn't know how long she'd been standing there. The ache in her chest was still fresh, but her fear wasn't sharp anymore.

She glanced toward the kitchen. Lucas stood there, rolling up his sleeves and poured a glass of whiskey

He hadn't said much since Sophia left. He'd given her space.

"Do you think he had help?"

Her voice came out softer than she expected.

Lucas looked up slowly, his eyes locking on hers. He took a quiet sip before answering.

"I don't *think,* Amelia. I *know.*"

A chill ran down her spine.

"How?" she asked, voice thinner now.

He set the glass down gently, like even his rage had discipline.

"Because I know men like him. I know how they think."

A pause. A weight behind his next words.

"And I know how to stop them."

The certainty in his voice didn't scare her.

It *settled* her.

Like a lock clicking into place.

She turned back to the window, her reflection ghostly in the glass.

"I should be more scared than I am," she whispered.

"You should," Lucas said, moving closer. He didn't touch her. He didn't have to. She felt him behind her steady, solid and just *there.*

"Why aren't you?" he asked.

She swallowed hard, heart hammering against her ribs.

Her eyes stayed on her reflection, on the woman she barely recognized.

"Because you're here."

Silence again. But this time, it wasn't empty.

Then his voice, low, rough around the edges.

"Come here, Amelia."

It wasn't a command. Not even a request. It was an opening. A door she could walk through *or not.*

She turned.

He stood there, watching her eyes darker than before.

He was offering himself. Not control. Not pressure.

Just presence and for the first time in a long time she stepped forward.

Because this time, it was *her* choice. And she was ready to make it.

The second she was within reach, he lifted a hand tucking a strand of hair behind her ear. His fingers lingered, just for a moment, before drifting down her jaw.

"You want to know what I meant," he murmured.

"About control?" she whispered.

Lucas nodded, his fingertips barely grazing the side of her neck. "Yes. About given control. About trust."

She didn't move. Didn't breathe.

"Let me show you."

Her pulse hammered. "How?"

Lucas's thumb brushed against her chin, coaxing it upward. "I want to take you to bed."

Heat pooled low in her stomach, but he wasn't done.

"Not to fuck you," he clarified. "To show you what it feels like to give me a little control. Just enough to know you're safe."

Amelia's throat went dry.

"And if I can't?" she whispered.

Lucas's gaze softened, but his voice remained steady. "Then we stop. And you'll know that when I say I'll never take more than you give… I mean it."

She should hesitate. She should walk away.

But she didn't. Instead, she exhaled slowly and said, "Show me."

Lucas studied her for a long moment as if making sure she wouldn't change her mind. He didn't rush her, didn't press, he just watched.

"Are you sure?" he asked, his voice steady, calm.

Amelia swallowed. She wasn't sure of anything.

But she wanted to be so she nodded.

Lucas reached for her hand slowly, like he was giving her a chance to pull away. She didn't.

"Come with me," he murmured.

He led her toward the bedroom. The door was already open, the space inside dimly lit with the soft glow of a lamp.

Once they stepped inside, Lucas turned to face her his grip on her hand never tightening, never demanding.

"I want to be very clear, Amelia," he said, his tone low and deliberate. "This is about trust, not control. You can stop at any time. You say the word, and we walk out of this room, no questions asked."

Her heart hammered against her ribs. This was different.

Ethan had never given her choices and never given her an out.

"What word?" she asked, her voice barely above a whisper.

Lucas's lips quirked slightly. "It can be anything. Something that wouldn't normally come up in conversation."

She thought for a moment. A word that meant safety.

"Lavender."

Lucas nodded once. "Good. If you say it, everything stops."

There was no hesitation. No testing. Just certainty.

"Now," he continued, stepping closer, "I'm going to ask you to do a few things, nothing you don't want to do. If anything makes you uncomfortable, let me know. If you want to stop, you stop. Understood?"

Amelia exhaled. "Understood."

Lucas reached up, his fingertips skimming along her jaw, before drifting down the curve of her neck and over her arm. When they brushed the inside of her wrist, her breath caught.

"Give me your hands," he murmured.

It wasn't a command. It was an invitation.

Her muscle memory trained to keep control, to hold herself tight and unreachable. But she had *called* him when she was afraid. She had come to *him* when she needed to feel safe.

So she offered him her hands.

Lucas took them slowly, his thumbs stroking lazy circles on the backs before guiding them behind her back. He didn't restrain her. Didn't force her into place. He just let her *feel* it, the surrender.

"Breathe," he said, his voice dark and grounding. "Relax your shoulders. You're not trapped. You're *giving* this to me."

She inhaled slow and trembling then let it out, a soft breath that melted down her spine.

He was right. She could move. She could walk away. But she didn't.

"Good," he whispered, the word brushing against her skin like silk. "Now, close your eyes."

Her pulse surged.

"Lucas..."

"Shhh." His tone was pure heat and restraint. "Just for a second. Feel it."

Feel what?

But her lashes fluttered shut anyway. And then every sense bloomed. The heat of his body in front of hers. The steady, anchored rhythm of his breath and the way his fingertips hovered just shy of touching her. Teasing the air between them.

Her skin buzzed, desperate and alive.

"Do you feel unsafe?" he asked.

"No," she breathed, instantly.

"Do you feel controlled?"

She paused, searching.

Her heart was racing, but she wasn't scared.

She wasn't powerless.

"No."

His voice lowered, wrapping around her like smoke.

"Do you feel taken care of?"

Her throat tightened, the truth rising so fast it nearly unmade her.

"...Yes."

Lucas released her hands.

She didn't move.

A low, pleased sound escaped him. Approval.

"You're doing well, Amelia."

Warmth spread through her chest, coiling down to places that had been locked tight for far too long.

Then his hand, brushing a strand of hair from her cheek, so gentle it made her ache.

"This," he murmured, voice like sin wrapped in silk, "this is what I meant. Control isn't a prison when you give it to someone who knows how to hold it."

Her breath hitched. "And do you?"

Lucas's gaze locked on hers, molten and unreadable.

"That's not for me to say," he said softly, darkly.

"That's for *you* to feel."

Silence stretched between them, thick with something unspoken.

Then, finally, Amelia whispered, "I think I want to try."

And for the first time, she meant it.

Amelia's heart was still racing.

She stood before Lucas, her hands tingling from where he

had just held them behind her. Her pulse was uneven, her body aware of him in a way it hadn't been before.

He hadn't forced her. He hadn't trapped her but he had taken her to the edge of something, and now she couldn't stop thinking about what it would feel like to fall.

Lucas observed her, his sharp blue gaze scanning her face like he was reading every thought, every hesitation she didn't even know she had.

"You did well, Amelia," he murmured, stepping closer.

She swallowed. "It felt… different than I expected."

"Different, how?"

She struggled to put it into words. "I thought I'd feel trapped. Like I was giving up a part of myself." Her fingers curled into her palms. "But I didn't. I felt… lighter."

Lucas's lips barely quirked. "Because you weren't holding everything together on your own for the first time."

The words hit deep, too deep. She sucked in a breath, looking away.

Lucas didn't let her retreat. He never did.

"Would you like to try something else?" he asked, his voice calm and patient. "Or do you need space?"

That was the difference. Ethan never gave her a choice. Lucas always did.

She hesitated just for a moment before whispering, "What do you want me to do?"

Lucas's expression darkened, not with cruelty, but with something more profound. Something primal.

"Kneel for me."

Her stomach clenched.

"Not because I tell you to," he continued, stepping closer. His fingers traced down her arm, barely touching. "But because I want you to feel what it's like to give yourself to me."

A shiver ran through her.

Kneeling. A position of surrender. Of vulnerability.

Amelia had spent so long fighting for control, gripping it like a lifeline. But Lucas wasn't asking her to give it up permanently. He wasn't demanding it.

He was asking her to trust him with it.

Her pulse thundered as she lowered herself to her knees.

It felt… strange at first. It was not humiliating, not weak just exposed. Her breath came fast as she stared at his shoes.

Lucas exhaled slowly like he'd been waiting for this.

"Look at me, Amelia."

She lifted her chin, her eyes locking with his.

Something flickered in his gaze. Pride. Possession. Desire.

"That's it," he murmured, brushing his fingers along her jaw. His touch was light, but it set her skin on fire.

"How does it feel?" he asked.

Amelia licked her lips, her throat tight. "I don't know."

Lucas's thumb traced the corner of her mouth.

"I think you do," he murmured.

The tension was thick now, wrapping around them like an unseen force. He wasn't touching her anywhere indecent, wasn't doing anything except looking at her like he could see straight through her.

And somehow, it was more intimate than anything she had ever known.

Her breath shuddered. "What happens now?"

Lucas's jaw flexed. He exhaled, and for a moment, she thought he would take it further.

But instead, he reached down and gently, so gently, slid his fingers through hers. He pulled her up, steadying her as she wobbled.

"Now," he murmured, his lips near her ear, "you go to bed."

Her stomach plummeted.

"What?"

Lucas smirked, brushing a strand of hair behind her ear. "You're not ready for what happens next, little one."

A flush spread through her chest, equal parts embarrassment and frustration.

"You think I can't handle it?" she whispered.

His gaze darkened. Pure heat. Pure control.

"I know you can't."

Her breath caught.

Lucas leaned in, his mouth a breath away from hers, so close, she could feel his heat and the control in his stillness.

"And when I do take you?" His voice was velvet and steel, wrapping around her like a promise. "You won't just handle it. You'll beg for it."

Heat surged through her, fierce and undeniable.

But Lucas stepped back before she could say a word and even process the sharp, aching need curling inside her.

"Goodnight, Amelia," he murmured.

Twenty-Two

Chapter 22

Amelia had barely slept.

She'd spent the night tangled in sheets and spiraling thoughts. The memory of being on her knees in front of him. The sharp focus of Lucas's gaze had settled over her like a command.

It hadn't been sex.

It had been surrender and it had wrecked her.

Just a taste. A flicker of something dark and consuming and then he'd left her there. Wanting. Needing. She hated him for that bur she also *ached* for him because of that.

By morning, the restless hunger in her chest had sharpened into resolve.

Lucas was waiting for her to come to him. Waiting for her to admit the truth.

But she was done waiting and done pretending she didn't crave what he offered.

Every step she took down the corridor to his office echoed like a promise.

When she knocked, she could hear him inside. The quiet shifting of papers, the soft clink of glass, the sound of his voice wrapping up a call.

Then silence.

She stepped inside.

Lucas looked up from behind his desk.

He saw it instantly. The heat in her cheeks. The way her fingers flexed restlessly at her sides and the tension humming just beneath her skin.

His eyes darkened subtle, but unmistakable.

"Amelia." His voice was smooth and controlled. Like he already knew why she was here.

She stepped forward, pulse hammering. "I want more."

Lucas tilted his head slightly, considering her. He didn't look surprised. If anything, he looked like he had been expecting this.

"More of what?" he asked, leaning back in his chair, fingers lacing together.

Amelia's breath quickened. He was making her say it. Good. She wanted to say it.

"What you did last night." Her voice was quiet but steady. "The way you......" She swallowed, gathering her courage. "The way you made me feel."

Lucas exhaled slowly, standing from his chair in one fluid motion. He walked around the desk, his movements measured and deliberate. When he stopped in front of her, he was close. So close she could feel his heat.

"And how did I make you feel, Amelia?"

She knew what he was doing, making her voice it and

making her own it.

"Safe," she admitted. "But also…" Her fingers curled at her sides. "Like I didn't have to be in control. Like I could let go."

Lucas's gaze flickered with something dangerous. Something knowing.

"You could." His voice was softer now, laced with something more profound, richer. "You still can."

A shiver ran down her spine. She wanted to.

"Show me," she whispered.

Lucas studied her for a long moment. Then, without a word, he reached out.

His fingers traced up her arm, slow and teasing, until they rested on the delicate column of her throat. He didn't squeeze or press, he just held her there, the warmth of his palm anchoring her in place.

"Breathe," he murmured.

She did. Shaky, uneven, but she did.

Lucas watched her closely, his thumb brushing against her pulse. "You don't know how beautiful you are when you surrender, do you?"

Her breath stuttered.

His other hand reached for her wrist, bringing it up between them. He turned it over, fingers grazing the sensitive skin of her inner wrist before guiding her hand behind her back.

"Stay like this," he instructed.

She obeyed.

It was small a simple act but the second her hands were behind her back, without him forcing them, without him holding them there a rush of heat pooled low in her stomach.

Lucas hummed in approval. "That's it. Feel that?"

She did.

He circled her slowly, his hand dragging lightly across her waist, her back and her hip. Never fully touching, just reminding her that he was there.

"Tell me what you feel."

"Exposed," she admitted, her voice barely above a whisper.

Lucas stopped in front of her again, his thumb brushing over her lips this time. Soft, teasing. Just a hint of dominance.

"Do you want me to stop?"

Amelia swallowed hard.

"No."

Lucas exhaled, slow and controlled.

There was tension in every line of his body, restraint pulled so tight it felt like it might snap.

"You're ready for more, aren't you?"

His voice was low, rough, dragging shivers down her spine.

He tilted her chin up, his fingers firmer now, holding her just enough to remind her who was leading this yet still letting her choose.

"Then beg me for it."

Her breath caught, eyes wide, heart crashing in her chest.

Beg?

Ethan had demanded. Taken. Broken.

But Lucas… Lucas wanted her *to give.*

To *want.*

And God, she did.

She hesitated, every nerve in her body screaming. Her hands stayed curled behind her back, her skin flushed, throat dry.

But her body already knew what her pride was too afraid to say.

"Please."

Just one word.

Soft.

Vulnerable.

Brave.

It felt foreign on her tongue, but right *so right.*

Lucas's breath left him in a low, approving exhale, and the look in his eyes turned molten.

"Good girl," he murmured and the praise scorched her to her core.

His mouth met hers, and everything unraveled.

It wasn't soft. It wasn't tentative. It was control and fire and everything she had been waiting for.

Lucas's hands stayed where they were one cupping her jaw, the other grazing the back of her neck, holding her in place but not caging her in. Just guiding.

And for the first time in her life, Amelia let him.

She let go.

Lucas broke the kiss first, his forehead brushing against hers, his breath warm against her lips.

"You want more," he murmured.

She did.

"Then kneel."

Her pulse jumped.

She knew she could say no. She knew she could walk away. But she didn't want to.

Slowly, deliberately, she sank to her knees.

The air shifted.

Lucas stood over her, watching her with an unreadable gaze, something dark and dangerously patient.

"Look at me."

Amelia lifted her chin, her eyes locking onto his.

Lucas made a low, approving sound.

"That's it." His fingers traced the curve of her jaw, slow and teasing. "Do you feel trapped?"

She swallowed. "No."

"Do you feel powerless?"

"No."

Lucas's fingers drifted down her arm, slow and deliberate, until they brushed the sensitive inside of her wrist. He guided her hands behind her again but this time, he didn't have to say a word.

Amelia moved willingly.

The moment her hands clasped behind her back, something deep inside her shifted.

Lucas saw it. Felt it. His smirk curled, dark and knowing.

"There it is." A shiver raced down her spine.

"Do you know what that feeling is?" he asked, his voice thick with control and promise.

She swallowed hard. "Tell me."

He leaned in, his lips a breath from hers, and when he spoke, it wasn't a whisper it was a *confession*.

"That's trust, little one."

The air fled her lungs.

"You've been holding on so tightly, for so long, you've forgotten what it feels like to let go. To let *someone else* carry the weight for a while."

She should've pulled away.

Should've protected herself but instead, all she could feel was *how right it was.*

"You think you're ready for more?"

Her breath hitched. "Yes."

He smiled.

Slow. Dangerous. Certain.

"No."

The word hit like a spark to dry leaves.

No?

Heat coiled tighter in her stomach, her frustration igniting. "Then make me ready."

Lucas's grip on her jaw tightened not cruel, just enough to make her still. To make her *feel.*

"Patience," he murmured, voice like a dark promise.

Her pulse jumped.

Her body betrayed her, a shiver running through her.

Lucas pulled back, his smirk lazy, confident.

"Go home, little one. And next time you come to me… be ready."

Chapter 23

The cafe was warm, filled with the scent of fresh bread and espresso, the afternoon rush buzzing softly around them. Amelia stirred her iced coffee absentmindedly, a small smile playing on her lips as Sophia studied her from across the table.

"Okay, spill," Sophia finally said, setting her fork down with a dramatic sigh. "What the hell is going on with you?"

Amelia blinked, snapping out of her daze. "What?"

Sophia leaned in, narrowing her eyes. "You're… glowing. Like suspiciously glowing. You look like someone who has been thoroughly…."

"Sophia!" Amelia hissed, cheeks flaming.

Sophia smirked, popping a fry into her mouth. "Oh my God, I knew it. It's Lucas, isn't it?"

Amelia bit her lip, but she couldn't help the way her smile deepened.

"I don't know what you're talking about," she murmured,

lifting her drink to her lips.

Sophia scoffed. "Please. You were a mess just a week ago, and now you're sitting here all dreamy-eyed, playing with your damn straw like some love-struck teenager." She leaned forward, eyes sparkling. "So? How is it? And don't you dare say 'it's complicated' because I will throw this fry at your head".

Amelia exhaled a small laugh, shaking her head. She had missed this, missed feeling light and missed feeling like herself.

"It's… different," she admitted. "With Lucas, I mean."

Sophia arched a brow. "Different, how?"

Amelia hesitated, choosing her words carefully.

"He makes me feel safe," she said softly. "But not just that. He makes me feel… free."

Sophia's playful expression softened. "That's a big deal, Ames."

"I know."

"And you trust him?"

Amelia didn't even have to think about it. "Yes."

Sophia studied her for a moment before sighing dramatically. "Well, damn. If I had known all it took to get you happy again was a brooding, possessive billionaire, I would have found you one myself."

Amelia laughed, shaking her head. "It's not like that."

"No?" Sophia smirked. "So he's not the type to ruin some poor waiter's life for looking at you too long?"

Amelia opened her mouth to deny it, then thought about how Lucas watched her, owned her with his gaze alone and told her she was his.

…Okay, maybe Sophia wasn't completely wrong.

"Shut up," Amelia muttered, picking up a fry.

Sophia grinned, but then her expression sobered slightly.

"But seriously, Ames… you deserve to be happy. And if Lucas makes you happy, I'm not going to give you shit about it."

Amelia smiled, warmth spreading in her chest.

"Thank you."

Sophia took a sip of her drink and then sighed. "That being said… we still need to talk about Ethan."

Amelia tensed. The warmth that had settled over her quickly faded, her fingers tightening around her fork.

"Sophia,"

"No, listen," Sophia interrupted, her voice more serious now. "I get that Lucas is handling things, and I know you trust him. But Ames, this is your life we're talking about. A man found you, stalked you, and left a note saying you belonged to him. And instead of going to the police, you're letting Lucas take care of it?"

Amelia looked down, her stomach twisting.

"It's not that simple."

"It kind of is," Sophia pressed. "I love you and know you feel safer with Lucas involved. But Lucas is not law enforcement. He can't make this go away legally."

Amelia exhaled, staring at her half-eaten lunch. "The police didn't do anything before, Soph."

Sophia's expression softened. "I know. And that was bullshit. But this is different. You have proof. You have a letter. If Ethan is still watching you, he will slip up, and the police need to be the ones dealing with him, not just Lucas."

Amelia swallowed, shaking her head. "Lucas won't let anything happen to me."

Sophia sighed, leaning forward. "I know. But you can't just disappear into his world and pretend the real one doesn't exist. You have to protect yourself, too."

That hit deeper than Amelia wanted to admit.

Because a part of her wants to disappear into Lucas's world, she doesn't have to make decisions; she can let him handle everything, and she doesn't have to be afraid.

But was that the right way to deal with this?

Sophia reached across the table, squeezing her hand. "Just promise me you'll think about it, okay?"

Amelia hesitated, then nodded. "Okay."

But even as she said it, she wasn't sure if she meant it.

Deep down, she knew Lucas was already handling it.

And somehow, that made her feel safer than the police ever had.

Amelia barely registered the elevator ride up.

Her body was humming from lunch with Sophia, the ache of unpacking Ethan, the thrill and terror of saying Lucas's name out loud.

She was caught in the middle. Logic pulling her one way, instinct pulling her another.

One voice told her to be smart. Call the police. File the report. Take control.

The other, quieter but stronger, whispered that maybe she already *was* taking control.

Because this, coming here this was *her* choice.

Letting Lucas protect her and letting him take control in a way that didn't choke her, but let her *breathe*.

She wasn't afraid. Not of him. She just needed *more*.

Her heart thundered, loud and unrelenting. She clenched her fists, released them. Again. Again. Trying to steady the tremble in her fingers.

Her mouth was dry. Her knees already unsteady.

She stepped into the penthouse.

Lucas was by the windows, city lights stretching out behind him like a kingdom he owned without trying. His phone was in one hand, jacket draped over the back of a chair.

Then he looked up.

The second his eyes met hers, his gaze darkened like he could see right through her skin, straight into her pulse.

"What is it?" His voice was low, steady. He knew her well enough now to see the shift in her.

Amelia hesitated but only for a second.

"Tell me to kneel."

Lucas stilled.

His entire body went rigid, his eyes sharpening like a predator who had just found its prey.

"Say that again."

She swallowed, heat pooling in her stomach at how his voice changed low and controlled.

"I want you to tell me to kneel," she repeated, softer this time, pulse-pounding.

Lucas exhaled slowly, setting his phone down. He was silent as he walked toward her, his movements slow and calculated. The air between them grew thick, charged with something she wasn't sure she could handle but desperately wanted to try.

He stopped in front of her, tilting his head slightly.

"Did Sophia put doubts in your head?"

Amelia inhaled sharply.

Of course, he could see through her. Of course, he knew exactly what had led her here, standing before him asking for something she didn't fully understand yet.

"She thinks I should go to the police," she admitted. "That I shouldn't just let you handle it."

Lucas let out a soft, dark hum as if he'd been expecting that.

"And what do you think?"

She licked her lips, searching for an answer, but the only thing she could think about was how badly she wanted him to touch her.

"I think…" She swallowed, her voice uneven. "I think I don't want to talk about Ethan anymore."

Lucas exhaled, his hand lifting but not to touch her. Not yet.

"And you think kneeling for me will take that away?"

"I think it will make me feel something else," she whispered.

For a second, Lucas just watched her. And then, finally, "Kneel."

The command slammed into her like a physical force.

Her knees hit the floor before she fully registered moving, her body surrendering even as her mind screamed doubts. *That this was dangerous. That she shouldn't give herself away like this.*

But the louder voice, was the one that whispered:

You're safe. You're his. And you're still free.

Lucas stepped closer, towering over her.

"Look at me."

She lifted her chin, meeting his gaze.

The approval there wrecked her more than any touch could.

"You want to give me control, Amelia?"

His voice was low, steady, a dark promise.

"Then you have to say it."

Her whole body trembled, pulse hammering, heart splitting wide open.

"I want you to take it," her voice breaking with the force of it.

Something in Lucas's eyes flared, something dark and desperate.

He leaned in, brushing his mouth across hers in a soft, devastating kiss.

And then the world tilted.

He stripped her slow, his touch reverent and ruthless at once, pulling down her bodysuit inch by agonizing inch.

Her skin pebbled under his hands, nerves screaming with every whisper of contact.

And she had never felt more alive. He knelt, his hands gripping her thighs, "You're mine tonight," he said, his voice low and commanding. Then he stood, taking her hand and leading her down the hall, each step deepening the anticipation that pulsed between them. She didn't ask where they were going. She already knew.

Inside the playroom, Lucas's smile was dark and deliberate as he moved to the restraints mounted on the wall. He turned back to her, his eyes burning with intention.

With slow, practiced ease, he secured her wrists and pulled them above her head, locking them into place.

She was now completely at his mercy.

Lucas stepped back, his eyes never leaving hers. He reached to the drawers, pulling out a flogger. The leather tails snapped against his palm, the sound echoing in the room. Amelia's eyes widened, her breath catching in her throat.

"Ready?" Lucas asked, his voice a low growl.

Amelia nodded, her body tense with anticipation. Lucas stepped forward, the flogger rising like a promise in his hand. The first kiss of leather across her back made her gasp, a bloom of pain and pleasure that left her shuddering.

Every strike painted another piece of her freedom onto her skin.

She cried out, sobbed, broke apart and yet she craved more.

Because with every mark, every kiss, every brutal, perfect touch Lucas wasn't just breaking her. He was putting her back together.

He didn't speak. He didn't need to. The rhythm of the flogger said everything.

Each snap of leather left another mark, each one louder, deeper. Proof of how far she'd let herself go. Of how far he'd taken her.

Her body was a canvas now, painted in heat and pain and pleasure, her moans echoing like music off the walls.

Then, silence.

Lucas stepped back, his breath uneven.

She barely had time to catch hers before the soft brush of leather ghosted across her face.

A blindfold.

Darkness claimed her as he tied it in place once sight was gone, her breath got shallow and every other sense stretched thin and waiting.

"You're doing so well for me," he murmured, his hand sliding down her side.

He didn't need to ask if she was okay. He could feel it in the way her body moved, still reaching for him, still begging without words.

Her skin buzzed with awareness, her breath shallow, body raw with anticipation.

Lucas traced his fingers down her side, a whisper-soft touch that only made her crave more. When he reached her thigh, he brought the paddle down again, sharp and precise. Another mark bloomed across her skin, and she shivered.

Each strike was a command. A promise. A test she was desperate to pass.

And she gave in to every one.

He moved higher, dragging the leather across her stomach before letting it fall again. Amelia gasped, her muscles tightening.

Lucas watched her, she was close. He could feel it in the way her body tensed, in the way she gripped the restraints like they were the only thing tethering her to the earth.

He moved to her breasts, the paddle striking sharp and sure. She cried out not just from the sting, but from the way it pulled something deeper out of her. Every sound, every mark, felt like proof that she could take it. That she wasn't broken. Not anymore.

Then his mouth replaced the leather.

His lips closed around one peak, sucking until it throbbed. Teeth followed grazing and teasing . She arched into him. He moved to the other, just as relentless. She whimpered, hips shifting, desperate for more contact.

Lucas pulled back only to capture her mouth in a kiss that was more possession than affection. His tongue invaded hers, hard, fast and rough, a mirror of the way she needed him inside her.

By the time he stepped back, she was trembling, wet, open and aching.

He spread her legs, hands firm on her thighs, his gaze drinking her in. Her arousal glistened between her thighs.

Then Lucas lowered his head, deliberate and unhurried.

His tongue met her clit in one slow, devastating stroke.

Amelia cried out, the sound torn from her throat, her hips instinctively bucking toward him, desperate and lost.

He didn't stop.

Two fingers slipped inside her deep, purposeful and relentless in rhythm.

There was no mercy in his touch, only precision.

She was unraveling beneath him, trembling with every breath, every thrust, every flick of his tongue.

"You're close," he murmured, voice thick with restraint. "I can feel it."

She whimpered, fingers clenching, her body begging.

"Come for me."

It wasn't a request.

It was an order rough, raw and laced with authority she'd given him freely.

Her release slammed into her like a storm, ripping through her with no room to brace.

She shattered spine arching, mouth open in a silent cry every piece of her coming undone in his hands.

And through the chaos of it, she felt the one thing she hadn't expected to find in surrender.

Freedom.

Lucas didn't let up. His fingers moved with cruel expertise, dragging her higher, pushing her past what she thought she could take, again and again. Every touch sent another jolt of heat spiraling through her, her body already aching from the intensity but craving more.

He shifted between her legs, his cock hard and pulsing as he aligned with her. One hand gripped her hip, steady and grounding. When Lucas finally entered her, her body welcomed him without hesitation, slick and open and desperate.

His movements were deep and relentless, every thrust shoving her closer to the edge of a cliff she couldn't stop herself from falling over.

Lucas began to move, deep and deliberate, his hips rolling against hers in a rhythm that made her lose all sense of time, of thought, of everything except *him*.

Amelia moaned, her body arching into his touch. Every thrust pushed her further into surrender, into that intoxicating space where she belonged only to him.

Lucas leaned down, his mouth claiming hers in a fierce, possessive kiss. His teeth scraped her lower lip before biting down, sharp enough to make her gasp.

He growled against her mouth, his hips driving harder, deeper, as if trying to imprint himself inside her.

His hand slid between them, fingers finding her clit without hesitation. The rough, unrelenting pressure made her cry out and she shattered around him, screaming his name, her whole body convulsing with the force of it.

Tears streamed down her cheeks as she came again. The release pure, raw, and soul-breaking.

And Lucas felt it, felt her fall apart around him, felt her trust, her surrender, her fire and it undid him.

Lucas's control shattered.

A guttural sound tore from his throat as he thrust into her one final time, his body locking tight, his release spilling into her in hot, broken pulses.

His breath was ragged against her neck not just from pleasure, but from the unbearable weight of everything she had just given him.

He collapsed over her, a harsh, shaking wreck of a man,

pressing his forehead to her shoulder like he needed her just to stay upright.

For a moment, he didnt move, didn't speak.

It was just them raw, ruined, and more alive than either of them had ever been.

Then he rolled to the side, still watching her, a satisfied smirk curling at his lips.

"You're mine," he said, voice low and rough.

"Completely. Utterly. Mine."

Amelia met his gaze, her body still trembling, her chest rising and falling with every sharp breath.

And she nodded. Because it was true. She *was* his. And in this moment, in this surrender, she had never felt more free.

Lucas eased her down onto the nearby chaise, grabbing a blanket from the corner and wrapping it around her shoulders. She was still trembling, aftershocks from everything he'd taken and everything she'd given.

He knelt in front of her, his hand gently stroking her thigh. "Color?"

She blinked, and then whispered, "Green."

His smile was small, but it lit something inside her. "Good girl."

Her eyes burned. Maybe from the pain. Maybe from the release. Maybe because in this moment, she didn't feel broken at all.

Twenty-Four

Chapter 24

Amelia woke slowly, her body heavy with warmth and exhaustion.

For a moment, she lingered in that fragile place between sleep and reality, cocooned in silence.

The weight of the blanket and the firmer, grounding weight of an arm draped across her waist.

Lucas.

And then the memories surged hot, sharp, electric.

The way he touched her. The way he *owned* every inch of her. The way she had given herself over, piece by piece, until there was nothing left but *want.*

Her throat tightened. Because now that the storm had passed, now that her body was no longer trembling with release fear crept in.

Not of him but of herself.

What did I do?

She should feel strong. Liberated. Empowered.

But instead, the voice inside her began to whisper.

You gave too much.

You let go.

You're just like before. Weak.

Amelia squeezed her eyes shut, fighting it back. *No. No, not this time.*

The bed shifted. Then Lucas leaned in, slow and sure, pressing a kiss to the back of her shoulder.

Not demanding.

Not possessive.

Just... *gentle.*

It melted something inside her.

A reminder. This wasn't like before. She hadn't been broken. She'd *chosen* this. And she was still whole.

"Good morning," he murmured against her skin.

She swallowed hard, blinking at the muted light spilling through the floor-to-ceiling windows.

"Morning," she rasped, her voice scratchy and uneven.

Lucas shifted, rising onto one elbow to look down at her.

His hand brushed a piece of hair away from her face, his fingers lingering at her temple.

"You're quiet," he said simply.

Not demanding. Not accusing. Just... noticing.

Amelia forced a smile that she knew didn't reach her eyes.

"Just tired," she lied.

Lucas didn't call her on it.

He just hummed softly, his thumb stroking a slow, grounding circle against her hip under the covers. And somehow, that broke her even more.

She blinked hard against the sudden sting in her eyes.

Lucas's gaze sharpened immediately.

Still, he didn't push. Instead, he shifted closer, tucking her against his chest like he knew she needed the contact more than the conversation.

Amelia let herself be held. Let herself breathe him in clean soap, expensive cologne, something uniquely him.

Let herself believe, just for this fragile, terrifying morning, that maybe she hadn't ruined anything.

That maybe she could be this girl, this woman, who could be touched and broken and put back together again.

Lucas pressed another kiss to her hair, silent and steady, like a vow he didn't have the words for yet.

Neither of them spoke.

They didn't need to.

Twenty-Five

Chapter 25

The city lights reflected long on the pavement as she stepped onto the quiet sidewalk.

She checked her phone.

Lucas: On a call. Be home soon.

Warmth curled in her chest. He always checked in and always knew where she was. I made her feel so safe. That was until she saw the car.

A black sedan. Parked across the street. Engine idling.

She slowed her steps.

The crack in the driver's side window was just wide enough to show the shadow of a man inside.

Not just any man.

Ethan.

Panic slammed into her chest.

No, no, no.

He wasn't supposed to be here.

He wasn't supposed to find her.

But there he was watching. Waiting.

Amelia's breath hitched, sharp and shallow.

The street around her felt wrong too quiet, too still, like the city had turned its back just for him.

She forced herself to keep moving.

Don't look.

Don't stop.

Her fingers tightened around her phone like a lifeline.

Do I run? Do I call Lucas?

Then she heard it.

The slow, deliberate creak of the car door swinging open.

"*Amelia.*"

Her blood turned to ice.

That voice.

Smooth. Charming.

Deceptive.

It was the voice he used before his hands turned cruel. Before the apologies turned into bruises.

She kept walking. Her steps getting faster and faster.

"Don't be rude," he called after her.

She heard his footsteps, calculated and calm, closing the distance like a man who had all the time in the world.

She glanced around.

The sidewalk was empty. No one to call out to. No one to see. And he knew *it.*

Her fingers shook as she pulled out her phone, dialing Lucas's number without thinking.

Ethan laughed. "Oh, come on. You don't need him."

Her stomach twisted. He knew.

Before Lucas even answered, Ethan spoke again, his voice

colder this time.

"You really think he can keep you safe forever?"

She felt it then, the moment he dropped the act.

The threat in his voice. The promise. Her blood turned to ice.

Lucas's voice came through the line. "Amelia?"

She turned the corner, breaking into a full run, dropping her phone on the pavement.

She didn't care if it looked ridiculous, didn't care that Ethan's laughter followed her.

She just knew she needed to get home.

To Lucas.

She sank into the wall outside the elevator, her lungs burning, her heart racing like it might crack her ribs. She'd seen that look in Ethan's eyes before. And she knew what it meant.

It wasn't over.

Amelia barely made it through the door before Lucas was on her.

The second she stepped inside the penthouse, he was there his hands gripping her arms as his eyes raked over her.

"What happened?" His voice was low and lethal, his entire body vibrating with restrained fury.

Her breath was still uneven, her pulse racing as she looked up at him.

"He was there," she whispered. "Outside my work. Watching me."

Lucas's jaw clenched, his grip tightening just enough for her to feel the controlled violence in him.

"Did he touch you?"

"No," she said quickly, shaking her head. "But he spoke

to me. He," She swallowed hard. "He said I couldn't be safe forever."

Lucas went entirely still.

A dangerous, frightening stillness.

Amelia had never seen him like this, his usual composure cracked, the mask slipping just enough for her to see the storm brewing underneath.

He released her arms but only to cup her face, tilting her chin up and forcing her to look at him.

"You listen to me, Amelia," he said, his voice like steel. "Ethan just made the biggest mistake of his life."

A shiver ran down her spine.

"Lucas……"

"No," he cut her off, his dominance wrapping around her like a cage. "I let him play his little games. I let him watch from a distance. That ends tonight."

She saw it then the shift from protector to predator.

"What are you going to do?" she whispered.

Lucas's thumb brushed her jaw, his touch almost gentle, at odds with the fury in his eyes.

"Whatever it takes."

A breath lodged in her throat.

"You're mine, Amelia," he murmured. "And he's about to learn exactly what that means."

Before she could respond, he was already moving. Lucas didn't waste time pulling out his phone.

It rang once before a voice answered.

"Graves."

"I need you to find someone."

A low chuckle came through the line. "It's been a while since you asked me to hunt down a ghost."

Lucas didn't smile. Didn't acknowledge the joke.

"His name is Ethan Walker," he said smoothly, deadly calm. "I want to know where he sleeps, where he works, who he talks to. Every move he makes."

The other end of the line went silent for a second.

"Understood. Does this ghost need to disappear?"

Lucas's grip on his phone tightened.

"Not yet."

A slow exhale. "That means you want leverage first. Good. I like it when you think like this."

Lucas's jaw flexed. He wasn't in the mood for games.

"How long?"

"Depends. Suppose he's been careful, maybe a few days. If he's sloppy, I'll have something for you by morning."

Lucas exhaled slowly, his fingers drumming against the desk. "I want it clean. No mistakes."

"It's always clean."

Lucas ended the call without another word.

He set his phone down, rolling his shoulders back, his mind calculating the next steps.

He could have ended Ethan tonight. One phone call, one word, and the problem would disapear. But Amelia wasn't ready for that. Not yet.

So he would do this her way for now.

But Ethan was already a dead man walking. He didn't know it yet.

Twenty-Six

Chapter 26

Amelia lay curled against Lucas's chest, her ear pressed to the quiet, grounding rhythm of his heartbeat.

His arm rested heavy around her shoulders, anchoring her there, while his fingers traced slow, absent circles down her spine, the weight of his touch threading comfort through her bones

The bedroom was dim, lit only by the faint glow of the city beyond the windows.

For the first time in a long time, she felt… safe.

Safe in a way she hadn't thought she could ever feel again.

Lucas murmured something against her hair, something soft, unintelligible but she was already slipping under, the rhythm of his heartbeat a slow drum against her ear.

She drifted into sleep tucked into him, surrounded by warmth, by strength, by the quiet certainty of him.

The darkness came quietly.

A shift in the air.

The slow bleed of warmth into cold.

The sheets roughening beneath her skin.

She tried to move, but her body felt heavy, uncooperative.

And then,

The door slammed.

A voice she hadn't heard in months rasped against her mind, low and cruel.

You thought you could leave me?

You think he can keep you safe?

Panic clawed up her throat.

Invisible hands clamped around her wrists, yanking her upright.

She kicked and struggled, but it was like fighting smoke.

You're mine, Amelia.

You'll always be mine.

The darkness pressed harder, tighter, suffocating.

She tried to scream, but no sound escaped.

"Amelia."

A voice, low, real, cutting through the terror.

"Amelia, wake up. It's okay. I've got you."

Strong hands gripped her shoulders, not rough, not restraining just steady and grounding.

She thrashed blindly, a broken sob tearing from her lips.

"Shh. Look at me, little one. Open your eyes. You're safe."

Lucas's voice, his hands and his scent bringing her back to reality.

She gasped awake, her body shaking violently.

Her fists swung out instinctively, but Lucas caught her wrists gently, pulling them to his chest.

"It's me. Just me. You're safe."

Amelia blinked wildly, heart hammering, the bedroom coming into focus through the haze of panic.

Lucas was sitting against the headboard, his body wrapped around hers, holding her gently but firmly against him.

"You're okay," he said again, his voice a low, steady rumble. "You're here. You're with me."

She pressed her forehead to his chest, gulping in air that felt too thick, too heavy.

Lucas shifted, adjusting her effortlessly into his lap, cradling her against him like she weighed nothing.

His hand stroked her hair, slow and steady, over and over again.

"I'm right here. I'm not going anywhere."

Tears flooded her eyes.

She hated this, hated feeling weak, hated the way the past could still crawl under her skin and rip her open without warning.

Lucas tightened his hold when she started to pull away.

"No," he murmured against her hair. "Don't run from me."

The broken sound that escaped her throat wasn't a sob, it was a release.

A surrender.

Her body slumped fully against his, every last thread of resistance unraveling.

Lucas rocked her slowly, the motion instinctive, protective.

"You survived him, Amelia," he whispered. "You survived. And you're safe now. I swear it."

The panic ebbed slowly, leaving only exhaustion and the tremor of aftershocks in its place.

Lucas didn't rush her.

He didn't speak again. He just stayed with her. Until her

breathing evened out. Until the tremors stopped. Until she was weightless again in his arms.

When he finally eased them back down onto the bed, he kept her tucked tightly against his chest.

His lips brushed her forehead in a kiss so soft she almost didn't feel it.

Almost.

"Sleep," he whispered.

"I'm here. I'm always here."

And this time, when Amelia slipped back into sleep, she did it knowing that if the darkness came again, she wouldn't have to face it alone.

Twenty-Seven

Chapter 27

Amelia woke slowly, tucked against Lucas's side, the soft early morning light spilling across the bed.

For a moment, she stayed still, listening to the steady thud of his heartbeat beneath her ear, letting the rhythm calm her scattered nerves.

The nightmare felt distant now. A shadow that had retreated in the face of the man wrapped around her like armor.

Lucas's fingers were stroking her hair lazily, as if he hadn't slept at all, as if keeping her tethered to him was more important than anything else.

"You're awake," he murmured.

She nodded against his chest. Neither of them moved for a long minute.

Finally, Lucas shifted carefully, brushing his lips against her forehead.

"I'll make coffee," he said, like it was a promise, like it was the first step in stitching her back together.

Amelia let him go reluctantly, her body already missing the heat of him the moment he moved away.

She pulled the blanket tighter around herself, watching as Lucas padded into the kitchen.

He made coffee like it was second nature, like taking care of her was something he didn't even have to think about.

When he returned, he handed her a mug and climbed back into bed beside her.

Amelia cradled the warmth between her hands, breathing in the rich scent, grounding herself.

"Whatever you need today," he said quietly, his gaze steady, "you have it."

Tears prickled behind her eyes again, but she blinked them away.

She didn't need to cry anymore.

She just needed this.

This man.

This moment.

This peace.

For a few minutes longer, she allowed herself to believe she could carry it with her,

even after she walked out the door. Even after the real world crept back in.

The moment Amelia had gotten to work that morning, her breath stuttered, sharp, shallow, useless.

She tried to steady herself, pressing a hand to her stomach, whispering the mantra she'd been clinging to since the night before: *You're safe now. Lucas is handling it. You're safe.*

But her body didn't believe it.

Ethan had been there.

Watching. Waiting. Smiling like he already knew how the story ended..

The elevator doors opened with a soft ding, and she stepped out into the lobby like a woman walking into a battlefield. Every sound was too loud. Every face a threat.

She made it through the day, somehow. Answered emails. Attended meetings. Smiled when she was supposed to. But inside, everything screamed.

Her heart never stopped racing.

She jumped every time the door opened.

She glanced out the window too many times to count, convinced she'd see that black sedan waiting across the street.

By five o'clock, she was raw. Empty. Worn down by the weight of holding herself together.

She stepped out of the building, heart pounding, eyes scanning instinctively. The sidewalk blurred around her, commuters, honking horns, the rush of wind but none of it mattered.

She was bracing for him.

For Ethan.

For that same sick smile. That same stillness before he lunged.

But what she saw instead made her legs nearly buckle.

Lucas leaning against his car like a storm in a suit, eyes locked on hers the second she stepped out.

Her breath hitched, not from fear this time but relief.

The kind that cracks you wide open because you didn't realize how tightly you'd been holding yourself together.

She walked straight toward him, not trusting her voice. Not trusting the tears that suddenly pricked her eyes.

Lucas opened the passenger door for her without a word. Just held it, watching her, reading everything she couldn't say.

And when she slipped inside, the door closing behind her like a seal, it hit her,

She was safe. For now.

Finally, his voice cut through the quiet as he sat beside her, low and controlled. "Say the word, and he disappears."

Her head snapped toward him. "Lucas,"

"I mean it." His fingers tapped once against the steering wheel, casually, as if he wasn't making a promise soaked in quiet violence.

A shiver ran down her spine. Not from fear. From something else.

She exhaled, shaking her head. "That's not how this works."

Lucas hummed a noncommittal sound. "No, sweetheart. That's not how you work." His gaze flicked toward her, unreadable. "But me? I don't play by the same rules."

Her stomach clenched. He wasn't bluffing.

Lucas was the type of man who could make Ethan disappear,and never lose a single hour of sleep over it.

The realization should have terrified her.

Instead, it made her feel safe.

Chapter 28

Amelia sat curled on the couch, legs tucked beneath her, Lucas's hoodie swallowed around her like armor.

It smelled like him leather, cedar and something grounding. Something safe.

But no matter how tightly she wrapped it around herself, the hum of anxiety still clung to her skin, quiet but constant. Like her body hadn't gotten the message that the danger had passed. Lucas entered the room, eyes finding hers immediately.

"You need a change of scenery," he said simply, like it was already decided.

Amelia blinked. "What do you mean?"

He stepped closer, crouching in front of her. "You've been holding your breath since yesterday." His fingers brushed along her knee soft, grounding. "Let me take you out. Somewhere quiet. Somewhere that's just us."

She hesitated. Her body was still wound too tight, her heart not quite ready to trust the stillness.

But then he said, "Wear that black dress you like. I'll handle the rest."

And somehow, just like that, the decision felt easy.

The restaurant glowed with soft candlelight, shadows stretching long across crisp white linen. Jazz curled through the air but the silence between them was heavier than the music.

Lucas hadn't touched his food. His drink sat untouched. His eyes hadn't left her once.

Amelia sat across from him, shoulders tight, hands wrapped around her wine glass like she might shatter without it. She hadn't said much since.

There was something hollow in her eyes something broken.

She looked like she was still trying to climb out of whatever had pulled her under.

Lucas leaned in, the candlelight catching the sharp angles of his face. His fingers toyed with the rim of his glass, slow and deliberate, but his eyes stayed locked on hers.

"I want to take you somewhere," he said, his voice like aged whiskey warm, dark, and far too smooth.

Amelia tilted her head, drawn in despite herself.

"Somewhere?"

The word slipped out softer than she meant, wrapped in breathless curiosity.

His mouth curved into that sinfully calm smirk that always made her knees weak.

"Yes. Somewhere that'll leave a mark. Something you won't forget."

Then his hand moved. Just a whisper of touch. The backs of his fingers grazed hers, and it was enough to send a shiver straight through her spine.

"I think you'll like it," he murmured, voice threaded with quiet command and something that sounded dangerously close to desire.

She didn't look away. Her heart pounded. Her body leaned into the tension tightening between them.

"Tell me more," she breathed, barely holding her voice steady.

Lucas studied her for a moment, his expression unreadable yet intoxicating. Then, he took a slow sip of his wine, savoring the taste before setting the glass down with deliberate ease. "Have you ever been to a place where desire is felt and indulged? Where fantasies aren't whispered in the dark but lived?"

Heat pooled low in her belly. "A sex club?" she asked, barely above a whisper.

He didn't flinch, didn't hesitate. He nodded. "Yes."

Her breath came faster now, anticipation mixing with nerves. "And you want to take me there?"

Lucas leaned in, his fingers tracing slow, lazy circles on her wrist. His touch was warm, deliberate. "Only if you want to go. No pressure, no expectations. Just an experience, a world of pleasure at your fingertips." His voice was silk and sin, coaxing her closer, making her want to lean into him, into the possibilities he was offering. "Say the word, and I'll show you things you've only dreamed of."

She swallowed hard, feeling the electric pulse between them. She had always been drawn to the unknown, to the edge of surrender where curiosity met need. And Lucas... Lucas was offering her a doorway into something thrilling, something forbidden.

She let her fingers slide along him. "What happens there?" she asked, voice husky.

His thumb brushed the inside of her wrist, setting off a flutter low in her stomach. "Anything you want," he promised. "You can watch, you can explore, you can feel. It's a place where pleasure is sacred, where every desire is honored."

Her lips parted, her breath coming uneven. The way he spoke, the way he touched her, it was intoxicating. Dangerous in the most alluring way. She felt her heart hammering against her ribs as a slow heat unfurled in her core.

"When?" she finally breathed, her resolve melting away under the weight of her hunger.

His smirk deepened, his fingers tightening ever so slightly around hers. "Friday night. Wear something that makes you feel powerful." His gaze dropped to her lips before lifting back to her eyes. "And trust me."

A slow smile played on her lips as she let the idea settle in. Excitement warred with nerves, but one thing was sure. Lucas had unlocked a hunger inside her she never knew she had.

The next few days were a blur of anticipation and uncertainty. She felt the pulse of excitement thrumming through her veins, an intoxicating rush that had her restless at night and distracted during the day. The thought of Friday, of stepping into that world with Lucas, sent shivers of thrill and trepidation down her spine.

Yet, there was a shadow she couldn't shake.

Ethan.

She hadn't seen him in weeks, but the feeling of being watched still lingered in the corners of her mind. Was he still out there? Waiting, watching? She tried to push the thought away and drown herself in the excitement of what was to come, but the anxiety gnawed at her edges.

Her phone buzzed, pulling her from her thoughts,a message from Lucas.

Counting down the days?

She smiled, fingers hovering over the keyboard before typing back.

You have no idea.

As Friday crept closer, Amelia found herself replaying that night with Lucas again and again. His voice, his touch, the way his words wrapped around her like a promise.

Pleasure. Power. Something deeper. Something real.

But late at night, when the world went still and shadows crept across her walls, her mind always drifted back to *him.*

Ethan.

Desperate for a distraction, Amelia messaged the one person who could pull her out of her spiral.

Sophia.

If anyone could help her find the perfect outfit and maybe talk her down from the emotional ledge it was her.

They met at their usual café, the one with the lopsided chairs and lattes big enough to swim in. The smell of cinnamon and espresso filled the air, familiar and comforting.

"You look like you're about to burst,"Sophia teased, stirring her coffee. "Spill. What's got you so wound up?"

She hesitated for a moment before exhaling. "Lucas invited me somewhere Friday night. Somewhere… different."

Sophia leaned in, intrigued. "Different, how?"

She bit her lip, the words hanging heavy before she finally admitted, "A sex club."

Sophia's eyes widened before a slow, knowing smile spread

across her lips. "Oh, this just got interesting. And you're going, obviously?"

She nodded, her nerves and excitement warring. "But I need something to wear. Something powerful."

"Say no more." Sophia grinned. "Shopping spree it is."

The next few hours were a whirlwind of fabric, lace, and indulgence. Sophia pulled her through boutique after boutique, rejecting anything that didn't scream confidence. They laughed, debated over lingerie sets, and even sipped champagne in a high-end store as they sorted options.

"This," Sophia said, holding up a black silk dress with a dangerously low neckline and a slit that ran high up the thigh. "This is the one."

She ran her fingers over the fabric, imagining Lucas's eyes darkening when he saw her in it. A thrill shot through her. "Yes."

The sunlight hit her face, the bags in her hands swinging gently with each step. For the first time in days, Amelia felt lighter. Not completely free, but close.

But then it changed. A knot pulled tight in her gut. That familiar prickle at the base of her neck. The unmistakable weight of eyes on her.

She froze. And then she saw him. Across the street. Leaning against a lamppost like he belonged there.

Ethan.

His arms were crossed, his body relaxed but his eyes, dark and unblinking, locked onto hers with razor precision.

And then That smirk. A silent threat dressed as a smile. A chill raced up her spine.

The air suddenly felt too thin. He had found her. Again.

Her breath caught in her throat, her grip on the shopping bags tightening. "Sophia…" she whispered, panic creeping into her voice. "He's here. Ethan. Across the street."

Sophia's expression darkened instantly. Without hesitation, she whirled around, eyes zeroing in on Ethan. "Are you fucking serious?" she shouted, her voice cutting through the noise of the street. "Do you have nothing better to do than stalk her, you creep? Get a damn life!"

A few pedestrians turned their heads, curious about the commotion. Ethan's smirk didn't falter, but something menacing in his stare made Amelia's blood run cold.

"Sophia, please," she begged, tugging on her friend's arm. "Let's just go. I don't want to do this here."

Sophia's jaw clenched, her protective nature warring with Amelia's plea. But after a tense moment, she exhaled sharply and nodded. "Fine. But if he follows us, I swear I'm calling the police."

Amelia didn't need another warning. She grabbed Sophia's hand, weaving them through the crowd, her heart hammering in her chest. Even as they disappeared into the bustle of the city, she couldn't shake the feeling that Ethan was still watching and still waiting, which terrified her more than anything.

Back at Amelia's apartment, she dropped her bags by the couch and ran a shaky hand through her hair. Sophia paced beside her, arms crossed, clearly still fuming.

"Are you going to tell Lucas?" Sophia asked, finally breaking the silence.

Amelia hesitated, chewing on her lower lip. "I don't know. He's been amazing with the whole Ethan thing, but…" she sighed, sitting down. "I like him, Soph. Maybe even love him.

And I don't want to scare him off. What if this is too much? What if he decides I'm not worth the trouble?"

Sophia scoffed. "Are you serious? Amelia, that man worships the ground you walk on. If anything, he'd want to know to protect you."

Amelia looked down, twisting her fingers in her lap. "Maybe. But for right now… I want to keep it to myself. At least until I figure out what to do."

Sophia exhaled sharply but nodded. "Alright. But if he so much as breathes near you again, we're going straight to Lucas. No arguments."

Amelia managed a weak smile. "Deal."

But even as she said it, doubt settled heavily in her chest. How long could she keep this from Lucas?

Later that night, Amelia stood before the mirror, her hands smoothing down the black silk that clung to her body like a secret.

The dress shimmered in the low golden light of her bedroom, each movement catching shadows and softness in all the right places.

She looked… different.

Stronger. Exposed. Ready.

But inside, her heart pounded, each beat a mix of nerves and electricity.

Anticipation coursed through her. Tonight wasn't just a date. It was a threshold and she was about to step over it.

Her phone buzzed, a message from Lucas.

Waiting downstairs. I can't wait to see you.

Taking a deep breath, she grabbed her clutch and entered the night.

The moment Amelia climbed into the car, Lucas looked over at her and for a second, he just *stared*. Not in that polished, practiced way she'd seen before. This was slower. Real. Like she'd caught him off guard.

"You look…" he paused, then smiled, "Breathtaking."

She gave a nervous laugh, brushing a hand down her dress. "You have to say that."

"I don't," he said, and took her hand, his thumb tracing the inside of her wrist before bringing it to his lips.

It was barely a kiss. Just warmth. Contact. But it sent her heart into a spiral.

She cleared her throat. "Ready?"

Lucas glanced at the road, then back at her, that familiar smirk tugging at his mouth. "I've been ready. You?"

She nodded, though her stomach flipped. "I think so."

As he pulled away from the curb, the city blurred outside the window.

She didn't know where this night would lead. What it would ask of her.

But for once, that uncertainty didn't scare her.

It *thrilled* her.

The bass pulsed through the floor, each beat climbing up Amelia's spine and settling deep in her chest. Lucas's hand tightened around hers steady and grounding.

This wasn't just a club. It was like another world.

Red lights bled across the walls, painting every silhouette in sin and shadow. Bodies moved together like they'd forgotten how to be alone. The air was thick, clinging to her skin with heat and want.

Her breath caught as Lucas guided her further in. Every step stripped something away.

Fear. Doubt. Control. And still, she followed not because she had to. But because a part of her wanted to see who she'd be… on the other side of letting go.

"You're safe with me," he murmured, his voice low and steady, cutting through the noise. His grip on her hand was firm, grounding her amid the sensory overload. She looked up at him, eyes wide. His face gave nothing away. It was calm and composed. But there was something in his eyes. Not cold. Not cruel.

Something steady. Grounded.

Was it control? Confidence?

Whatever it was, it made her feel like she could breathe again… even as her heart raced.

"Is this… okay?" she asked, her voice trembling slightly. She wasn't sure if she was asking about the club, the people or how her body seemed to hum with anticipation.

Lucas didn't answer right away. He leaned in slowly, his breath warm against her ear.

"You're in control, Amelia. You say what's okay. This night belongs to you."

His voice was low, steady, meant to calm her but it lit a fire beneath her skin.

They moved through the crowd, Lucas's grip firm but steady.

She felt the stares on her. Curiosity? Desire? Maybe even judgment. It didn't matter. It still made her skin prickle. But Lucas didn't pause, didn't even look back.

He led her to a platform bathed in low light, where others moved together like the world beyond them didn't exist.

And for a second, Amelia wondered if she was about to disappear, too. Into him, into this.

And if she did… would she come back the same?

"Here," he murmured, voice deep and steady, turning her gently until their bodies aligned. His hands rested at her hips, not to possess but to hold her steady. "This moment is yours. You choose what happens next."

Her pulse thundered in her ears, louder than the music, louder than reason. She parted her lips, breath catching. "Lucas, I—"

He silenced her with the softest touch. His thumb grazing the edge of her hip, a touch that spoke volumes. "Don't explain. Don't hold back. Just look at me."

The nearness of his body, the heat of his skin, the quiet reverence in his eyes made her feel like this wasn't about control. It was about surrender but only if she chose to.

"You're in control," he repeated, his voice a low growl. "Show me."

Her hands trembled as she reached up, her fingers brushing against the collar of his shirt. She could feel the muscles beneath the fabric, his chest's steady rise and fall. Slowly, she unbuttoned his shirt, her movements hesitant at first but growing bolder with each passing second. She could feel his eyes on her, watching her every move and the intensity of his gaze made her cheeks burn.

When the last button was undone, she pushed the shirt off his shoulders, letting it fall to the floor. His chest was bare now, his skin glistening in the dim light. She let her hands roam over his torso, feeling the hard planes of his muscles beneath her fingertips.

"Good," he murmured, his voice low and approving. "Now, show them."

Her breath caught in her throat as she realized what he meant. The people around them were watching, their eyes glued to the two of them. She could feel their gazes like a physical touch and it made her skin crawl with a mix of embarrassment and excitement.

But Lucas's hands were still on her hips, grounding her, reminding her of his presence. "You're in control," he reminded her, his voice steady. "This is about reclaiming your strength."

She nodded, her throat tight. Then, with trembling fingers she reached for the hem of her dress. Every breath felt heavier as she began to lift it, the soft fabric sliding slowly over her thighs. Her skin prickled under the cool air and under his gaze.

Her heart pounded so loudly it drowned out everything else.

When the fabric reached her hips, she froze. Just for a second, the weight of vulnerability hit her hard. But so did something else. Trust. So she took a breath and kept going.

"Don't stop," Lucas urged, his voice low and commanding.

She pulled the dress over her head with a deep breath, letting it fall to the floor. The cool air kissed her skin, making her shiver but Lucas's hands were warm and steady on her hips. She could feel his eyes on her, tracing every curve.

"Beautiful," he murmured, his voice rough with desire. "Now, show them who you are."

Her hands trembled as she reached for the clasp of her bra, but she forced herself to keep going. The fabric fell away, revealing her breasts to the room. She could feel the heat of their stares but kept her eyes locked on Lucas, letting his presence ground her.

"Good girl," he praised, his voice low and approving.

Her breath caught as she slipped her panties down, pooling at her feet.

She stood there bare and exposed. But not small. She felt powerful. Chosen. Seen.

Lucas's hands found her waist, warm and steady. He drew her in, his eyes never leaving hers, like she was the only thing that mattered.

Her fingers moved slowly, hesitating just above his belt. She could feel the heat radiating off him, the quiet tension in the air thick enough to steal her breath.

When she finally reached for the buckle, her hands trembled.

Lucas watched her with a stillness that made her chest ache.

"Good girl," he murmured, voice low. "Take your time."

The click of the buckle echoed between them, louder than it should've been. Her breath caught as she eased it open, her movements careful, almost shy.

She could feel the hard press of him through his pants and her pulse kicked up, her heart thudding wildly in her chest.

Slowly, she unzipped him. His pants slid down, pooling at his feet, leaving him bare before her. Undeniably exposed, but still so in control. That paradox… it did something to her.

She swallowed, eyes dragging over the lines of his body. The way his muscles tensed beneath the weight of her gaze. The way he let her lead, even now, even like this.

Her hands hovered for a moment, the air buzzing with anticipation.

And then she touched him. Her fingers brushed his skin and something inside her cracked open. The fear. The hesitation. The memory of someone else's roughness… replaced with this.

With him.

Her hands shook, but she didn't stop.

Lucas exhaled a breath that sounded like restraint and something close to worship.

"You're safe," he said softly, barely a whisper. "With me, you always are."

"Lucas," she whispered, her voice trembling with need. "I…"

"Don't overthink it," he murmured, his voice low and steady. "Just feel."

She nodded. Slowly, she wrapped her hand around his cock, feeling the heat of him in her palm. He was hard. So hard it made her chest ache and her legs feel unsteady. "Good girl," he murmured, his voice rough with desire.

She tightened her grip, her palm sliding up his cock in a slow, deliberate motion.

Lucas inhaled sharply, the muscles in his abdomen tightening under her touch. She swallowed, her pulse thudding in her ears as she tightened her grip. Her palm moved slowly, deliberately, dragging up the length of him with aching precision.

His head fell back slightly, a low groan slipping from his throat.

That sound made her bolder. The crowd seemed to hold their breath, glued to the scene unfolding before them. She could feel their gazes on her, the weight of their attention making her skin burn. But instead of shying away, she leaned into it, her movements becoming more confident as she worked him. Her hand moved with confidence now, wrapped around the length of him, each stroke deliberate, sure. The rhythm was slow at first, steady, like she was learning him through touch alone. Feeling the pulse of him under her palm. The way he tensed. The way he *watched* her.

Her thumb brushed over the head, catching the most sensitive part of him on every upward glide.

Lucas exhaled a harsh breath. "That's it," he growled.

His hand slipped into her hair. Not rough, but firm. His fingers curling at the nape of her neck. Anchoring her. Guiding her.

Every time she paused, hesitated, his grip tightened just enough to remind her who he was.

"Don't stop."

She didn't. Her hand moved faster now, each stroke slick. Fueled by the heat radiating off him. She could feel him getting closer, the tension winding tighter with each passing second. His abs flexed. His thighs trembled. The quiet curse he muttered under his breath made her stomach twist in the best way.

Then his fingers tightened in her hair. He pulled her head back just enough to make her eyes meet his.

And when they did? It stole her breath. Her spine tingled. Her skin flushed. She couldn't look away if she tried. Because in that moment, it wasn't just about power or pleasure.

It was about being *seen* completely. And by him? It felt like being devoured and protected all at once.

The world around them dissolved. The crowd. The lights. The music. Gone. All that remained was *him*.

His breath. His body. His eyes dark, unblinking, locked

on hers like she was the only thing anchoring him to this moment.

Her hand moved with desperate precision, driven by the way he looked at her.

Each stroke dragged him closer. She felt it in the way his muscles pulled tight beneath his skin, in the way his abdomen clenched under her touch.

He was right there on the edge. A low, ragged sound tore from his throat as his grip in her hair tightened, grounding himself with her.

"Fuck," he growled, voice shredded and desperate, his hips jerking forward into her palm.

"Don't stop. Don't you fucking dare stop."

She didn't. Her hand moved faster slick, steady, relentless. Gliding over him with practiced urgency. She could feel him unraveling under her touch, every inch of him wound tight and ready to snap.

Lucas pulled the chair closer, sat down, and gripped her waist tight, his touch both commanding and reassuring. She could feel the heat of the crowd's gaze on her skin, but it didn't make her falter. Instead, it fueled her, the weight of their eyes pushing her to claim this moment, to claim him.

His hands shifted, guiding her to straddle him, their bodies aligning in a way that made her breath catch.

Slowly, she lifted herself, feeling the heat of him against her. The crowd's murmurs faded into the background, replaced by her heartbeat and Lucas's strained breathing.

She lowered herself, inch by agonizing inch until they were fully connected. A soft gasp escaped her lips, and she heard Lucas's sharp intake of breath. His hands gripped her hips, but he didn't move, didn't take over. He was letting her lead, and the power of that, sent a thrill through her.

She began to move, rolling her hips in a slow, deliberate rhythm. The sensation was overwhelming; every nerve in her body alight with pleasure. She could feel how Lucas's body responded to her, his muscles tense, his breath coming in short, ragged bursts. She leaned back, her hands resting on his thighs for balance, and let her head fall back, her eyes closed.

She focused on the way their bodies moved together, the way he felt inside her, the way her own pleasure built with every movement. But then she opened her eyes, and the reality of where they were crashed back into her.

The crowd was watching, their eyes locked on her. She could see the hunger in their gazes, the envy, the admiration. And it didn't scare her. It empowered her.

She let out a low moan, her movements becoming more deliberate, more forceful. She could feel Lucas's grip tighten on her hips, but he still didn't take control. He let her set the pace, allowing her to claim this moment.

"Lucas," she breathed, her voice trembling with the intensity of her pleasure. "I…"

"Don't stop," he growled, his voice rough with need. "Take what you want."

His words sent a shiver of excitement through her. She leaned forward, her hands resting on his chest, and increased her pace, her hips moving faster, harder. The pleasure was building, spiraling out of control, and she could feel herself getting closer to the edge.

"Look at them," Lucas murmured, his voice low and commanding. "Let them see you."

She hesitated momentarily but lifted her head, her eyes

meeting the crowds. She could see the way they watched her, the way they were captivated by her, and it only fueled her more. She felt powerful and in control. The knowledge that they were all watching her, all witnessing her claim Lucas, sent a thrill of excitement through her.

She let out a low moan, her movements becoming even more frantic as she approached her climax. She could feel Lucas's body tense beneath her, and she knew he was close, too.

"Lucas," she gasped, her voice trembling with need. "I'm... I'm going to..."

"Let go," he growled, his voice rough with need. "Take it."

And with that, she tipped over the edge, her body convulsing with pleasure as she came, her cries filling the room. She could feel Lucas's release a moment later, his body tensing beneath her as he found his climax.

For a moment, everything was still, the world seeming to pause as they caught their breath. Then Lucas's hands shifted, pulling her closer, and she leaned into him, her body still trembling with the aftershocks of her pleasure.

"You were incredible," Lucas murmured, his voice low and warm.

She smiled, a sense of pride washing over her. She had done it. She had taken control, claimed this moment, and never felt more powerful.

The crowd was still watching, their eyes locked on her, but she didn't care. She had claimed this moment and Lucas, and she had never felt more alive.

But then Lucas's grip on her waist tightened, and he leaned in, his lips brushing against her ear. "Ready for more?" he whispered, his voice low and teasing.

Her heart skipped a beat, and she felt a thrill of excitement course through her. "More?" she asked, her voice trembling with anticipation.

Lucas smirked, his eyes dark with promise. "Oh, yes," he murmured. "Much more."

Lucas's smirk was a dare, a challenge that sent a shiver down her spine. She could feel the heat of his breath against her ear, the weight of his words settling in the pit of her stomach. More. The word echoed in her mind, igniting a fire that had already been stoked to a roaring blaze.

Lucas's fingers trailed up her arm, leaving a trail of goose-bumps in their wake. "The kind that will make you forget everything else," he murmured, his voice dripping with sensuality. He leaned in again, his lips brushing against her neck. "Trust me."

She swallowed hard, her pulse quickening. Trust. That was the key. She had trusted him this far, and he had led her to a place of power, of control she hadn't known she possessed. But this… this felt different. This felt like he was about to push her to the edge, where she would have to let go completely. And yet, the thought excited her more than it frightened her.

"Okay," she whispered, her voice trembling but resolute.

"You're not going to back out now, are you?" His voice was low, a deep rumble that sent shivers down her spine. His hand tightened around her wrist, pulling her closer until their bodies were pressed together. She could feel the heat radiating from him, how his chest rose and fell with every breath. His eyes held hers, dark and intense, demanding her submission.

"I'm not scared," she whispered, though the tremor in her voice betrayed her. She wasn't sure if fear or anticipation made her heart pound, but she knew one thing for sure,she wanted this. She wanted him.

He smirked, a devilish curve of his lips that made her stomach flip. "Good. Because I'm not going to be gentle."

Before she could speak, he spun her around in one fluid motion, her back colliding with the solid heat of his chest.

Her breath hitched. His arm wrapped around her waist, pulling her tight against him, and the other hand, God, that hand roamed with purpose. Skimming up the curve of her hips, tracing the outline of her ribs, then higher claiming the weight of her breast like it already belonged to him.

His touch wasn't gentle. It was *possessive.*

She felt the hard press of him against her, thick and pulsing with need, and her knees almost buckled.

Then his mouth dipped to her ear, his voice a growl that burned down her spine.

"Look at them."

Her eyes fluttered open, dazed, heavy with lust. And when she looked?

She saw them.

A sea of faces, eyes locked on her like she was something forbidden. Something worshipped.

They weren't just watching, they were *starving.*

"They're watching us," Lucas whispered, breath hot and wicked against her skin. "Every single one of them."

A shiver rolled through her, dark and heady.

"Do you like that?" he asked, voice rough with control, with ownership. "Knowing they all wish they were me right now? That they're imagining what it would be like to have you beneath them?"

She couldn't speak. Could barely breathe.So she nodded.

Once.

It was like a confession and surrender all at once.

His hand slid lower, fingers digging into the soft flesh of her ass, pulling her tighter against him.

She gasped louder than she meant to. And the sound made his eyes darken.

"Good," he murmured. "Let them watch."

"Tell me what you want," he demanded, his fingers teasing her clit.

"I want you," she breathed, her voice barely audible over the pounding music. "I want you to take me. Right here. Right now."

He chuckled a low, dark sound that sent a shiver down her spine. "That's my girl."

She whimpered, her body trembling with anticipation. His fingers dipped inside her, coating themselves in her wetness before he pressed one against her asshole. She tensed, the sensation foreign yet somehow thrilling.

"Relax," he commanded, his voice firm but reassuring. "I'll make it good for you."

She took a deep breath, trying to steady herself as he slowly pushed his finger inside. The stretch was intense but not unbearable. She could feel her body adapting, opening up for him.

"That's it," he praised, his voice a low growl. "Take it."

He added a second finger, stretching her further. The pain started to give way to pleasure, a strange, intoxicating mix that made her writhe against him. She could feel herself growing wetter, her body responding to his touch.

"You're so fucking perfect," he muttered.

Her breath caught as he slowly pulled his fingers free, the

sudden emptiness making her body tremble left raw, aching and open.

Then she felt him. The blunt heat of him pressing against her slow, deliberate. The weight of it made her pulse stutter. Every nerve ending lit up.

She braced herself, hands gripping the nearest surface, heart thudding in her throat.

Lucas leaned in, his voice a dark whisper against her ear.

"You ready for me?"

She nodded, breathless. "Yes."

There was no hesitation in him.

With one sharp thrust, he filled her deep, relentless and unforgiving. The stretch stole the air from her lungs, a sharp, searing burn that tore a cry from her throat.

It hurt. God, it *hurt*. But then it shifted. The pain dulled, blurring into something else.

Something darker. Deeper. A pleasure she couldn't name, couldn't stop.

"Fuck," he growled, his fingers bruising into her hips as he sank all the way in, buried to the hilt.

"So fucking perfect," he rasped, voice raw with praise and possession.

She could feel every inch of him inside her, stretching her, filling her in a way she had never experienced before. The sensation was overwhelming, almost too much, but she didn't want it to stop.

With a growl, he pulled back, then thrust forward again, harder this time. The pain was still there, but it was mingling with pleasure now, a heady mix that made her body tremble.

"That's it," he grunted, his thrusts growing faster, more forceful. "Take it. Take all of me."

She could feel herself unraveling, the pleasure building with every thrust. Her body was on fire, every nerve ending alive with sensation. She could hear the sound of flesh meeting flesh, the low moans escaping her lips, the growls coming from him.

"You feel so damn good," he growled, his hands tightening on her hips.

She could feel herself getting closer, the pressure building inside her. Her body was trembling, her breath coming in short, ragged gasps.

"I'm close," she whispered, her voice barely audible over the pounding music.

"Not yet," he commanded, his voice rough with need. "I'm not done with you."

He reached around, his fingers finding her clit and she let out a strangled cry as he started to rub. The sensation was almost too much, the pleasure overwhelming. Her body was on fire, every nerve ending alive with sensation.

He stepped back, his hand still lingering on her hip, and she felt the absence of his body like a cold draft. His eyes locked onto hers, an unspoken challenge simmering between them. The club's dim, crimson glow painted him in shadows, making his stern features even sharper, more predatory.

"Come," he said, his voice low but commanding, a tone that brooked no argument.

She hesitated, her breath catching in her throat. He led her toward the club's center, where a large, sturdy cross stood, its polished wood gleaming under the ambient lights. The crowd parted as they approached, whispers and murmurs rising like a tide. She could feel their eyes on her, their curiosity, their hunger. It made her skin prickle, a strange mix of vulnerability and arousal coiling in her stomach.

This is insane, she thought, but her feet kept moving, her body drawn to the cross as if it were inevitable.

He stopped in front of it, his gaze never leaving hers. "Stand here," he instructed his voice firm. She obeyed, her back pressing against the cool wood. Her hands instinctively reached for the edges, gripping them for support.

He stepped closer, his fingers brushing against her cheek before trailing down her neck, collarbone, and chest.

She should have felt ashamed and humiliated but felt… alive instead.

He stepped back, his gaze raking over her like a predator appraising its prey. "Beautiful," he murmured, the word almost reverent.

Her cheeks flushed, but she held his gaze, refusing to look away.

He reached for a small vial of oil on a small table beside him, the liquid catching the light as he uncapped it. He poured a generous amount onto his fingers, the scent of lavender and something spicier filling the air.

"Relax," he said, his voice softer now, almost tender. His fingers brushed against her entrance, the oil warm against her skin. She tensed, her body instinctively recoiling, but he was patient, his touch gentle as he began to massage the oil into her.

The sensation was strange at first, but then it turned into something else, something intense. His fingers pressed deeper, stretching her slowly, deliberately. Her breath came in shallow gasps, her body trembling as he worked her open.

"That's it," he murmured, his voice a soothing hum. "Let me

in."

She bit her lip, a whimper escaping her throat as he added a second finger. The stretch was almost too much, but it was so good at the same time. Her body was betraying her, responding to him in ways she couldn't control.

She gasped, her nails digging into her palms as he filled her, inch by agonizing inch. The crowd's whispers grew louder, their excitement palpable, but all she could focus on was him, the feel of him inside her, the way he stretched her almost to the point of pain but not quite.

Her cheeks burned with humiliation and desire, but she couldn't look away from the sea of faces watching her. Their gazes were like fire, licking at her skin, making her feel more exposed than ever. She moaned, the sound escaping her lips before she could stop it.

He withdrew his fingers, and she whimpered at the loss, but before she could protest, he was pushing her forward, bending her over a low table. The cool surface pressed against her chest, and she gasped as he spread her legs wider, positioning himself behind her.

"You're mine tonight," he said, his voice dark and possessive. "And everyone here is going to watch."

She closed her eyes, but he gripped her hair, yanking her head back. "Open them," he commanded, and she obeyed, her gaze locking onto his.

Without warning, he thrust into her, and she cried out, the sensation overwhelming. He was rough, his movements erratic and desperate, and she could feel every inch of him as he pounded into her. The table creaked beneath them, and the sound of skin against skin filled the room.

The crowd erupted into cheers and whistles, their excitement palpable. She could feel their eyes on her, their lust feeding into her own. She moaned, her body responding to him in ways she didn't think possible.

"That's it," he growled, his hands gripping her hips so tightly she was sure there would be bruises. "Take it. Take all of it."

She could feel herself unraveling, her body tightening around him as he drove her closer to the edge. Her breath came in short, sharp gasps, and she could feel the heat building inside her, threatening to consume her.

"Please," she begged, her voice broken, her body trembling.

He didn't respond. His movements becoming more frantic and desperate. She could feel him losing control, and it only fueled her own desire. The room blurred around her, the sounds of the crowd fading into a distant hum as she focused on the sensation of him inside her.

And then with one final, brutal thrust she shattered.

Her cry broke the air, raw and unfiltered, as her body convulsed around him.

Pleasure ripped through her in violent waves, too much and not enough, a crashing release that left her breathless, unraveling in his hands.

Lucas wasn't far behind. He let out a harsh groan, his grip on her hips tightening as he surged forward and spilled deep inside her. The sound of his release, of her name torn from his throat was something she would never forget.

Then... silence.

Not in the room *inside her.*

Like the noise had been chased out by the intensity of it all, leaving only the echo of what they'd just done.

And then applause.

The crowd erupted, the room swelling with whistles, cheers,

shouts of approval. The roar of attention came rushing back, crashing into her like cold water.

But she couldn't move. Could barely *breathe*.

Her legs trembled. Her heart thundered.

Lucas leaned in, still inside her, still surrounding her. His breath ghosted across her ear, low and warm.

"You were perfect," he whispered, voice thick with pride.

She didn't respond. Couldn't. But as her eyes fluttered closed and her trembling began to ease, she realized something. For the first time in forever, she didn't feel like she was disappearing. She felt *alive*.

The night air bit at Amelia's flushed skin, cool and crisp, a sharp contrast to the heat still simmering beneath her surface. Her heels clicked softly against the pavement, a quiet rhythm to everything that had just happened.

Her body still thrummed with adrenaline. With power. The city felt different now.

Less like a cage and more like a place where she could finally stop shrinking.

A place where she could *be*. Be bold, unapologetic and seen.

She had never felt this before. Not like this. Alive. Electric. *Unbreakable.*

Lucas walked beside her, not speaking, not rushing. Just *there*.

His fingers brushed the back of her hand. No pressure. No demand. Just an offering.

And she took it. Her fingers threaded through his, and something inside her settled. Not in surrender but in knowing. She had taken control tonight.

And then she saw him.

Not Ethan, but a man. Standing across the street beneath the dull glow of a street lamp.

He wasn't doing anything, just watching. Her pulse stumbled. The easy confidence she had felt seconds ago cracked, then fractured completely.

Lucas was talking about taking her home and getting her something to eat, but she couldn't focus. Not when the man was still there, like he had been waiting for her.

She swallowed hard, forcing herself to look away. *It's nothing, just a random guy.*

She told herself that, but her body didn't believe it.

The rush of power she had felt inside the club, the fire, the confidence, it didn't matter if one shadow on a street corner could make her feel like prey all over again.

Lucas's grip on her hand tightened. "Amelia?"

She blinked up at him, realizing how tense she had become. "Yeah?"

His gaze flickered toward where she had been looking, his sharp instincts picking up on something even if she hadn't said a word. The playful warmth from earlier was gone now replaced with something colder, something lethal.

"Do you know him?" Lucas asked, his voice unreadable.

She forced a breath and shook her head quickly. "No. I….it's nothing."

Lucas didn't look convinced, but he didn't press. Instead, he wrapped an arm around her waist and led her toward the car. She let him, leaning into his warmth, trying to shake off the feeling that she was still being watched.

By the time they reached her apartment, the unease had settled deep into her bones, impossible to ignore.

But she wasn't prepared for what was waiting inside.

The moment she flicked on the light, her breath vanished. The envelope sat on the coffee table. Plain. White. Waiting. For a second, all she could do was stare at it.

Her fingers went cold. Her breath wouldn't come.

No. No, no, no.

Lucas saw it the exact moment she did, his entire body going rigid beside her. He moved first, stepping in front of her like a human shield as he approached the table. His movements slow, calculated, like he was preparing for a fight.

He picked up the envelope tearing it open without hesitation. His shoulders tensed, his jaw clenched so tight she could see the muscles working.

Then, he spoke.

"Did you really think I'd let you forget me?"
Ethan.

The room spun. Her stomach twisted into knots so tight she thought she might be sick.

He had been here. Inside her apartment. Her knees buckled, and Lucas instantly caught her before she could fall. His hands were firm and grounding, but nothing felt real anymore. The walls felt too close, the air too thin, her body too small, too vulnerable.

"I need….." Her voice cracked. She swallowed hard, trying to pull herself together but the panic was squeezing around her throat.

Lucas cupped her face, forcing her to look at him. His eyes weren't just protective, they were dangerous. Filled with a quiet fury that could burn cities to the ground.

"You're not staying here tonight," he said, his tone absolute.

Uncompromising. "You're coming with me."

She could only nod because there was no arguing, no convincing herself that this was nothing.

It was real. Ethan was real. And no matter how much she had reclaimed herself tonight, he was still out there, trying to take it away.

Twenty-Nine

Chapter 29

Amelia barely slept that night. Even wrapped in Lucas's strong embrace, her mind refused to quiet, replaying every possible scenario in which Ethan had entered her apartment. Had he been there while she was out? Had he watched her sleep? How long had he stood in her home, touching her things, leaving that note as a sick reminder that she would never be free of him?

By the time the sun rose, exhaustion weighed on her but she couldn't close her eyes without feeling his presence lurking in the shadows.

Lucas stirred beside her, sensing her unrest. He brushed a hand over her arm. "You didn't sleep."

She shook her head. "I couldn't."

His jaw tightened, and she saw the flicker of anger in his eyes. "We'll figure this out. He won't touch you."

But Amelia wasn't so sure. Because Ethan wasn't just a

threat looming in the distance anymore, he was here. He had breached the last barrier of safety she had.

The day passed in a haze. Lucas refused to let her out of sight, insisting she stay at his place.

That night, Amelia returned to her apartment to grab a few essentials. Lucas hesitated but agreed to go with her.

A chill crawled over her skin the moment Amelia stepped into her apartment. The air felt heavier, charged with something unseen, something wrong.

She froze just past the threshold, gripping the strap of her purse so tightly her knuckles ached. Something felt off. The space was exactly as she had left it. Her coat draped over the armrest, a mug from the other morning still sitting on the counter. But the silence was different. It wasn't the comforting quiet of home.

Lucas stepped in behind her, solid and silent. Still, her pulse jumped. Something felt off.

Then she saw it her bedroom door. Ajar.

She never left it like that.

Her breath caught. Her chest tightened.

"Lucas…" It came out rough, but soft. Not even a full word, more a plea.

He followed her gaze and moved in front of her without a word.

She didn't breathe. Couldn't. Her body locked up as he pushed the door open.

The bed sat undisturbed. No signs of entry. Nothing broken. Nothing out of place.

Except the rose.

A single red rose, right in the center of her pillow. Perfect. Precise.

And beneath it folded paper.

Her stomach twisted. The edges of the room bent. Her hand caught the doorframe just in time.

Lucas moved fast. He crossed the room, snatched up the note and opened it in one motion.

He read but he didn't speak. His grip tightened. His jaw clenched.

Amelia stepped forward. It took everything.

"What does it say?" she asked.

He didn't answer right away.

And that silence?

It was worse than anything she could imagine.

Finally, he turned, meeting her eyes as he held the note.

"You look so beautiful when you sleep."

The world narrowed. Her vision tunneled. The floor felt like it was falling away beneath her feet and a wave of nausea rolled through her, sharp and sudden.

She sucked in a breath, too fast, too shallow. Her knees buckled, but Lucas instantly caught her before she could fall.

He pulled her against him, his grip steady, grounding. "Breathe, Amelia," he murmured, his voice low, controlled. "I've got you."

But she couldn't breathe. She couldn't think. He had been here.

Not just in her apartment. Not just leaving notes. Watching her while she slept.

Had he stood at the foot of her bed, watching in the dark? Had he touched her? Had he whispered things she couldn't hear?

Her stomach twisted painfully. She pressed a hand to her

mouth, fighting the wave of panic that clawed at her throat.

This was her home. Her safe space and he had poisoned it.

Lucas's grip on her tightened, his body coiled with barely restrained fury. "We're leaving. Now."

She barely registered his words or anything beyond the suffocating realization that Ethan had been closer than she ever imagined.

And he wanted her to know it.

The following day, Amelia forced herself to go to work. Every step felt like walking through mud, heavy and reluctant, but she did it anyway. Hiding wasn't an option. She'd lived that way once shrinking, avoiding, surviving in the shadows and she refused to go back.

Ethan had taken enough from her. He didn't get *this*, too.

Lucas had insisted on driving her. He didn't say much just opened the door, waited in silence, and didn't leave until she was safely inside.

His presence lingered long after he drove away.

The office buzzed with the usual noise phones ringing, keys clicking, someone laughing two desks over. And for a few hours, Amelia lost herself in it. She answered emails. Filed reports. Pretended everything was normal.

It almost worked. Until her phone buzzed. A single notification.

New email.

She glanced at the screen. No subject. No sender. Her pulse stuttered.

Then she tapped it open.

And the world dropped out beneath her.

There were photos. Grainy. Dark. But clear enough.

Her bed.
Her body.
Sleeping.
The sheets twisted around her legs. Then close ups of her lips, slightly parted.

Her neck, exposed. The soft dip of her collarbone.

Her fingers trembled. Her stomach twisted into knots.

She hadn't slept at her apartment last night. Lucas had insisted she stay with him.

So these… these weren't from then.

They were older. He'd been watching her long before she realized.

The bile rose in her throat. She couldn't breathe. Couldn't blink. The walls of the office closed in, her coworkers' voices reduced to white noise behind the sharp scream of silence in her head.

And then she saw it beneath the images, a single line of text.

I miss watching you dream.

That was it.

No signature. No threat. Just… that. Like a ghost whispering at the edges of her sanity. Like he'd never left.

Her hands clenched around the phone. Her lungs refused to work. She wanted to scream. To disappear. To just wake up and realize this was just a nightmare she could shake off.

But she was wide awake.

And Ethan… Ethan was still out there. Watching her.

She felt sick and violated. Her chair scraped against the floor as she stood abruptly and pushed away from her desk. The walls of her office felt like they were closing in.

She had to get out. She had to tell Lucas. But before she could move, another email arrived.

Don't run from me, Amelia. You know I always find you.

Terror rooted her to the spot. Her heart pounded so violently that she thought she might pass out.

Ethan wasn't just watching. He was taunting her.

The rest of the day was a blur. Amelia couldn't concentrate, couldn't function. Every sound, every flicker of movement in her peripheral vision, sent a jolt of fear through her. She kept checking her phone, half-expecting another message, another reminder that she was never alone.

When she finally left work, she hesitated at the front door of her office. The street outside was dimly lit, the faint glow of streetlamps casting long shadows. She scanned the sidewalk, her heart hammering in her chest. Was he out there? Watching?

Lucas had told her to call him when she was done, but she didn't want to feel like a prisoner in her own life. She gripped her keys, forcing herself to step outside. The air was crisp, but she was suffocating.

Then she saw him.

A dark figure across the street standing beneath a flickering streetlight. He wasn't moving, just watching.

Her blood ran cold. Her legs locked in place. She couldn't breathe.

Ethan.

She wanted to scream, to run, to do anything but fear rooted her in place. Then, slowly, he lifted his hand and waved.

A mocking, casual wave. As if they were old friends greeting each other on the street.

Amelia stumbled backward, nearly dropping her purse. Her breath came in ragged gasps as she fumbled for her phone. By the time she looked back up, he was gone.

Had she imagined it? Was her mind playing tricks on her? *No. He had been there.*

Shaking, she dialed Lucas's number with trembling fingers.

"Lucas," she whispered the moment he answered. "He was here."

"Where are you?" His voice was sharp, all business now.

"Outside work. I saw him across the street, and then he was just,gone."

"Stay where you are. I'm coming to get you."

Amelia clutched her phone tightly, glancing around, every nerve in her body on edge. The street felt too empty, too exposed. She backed against the wall of her office as if pressing herself into the building would make her disappear.

Minutes stretched into an eternity before Lucas's car screeched to a stop in front of her. He jumped out, scanning the area before his eyes landed on her. He was at her side in seconds, his hands cupping her face.

"Are you okay?"

She shook her head, tears spilling over. "He was here, Lucas. He waved at me like it was some game."

Lucas's jaw clenched, fury simmering just beneath the surface. "We're going to end this, Amelia. I swear to you, he will never touch you again."

The penthouse had become her sanctuary.

Up here, above the noise and neon, Amelia could almost pretend she was safe. That behind the floor-to-ceiling glass and marble silence, the past couldn't reach her.

That he couldn't reach her. But safety was a lie. And Ethan was getting closer.

It began as static. Unfamiliar numbers. Blank messages.

She blocked them all, only for more to appear, each one more persistent than the last.

Then came the calls. Always from "No Caller ID." Always the same: silence.

Until the *third* ring that night. When she picked up and heard it.

A laugh.

Warped. Low. Slipping through the speaker like smoke.

A sound she'd prayed she'd never hear again. And now... it wasn't just in her head.

Now, he was *letting her know.* He was close.

Amelia sat curled on Lucas's couch, swallowed by the oversized cushions, his black shirt draped over her like armor that didn't quite fit. The city lights bled into the penthouse like ghosts behind glass, but even the glittering skyline felt cold tonight.

She stared at her phone.

Motionless.

Empty.

Waiting.

Another email.

A towel slung around his neck, Lucas walked in from the bathroom, shirtless, damp hair tousled. The sharp scent of soap and steam clung to his skin. But the moment he saw her, saw the way she sat he stopped. Still as stone.

"Amelia."

His voice was low. Firm. But gentler than usual. A soft edge wrapped around steel.

She didn't speak. Just turned the phone toward him with trembling fingers.

He stepped closer, gaze locking on the screen.

Miss me, sweetheart?.

Lucas stared at the screen, jaw ticking, muscles coiling beneath his skin like he was holding back something violent.

But Amelia she couldn't move. Couldn't breathe.

Because Ethan wasn't just reaching out. He was *hunting* her again.

And this time, she could feel his breath at the back of her neck.

Lucas's jaw clenched as he took the phone from her, his body going rigid with barely restrained anger. He scrolled through the email, his expression darkening with every word.

"You can hide in your little penthouse with your rich boyfriend, but we both know the truth. You belong to me. I will always find you."

Lucas exhaled sharply, his fingers tightening around the phone before he forced himself to relax. He sat down beside her, cupping her face gently, his touch a stark contrast to the fury simmering in his eyes. "He doesn't own you, Amelia. He never did."

"I know," she whispered, though the fear in her voice betrayed her. "But he's not stopping, Lucas. I don't even know how he got my new email. What if….."

"He's not getting near you." His voice was resolute, his grip on her hand strong and reassuring. "You're staying here. I'm not letting you go back there alone."

She nodded, pressing her forehead against his shoulder,

seeking the comfort only he could provide. "I hate this. I hate that he still has this power over me."

Lucas pulled her closer, his fingers threading through her hair. "He doesn't have power over you, Amelia. He's a coward hiding behind threats. And I promise you, he will regret ever thinking he could scare you."

Then a knock came like a gunshot. Sharp. Sudden. Too loud in the stillness of the penthouse.

Amelia jolted, her breath catching mid-chest, heart slamming hard against her ribs.

Lucas was on his feet before she could blink.

One hand out, shielding her behind him. The other already curled into a fist.

There was no buzz. No warning. No call from the front desk.

His security wouldn't have let *anyone* up without alerting him first.

He approached the door with silent precision, every step controlled, lethal.

Checked the peephole and then unlocked it.

Outside stood one of his security detail, face grim, suit slightly rumpled like he'd just ran to get here. Something in his expression made Amelia's blood go cold.

"Sir," the man said, voice low. "We have a problem."

Lucas's posture shifted. Tensed. His shoulders squared like armor.

"What kind of problem?" he asked.

The guard hesitated, then extended a small, cream-colored envelope.

"No return address. It was left with the doorman, delivered

by courier. No name."

Lucas took the envelope, eyes narrowing.

He turned it over in his hands like he already knew it wasn't just a message.

It was a threat.

He opened it carefully. Pulled out a single folded page.

As his eyes scanned the note, his entire body went still.

Too still.

And then his jaw clenched ice creeping across his features.

He handed the paper to Amelia without a word.

Her hands shook as she took it.

The page was cold against her skin and the moment she unfolded it, her breath left her in a broken gasp.

Still think he can protect you?

No name.

No signature.

Just that.

Just *him*.

She didn't need to ask.

She felt it. Ethan was somewhere close. Really close. Close enough to slip a message past security. Close enough to *know* she was finally starting to feel safe. And now, he wanted to take that away.

He wanted her afraid again.

Lucas didn't waste a second. The moment Amelia read the note, he was already making calls. His voice was low and lethal, the calm fury of a man who would stop at nothing to protect what was his.

Amelia stood, her arms wrapped around herself as she stared at the glittering city skyline.

Behind her, Lucas was on the phone, his voice low but

firm, discussing security measures with someone from his team. She felt his gaze flicker toward her every few seconds, watching, waiting.

She knew what was coming. The conversation they were about to have.

And she already hated it.

Lucas ended the call with a clipped, "I'll let you know when we finalize the details," before setting his phone down on the counter. Then he turned to her.

"You need a bodyguard."

The words landed like a stone in her chest.

Amelia closed her eyes, her jaw tightening. Of course he wasn't going to ease into it.

"I don't…" The protest caught in her throat. She exhaled hard, steadying herself before turning to face him.

"Lucas," she said softly, "I can't have someone shadowing me. Watching me. Tracking where I go, what I do. I've *lived* that before. I barely survived it."

Her voice cracked, just a little. But she didn't look away.

"I can't….won't live like that again."

Lucas's features softened. His hands clenched at his sides like he was resisting the urge to reach for her. To fix it. To fix *her*.

But he didn't back down.

"This isn't about control," he said, voice low and steady. "It's about *keeping you safe*."

Safe.

The word made her chest ache.

She used to believe she could *build* safety brick by brick, lock by lock.

If she changed her routines. Double-checked every door.

Avoided the wrong streets. Never let her phone die.

But Ethan had shattered that illusion.

"I just…" Her arms wrapped around herself, and suddenly the room felt too big.

Too quiet. Too exposed.

"I don't want to feel like a *prisoner* again."

Lucas stepped forward, slow and careful, like he was approaching something broken.

"You're not," he said gently.

But her silence said everything. Because sometimes the worst cages were the ones you couldn't see, the ones that followed you even after the locks were gone.

Lucas stepped closer, careful, as if sensing how close she was to breaking. "Amelia." His voice was softer now, coaxing. "Having protection isn't a prison. It's power."

She swallowed hard, shaking her head. "It doesn't feel that way. It feels like admitting I've lost. That he still has control over me."

Lucas's jaw clenched, and he didn't speak for a moment. Then, with a quiet but unwavering intensity, he said, "No, it means you're fighting back. He wants you to feel vulnerable. Wants you to be afraid to live your life. You getting a bodyguard? That's you telling him he doesn't get to win."

Her chest ached with the weight of his words. Was that what she was doing? Letting Ethan win by resisting the help she so obviously needed?

She wanted to be strong. Independent.

But wasn't true strength knowing when to accept help?

She let out a slow, trembling breath. Her nod was barely there a flicker, a surrender so quiet it could've been missed.

But Lucas saw it. He always did. He stepped closer, his

presence steady and warm, like something she could lean into if she let herself.

His fingers brushed gently against her face, tucking a loose strand of hair behind her ear. The touch lingered, soft against her skin, grounding her when everything else felt like it might fall apart.

"I promise," he murmured, voice low and filled with a kind of quiet desperation. "It'll be someone you trust. Someone discreet. Invisible, if you need them to be. But I *need* to know you're safe, Amelia. Please."

The plea cracked something in her.

She'd fought so hard to hold on to control. To prove to herself, to the world that she wasn't weak. That she didn't need saving. But that wasn't what this was. This wasn't about surrendering power. It was about choosing to *live*.

To stop looking over her shoulder. To stop pretending she could outrun a man like Ethan alone.

Her lips parted. And for a long, agonizing moment, she said nothing her silence a final battle cry from the fractured part of her still chained to the past.

Then… she exhaled.

"Okay," she whispered.

One word.

But it held *everything*.

The fear. The trust. The quiet devastation of admitting she couldn't do this alone.

Lucas nodded, jaw tight, eyes soft. The relief in his face was subtle but deep.

He didn't say *thank you*. Didn't push or press.

He just reached for her hand, threading his fingers through hers. Holding on.

Like a promise. Like he wasn't going anywhere.

Within the hour, the penthouse had been transformed. More security cameras installed. Extra guards were stationed outside the building and on their floor. Access to the penthouse was now strictly controlled. No one got through without Lucas's approval.

But that wasn't enough.

"You'll have someone with you at all times," Lucas said, his tone leaving no room for argument. "I don't want you going anywhere alone, especially to work."

Amelia blinked, absorbing the shift in his demeanor. He had always been protective, but now he was in complete command mode. His dominance was unmistakable.

Lucas stepped forward, cupping her face in his hands. His thumb brushed against her cheek as he searched her eyes. "I need you to trust me on this."

Her heart clenched at the intensity of his gaze.

"I do trust you," she whispered.

His lips pressed a lingering kiss to her forehead before he pulled back. "Good. Because I'll do whatever it takes to keep you safe."

Thirty

Chapter 30

Amelia woke to the quiet hush of morning, the kind of stillness that only came before the city fully stretched awake. But even wrapped in the warmth of Lucas's arms, there was a tightness in her chest. Not panic. Just the shadow of it.

It was always there now. Like her body hadn't gotten the message that she was safe.

She stared at the ceiling, her breath steady but shallow, and tried to will the weight away.

Lucas didn't stir behind her, not at first. His arm remained snug around her waist, his body warm, solid, present. It should have been enough.

But something about the silence made it worse. As if Ethan had slipped through the cracks of her sleep, burrowed into her skin, and left behind his fingerprints.

She turned, needing to see him. Lucas.

Even in sleep, he looked like protection made flesh. His jaw slack but capable, arms loose but ready. He didn't move when she touched him, not right away. But a breath later, his eyes opened, alert, like he'd been halfway to her before he even woke.

"You okay?" he murmured, voice low, unguarded.

Her fingers grazed his chest, resting there like an anchor. "I don't know."

He pulled her close, no questions. Just closeness.

But still there was that ache inside her. That sense of loss for the version of her life she could never go back to.

"I miss how simple it used to be," she said, voice barely audible. "I miss not thinking about locks and shadows and escape routes."

Lucas didn't flinch. He just held her a little tighter.

"You don't have to carry it alone anymore," he said quietly.

She wanted to believe that. She wanted it more than anything.

But somewhere deep inside, where the old wounds hadn't closed, she still felt like something hunted. Something Ethan had marked.

And even in the safest arms she'd ever known, a part of her still listened for footsteps in the dark.

Lucas sat up slowly, dragging a hand down his face before glancing at his phone. "Mason's already downstairs. I want you to go straight to the elevator and into the car. No stops. No wandering."

Amelia sighed, pulling the blanket tighter around her. "You make it sound like someone's waiting outside with a net."

His jaw tightened. "I don't gamble when it comes to people I care about."

The words hit her chest like a spark. Sharp, unexpected and

warm.

People he cared about. She reached for his hand, lacing her fingers through his. "Okay," she said softly. "I'll do it your way."

Something in his shoulders relaxed. He brought her hand to his lips, pressing a kiss to her knuckles soft and lingering before sliding out of bed. "I'll have coffee waiting."

Amelia watched him disappear into the kitchen, heart thudding, torn between fear and the fierce, unfamiliar feeling of being protected.

By the time Amelia stepped out of the bedroom, she was armor-clad in the only way she knew how. A black pencil skirt that hugged her like a shield, a white blouse buttoned to precision, and heels that made her feel taller than she felt. Stronger than she was.

Lucas stood in the kitchen, sleeves rolled up, pouring coffee with calm efficiency. He looked so solid. So steady. Like nothing could touch him.

"Breakfast?" he asked, offering the cup.

She shook her head, her voice tight. "Too nervous."

He didn't argue. Just handed her the cup and leaned in, brushing a kiss against her mouth gentle and grounding. "Be safe. I'll see you later."

She nodded, forcing a smile before stepping into the elevator. Her stomach churned.

When the doors opened in the lobby, Mason was already there. He just opened the door of the waiting car with a quiet nod.

"Morning, Monroe," he said as she slipped in.

Amelia offered a small, tired smile. "Morning."

As the door shut, she let out a breath she didn't know she'd been holding.

This was it now. Her life, rewritten.

Mason pulled into traffic, glancing once in the mirror. "I'll keep my distance. You won't notice me."

She huffed, a faint laugh. "Pretty sure that's impossible."

She didn't miss the ghost of a smirk twitching at his lips. A quiet, human crack in the armor.

And oddly... it helped.

Amelia stepped out of the car, her heels clicking softly on the pavement. Mason shadowed her with quiet precision, always close but never intrusive.

Inside the lobby, the world buzzed as usual. Phones rang, keyboards clacked, voices drifted. But Amelia's pulse beat louder than all of it.

Sophia looked up from her desk and froze. Her eyes flicked from Amelia to the man behind her, then back again. "Uh... who's the human tank?"

Amelia exhaled, dragging a hand through her hair. "Lucas hired him. For protection."

Sophia's smirk vanished in an instant. "Ethan?"

Amelia nodded, throat tight. "He left a note. At the penthouse."

Sophia's jaw clenched. "Son of a bitch" She lowered her voice. "You okay?"

"Lucas is... taking care of it."

Sophia reached out, gently curling her fingers around Amelia's arm. "I hate that this is your life right now. But I'm glad you're not facing it alone."

Amelia gave her a grateful, shaky smile. "Me too."

Amelia spent the entire day at work trying to ignore the weight pressing down on her. She stole glances toward the front entrance more times than she wanted to admit, half-expecting to see his figure lurking outside the glass doors. Mason stood near the exit, stone-still, his eyes scanning every corner of the street like a man who expected war.

Amelia should have felt protected.

Instead, her skin crawled.

The fear didn't sit in her chest, it slithered, coiled low in her stomach, growing tighter with every breath. Her hands trembled as she shoved her things into her bag, trying not to notice how her coworkers laughed in the background, oblivious. Normal.

God, she wanted normal.

Sophia's voice was soft, hesitant. "Do you want to go somewhere first? Just… breathe for a minute?"

Amelia blinked, throat thick. She wanted to say yes. To chase down a barstool and a glass of wine and pretend Ethan's ghost wasn't following her.

But she couldn't lie to herself.

What she needed was the only place she felt untouchable.

"I just want to go home," she whispered. "To the penthouse."

Sophia didn't push. She just nodded, hugging her gently. "Call me. Please."

When Amelia stepped through the doors, the outside world felt sharper. Colder. The air bit at her skin.

Mason was already waiting. His expression unreadable, his body rigid. The dark sunglasses made him look more machine than man.

As he opened the door, Amelia climbed into the back seat, the click of it shutting behind her too loud, too final.

And as the car pulled away from the curb, her fingers curled into fists in her lap.

Because she wasn't breathing easier.

She was holding her breath.

The moment Amelia stepped inside, her body began to loosen like it had been bracing against the world all day, and only now remembered how to breathe.

The penthouse was dim, quiet. Sandalwood clung to the air, warm and familiar, like the memory of safety.

Lucas stood by the bar, his sleeves rolled, tie loosened, shirt unbuttoned just enough to make her heart stutter. When his eyes met hers, everything else dropped away.

He didn't speak.

Just crossed the room in a few long strides and wrapped his arms around her, firm and sure. His body was warm, solid. A fortress.

"How was work?" he murmured, voice low against her temple.

She didn't answer right away. Just buried her face in his chest and breathed him in.

"I couldn't focus," she finally whispered. "Every time the elevator dinged, I flinched. Every time someone looked at me too long, I thought….what if it's him?"

Lucas held her tighter.

And for a moment, just a moment, she let herself believe he could hold the fear at bay.

"He won't get near you, Amelia. I won't let him."

She closed her eyes. "I hate feeling like this. I hate that he still has power over me."

Lucas tilted her chin, forcing her to look at his piercing gaze.

"He doesn't. You're here. You're safe. And I promise you, I will not let him win."

A shiver rolled through her not from fear, but from the way his voice wrapped around her like a promise. The way his presence steadied her, tethered her to something real. Something safe.

Lucas dipped his head, his lips brushing her temple, feather-light. Then lower. A breath. A whisper. "Let me take your mind off him."

She tensed, a protest on the edge of her lips. "Lucas…"

"I want you to feel like yourself again," he said softly, like he was speaking to the most fragile part of her. "Not the girl he broke but the woman you are."

Her chest tightened. Her breath stuttered.

He kissed a line down her neck, each press of his mouth soft. His hands moved over her back with purpose.

The fear didn't vanish.

But it loosened.

"Come with me," he murmured, voice low, calm, but laced with something that made her knees weak.

Amelia followed, her fingers threading through his, the steady rhythm of his footsteps grounding her as they moved through the shadows of the penthouse. Every step away from the chaos outside felt like shedding armor.

In the bedroom, he turned to her. His fingers found the zipper of her skirt, slow and steady, eyes never leaving hers. The fabric slid over her hips, and his lips ghosted over her ear.

"Let me take care of you tonight," he whispered.

He moved to her blouse, undoing each button with aching care. Not to undress her, but to peel away everything the world had laid heavy on her skin.

Her heart skipped as he peeled the fabric away, letting it slip down her body, pooling at her feet. The cool air kissed her skin, but Lucas's warmth surrounded her, grounding her.

He stepped back just slightly, eyes dark with desire as he took her in. "So beautiful," he murmured, his fingers ghosting over her bare shoulders.

She reached for him, fingers fumbling at his shirt buttons, aching to feel his skin. To ground herself in the solid, steady warmth of him. Lucas didn't stop her. He let her touch, let her need. .

"Sit," he said, voice low, firm, but gentle.

She obeyed without hesitation, perching herself on the edge of the mattress, her hands resting on her thighs. Lucas stood before her, his towering frame casting a shadow over her. Without a word, he reached into the nightstand. Her breath caught when he pulled out a length of deep black silk. Something low and electric flickered in her chest. Anticipation.

He held the rope loosely in his hands, then looked at her, *really* looked.

"Do you trust me?" His voice was low, rough velvet.

Amelia's heart pounded, her skin already warming beneath the weight of his attention.

She swallowed hard, her lips parting. "Yes," she whispered, her voice shaky not with fear, but with *want*. With surrender. With the delicious ache of giving up control and knowing she was safe.

Her answer hung between them, quiet and powerful.

"Good," Lucas said, a smirk playing on his lips as he knelt before her. His hands moved one gripping her ankle while the other began to loop the rope around her wrist. The silk was cool against her skin. Lucas's fingers didn't fumble. They moved with purpose.

The first loop of silk cinched around her wrist like a promise. The second followed, his touch steady as he bound her with deliberate care, lifting her arms above her head, anchoring her to the bedpost.

The position left her utterly open. Exposed....The kind of exposure that stripped her bare from the inside out.

Her breath caught. She could feel her heartbeat everywhere. Against the silk, in her throat, between her thighs. Desire curled through her veins,

"Lucas..." she whispered, her voice a fragile thread of sound.

He leaned in, the heat of his body brushing hers, his fingers gently trailing along her jaw. "Shh," he breathed, his lips grazing her cheek. "Let me have you tonight."

Her eyes fluttered shut the moment his mouth met hers.

The kiss was slow, like he was worshiping her with every brush of his lips.

Every pull of his mouth unraveled her thread by thread, until she was floating in that space between surrender and need.

His hands followed. One slid along the curve of her throat, his thumb brushing over her pulse like he needed to feel the proof that she was real. Alive. *His.*

He traced her collarbone with maddening patience, then moved lower, fingers spreading across her chest cupping the swell of her breasts like he could feel the ache building beneath her skin.

There was hunger in his touch, yes but also something gentler. Like even in his desire, he *honored* her. Like breaking her apart was an act of devotion.

She arched into his touch instinctively, every nerve in her body begging for more.

When he pulled back, his eyes were pure heat, dark and devouring. "You don't know what you do to me," he rasped, drinking her in like a man starved. "You're mine like this… utterly, beautifully mine."

His fingertips ghosted along her ribs, down the curve of her waist, before settling on the inside of her thighs. A low gasp escaped her lips. Her muscles tensed beneath his touch, the anticipation unbearable. Lucas didn't speak, he didn't need to. His actions were a language all their own.

He leaned in, his lips brushing along her inner thigh, igniting a trail of fire with every kiss. She trembled, her body already aching. When his breath hit the damp heat between her legs, her hips jerked toward him.

He chuckled, dark and low. "So eager," he murmured against her. "So fucking perfect like this."

Her panties were barely a barrier, but he teased her through the fabric anyway. His tongue pressing gently, until her moans filled the room.

"Please…" she breathed, her voice barely a sound just a shiver of want caught between her lips.

She didn't even know what she was begging for.

Release. Relief. Or maybe just more of *him.*

Lucas stilled between her thighs.

"Please what?" His voice was pure sin.

She felt his breath before she felt his touch, warm and slow against her aching clit. The anticipation made her hips jerk, a quiet, desperate motion she couldn't contain.

"Tell me, sweetheart," he murmured, his lips so close she could feel the shape of his words. "Tell me exactly what you need."

Amelia's body trembled under the weight of her need. Her wrists pulled gently against the restraints, her chest rising and falling in rapid, shallow breaths. "I want your mouth," she whispered, shame and desire blending into something wickedly raw. "Please, Lucas…"

A groan vibrated in his throat, low and primal. "That's my girl."

He didn't make her wait this time.

His mouth claimed her through the soaked fabric. One slow, devastating stroke of his tongue that made her hips jerk off the mattress. Then another, firmer, more insistent. Her moan turned into a cry, her fingers curling into fists.

He hooked his fingers into her panties, dragging them down her legs with agonizing slowness, baring her completely. The cool air kissed her wet heat, and then his tongue return.

Lucas ate like a man starved. He licked and sucked, alternating between gentle swirls and punishing flicks of his tongue against her clit until she was writhing, moaning and panting his name.

Lucas…..oh God….*Lucas*," she gasped. The sound broken, desperate and pouring from her like a confession.

And then he was inside her. Two fingers slid in without warning. Deep, deliberate. Curling in just the right way to tear another cry from her throat.

The stretch was sharp, intoxicating. Pain-laced pleasure that shattered any thoughts she had left.

His mouth never left her. Tongue wicked and unrelenting, moving in rhythm with his fingers, coaxing her higher and dragging her apart one trembling breath at a time.

She was unraveling fast.

A heartbeat of heat and sensation. Of fingers and tongue. And by the time she realized she was begging again, she was already on the edge.

"I can feel you shaking," he growled against her. "Let go for me. Now."

And she did. Her orgasm tore through her like a storm. Her body bowed off the bed, back arched, a scream ripping from her throat as the world shattered in white-hot pleasure. Lucas didn't stop. His fingers working her through it, drawing every last ripple from her until she was a trembling mess.

When he finally pulled back, his mouth glistened with her, his eyes dark and wild.

"Beautiful," he said, brushing the backs of his fingers along her inner thigh. "But I'm not finished."

He climbed up her body slowly. Trailing open-mouthed kisses along her stomach, her ribs, the swell of her breasts. When he reached her mouth, he kissed her deeply. Letting her taste herself on his tongue.

"Lucas…" she gasped when he broke the kiss, her body still trembling.

"Shh." He undid the bindings, kissing each wrist as it was freed. "You gave me everything. Now let me give you more."

He flipped her gently onto her stomach. She felt his hands on her hips, his fingers digging in just enough to bruise. His cock, hard and heavy, pressed between her thighs.

"Ready for me?" he asked, his voice wrecked with restraint.

She nodded, cheek pressed to the mattress. "Yes… please."

His growl was the only warning she got before he slammed into her. Deep and hard. Her moan was guttural, broken. He thrust again and again and again His hands gripping her hips, dragging her back into each stroke like he needed to be buried in her completely.

Lucas leaned forward, his chest against her back, his hand sliding up her throat to tilt her head just enough for his mouth to find her ear.

"You feel that?" he rasped. "That's how I own you. Every inch of you. Every sound you make. Every time your body begs for mine."

His hand slid lower, finding her clit again. The pressure inside her built like an inferno.

"I want you to come around me again," he growled. "I want to feel you fall apart while I'm inside you."

Amelia cried out, the second orgasm crashing over her like fire and thunder. Her muscles clamped around him, her body trembling like she might come undone.

Lucas lost control. With a low, feral snarl, he drove into her one final time. His body shuddering with the force of it.

His grip on her hips tightened, bruising and desperate. Like letting go of her would mean unraveling completely. His rhythm broke. It was no longer measured, no longer composed. Just pure need. And then he was coming inside her. He held her there. Buried in her, his entire body trembling with the force of it. His jaw clenched like he was barely holding himself together. Because this wasn't just release.

It was surrender. And it wrecked him.

They collapsed together, tangled in heat, breathless and spent.

For a long time, the only sound was their ragged breathing.

Lucas's hand slid up her spine, tender now, as he pressed a kiss to her shoulder blade. "You're mine," he whispered.

"Nothing and no one, is ever taking you from me."

Amelia closed her eyes, her body sore and throbbing in the most beautiful way.

She lay curled against Lucas's chest, listening to the steady rhythm of his breathing. His hand traced lazy circles on her back, his warmth keeping her anchored.

"Are you okay?" he asked softly, his voice thick with sleep.

She nodded against him. "Better than okay."

Lucas pressed a kiss to her hair. "You're stronger than you think, Amelia."

She closed her eyes, soaking in the safety of his embrace. Maybe she was. Maybe, with Lucas by her side, she could finally believe it.

Amelia woke to the soft glow of the city lights spilling through the massive windows, her body still tangled with Lucas's. For a moment, she let herself savor the warmth of his arms around her, the steady rise and fall of his chest beneath her cheek. But then her phone buzzed on the nightstand, shattering the peace.

She stiffened.

Lucas felt it immediately, his grip tightening around her waist. "What is it?"

Heart pounding, she reached for the phone, fingers trembling as she unlocked the screen. A chill ran down her spine.

Another message.

Did you think staying with him would keep you safe? You're still mine. You always will be.

The air caught hard in her throat, sharp and sudden, as if the message itself had stolen her ability to breathe.

She didn't speak. She simply thrust the phone into Lucas's

hands, her fingers shaking so violently she nearly dropped it.

He read the message in a heartbeat. His body going rigid, jaw locking like a trigger pulled tight.

"Ethan." His voice was cold. Flat. Deadly.

Amelia scrambled upright, dragging the sheets with her and wrapping them around her body like armor that couldn't quite keep the panic out.

"He knows I'm here."

Her voice was thin, broken. "Lucas... *how does he know?*"

Her thoughts raced faster than she could catch them.

Was Ethan watching the building?

Had he followed her?

Had he been outside this whole time, waiting for her to let her guard down?

The walls felt like they were closing in.

Lucas was already in motion, grabbing his phone with the kind of calm that only came from fury held on a tight leash.

"I'm calling my team. We lock everything down now."

His voice was clipped, controlled, but she saw it in his eyes.

The rage. The promise of violence.

But it wasn't enough to stop the cold from seeping into her bones.

Because it wasn't just a message. It was a reminder.

Ethan still had reach. Still had power. And even here, wrapped in silk sheets and Lucas's arms, surrounded by locked doors and guards she wasn't safe.

A sharp knock at the front door made her jump. Lucas was on his feet instantly, pulling on his pants as he strode out of the bedroom. Amelia hesitated, before following.

When Lucas opened the door, his head of security, Damien, stood there. His expression grim.

"Sir, we found something."

Lucas let him inside. "What is it?"

Damien pulled out his phone and swiped to the security camera stills. "He's been outside the building. This was taken two hours ago."

Amelia stepped closer, and the air rushed from her lungs. Ethan. He was standing across the street, staring up at the penthouse, his face partially hidden by the hood of his jacket.

Her stomach twisted. "Oh my God…"

Lucas wrapped an arm around her, pulling her close. "We're upgrading security. More men, more cameras. And you're not going anywhere alone."

Amelia swallowed hard, her fingers gripping his arm. "Lucas… he won't stop. He's getting bolder."

Lucas's expression darkened. "Then we make sure he has nowhere to run."

The walls of Lucas's penthouse, once her sanctuary, now pressed in around her like a cage. Everything was beautiful but it felt hollow now. Too quiet. Too *watched*.

Amelia moved through the space on bare feet, her steps slow and deliberate Her senses sharpened to a knife's edge. She knew the security team was there hidden behind screens, cameras, encrypted feeds. She felt them. Eyes she couldn't see tracking her every movement.

And still, she listened. For footsteps that didn't belong. For breath where there should be silence. For *him*.

Lucas had reinforced everything. Additional guards. Upgraded surveillance. A private elevator now secured with biometrics. The penthouse was a fortress.

It should have made her feel safe. But it didn't.

Because all the new locks, all the eyes on her, weren't a

comfort. They were a *reminder*.

Of how close Ethan had come. Of how little space there was left between her and the version of her that had once begged to disappear.

The silence here wasn't peaceful anymore.

It was loaded. Every shadow a threat. Every creak a question.

She didn't feel safe. She felt *contained*.

Like prey kept on display. Protected, yes but only because something outside the glass still wanted to break in and finish the job.

Ethan was out there. Watching. Waiting.

The messages kept coming, each one more disturbing than the last.

You look good with him, but we both know you belong to me.

The text came with a photo.

Taken earlier that day.

Amelia, stepping out of the café with Sophia. Smiling. Unaware.

Her blood turned to ice.

She stared at the image, her fingers clenching around her phone. The angle was close. Too close.

He had been there. Watching her. Close enough to touch.

Her stomach twisted violently. She stumbled back, hitting the edge of the kitchen island with a sharp thud. The nausea crawled up her throat as the world tilted around her.

Lucas was at her side in an instant. "What is it?"

She couldn't speak, just handed him the phone, her hand trembling.

His eyes scanned the screen. His jaw locked. Then his whole body stilled in that terrifying, simmering way she recognized,lethal restraint.

"He was there," she whispered, voice thin with panic. "He's following me. Lucas, he's… *right there.*"

Lucas inhaled slowly, as if holding back something volcanic. "Mason," he barked. "We need eyes on every street camera near that café. Get me facial recognition. Anything."

Mason, didn't waste time with questions. "On it."

Lucas turned back to her, his hands landing firm and steady on her shoulders. "From now on, you're not stepping outside without me or Mason. Not even to get coffee. You hear me?"

Amelia's voice cracked. "I can't live like this, Lucas. I can't breathe with him always watching. I keep wondering… what if next time he doesn't just take a picture?"

Lucas's gaze burned with something cold. Dangerous. His hands slid up to frame her face. "He won't get that chance."

"I want to believe you," she whispered. "But he's not afraid. He's getting bolder."

Lucas's grip tightened slightly, his voice low and razor-sharp. "Then we stop playing defense."

She blinked. "What do you mean?"

"I mean we find him before he finds you. And when we do…" His tone dropped, a promise edged in fury. "I make sure he never comes near you,or anyone ever again."

Amelia swallowed hard, something trembling deep in her chest.

Because she believed him.

Not just that Lucas would fight for her.

But that he would end this.

For good.

Thirty-One

Chapter 31

Lucas sat at his desk, fingers drumming against the polished wood, his patience wearing thin.

The clock on the wall read 11:42 PM.

By now, he should have known where Ethan lived, what car he drove and what he ate for breakfast.

Instead? Nothing.

The phone finally buzzed. He answered immediately.

"Tell me you have something," he said, his voice like ice.

A sigh came from the other end of the line.

"I have… pieces," the investigator admitted. "But tracking this guy down is turning out to be harder than I expected."

Lucas's fingers curled into a fist.

"Explain."

"He's careful," the investigator continued. "There's no digital footprint. He has no credit card activity and no official lease in his name. I checked old addresses and past employers, nothing. It's like he's living off the grid."

Lucas's jaw clenched. That wasn't possible. Everyone left a trail.

"That's not all," the investigator added.

Lucas's grip on the phone tightened. "Keep talking."

"I ran background checks on him. A few minor altercations, a harassment complaint that never went anywhere but something doesn't add up. His employment records are patchy. Inconsistent. Every few months, he moves. He disappears. Almost like he's used to being watched."

Lucas exhaled sharply. That meant one thing.

"He's done this before," he muttered.

"It looks that way."

A slow, dark fury settled in Lucas's chest. Ethan wasn't just an obsessed ex. He was a predator.

"Find him," Lucas said, his voice dangerously calm. "I don't care how long it takes. I want know every single place he's been in the last six months. I want to know who he talks to, where he sleeps, what fucking toothpaste he uses. Do you understand me?"

"Understood," the investigator said quickly. "I'll keep digging."

Lucas ended the call, his mind already calculating his next move.

Amelia was sitting on the bed, curled under the blankets but she hadn't slept.

She had heard the edge in Lucas's voice through the walls, the barely restrained anger.

When he walked into the room, she could still feel it radiating off him. His frustration, his need to fix this, find Ethan and end this threat before it touched her again.

She swallowed hard. "Was that about him?"

Lucas sat down at the edge of the bed, his back to her, hands clasped together as he exhaled slowly.

"He's harder to track than I thought," he admitted. "He knows how to disappear."

Her stomach twisted.

"What does that mean?" she whispered.

Lucas turned his head slightly, his gaze piercing, unwavering.

"It means he's not done with you yet."

A chill ran down her spine.

She knew Ethan was dangerous. But she had hoped this would be over quickly. That Lucas would find him, shut him down and make it stop.

Instead, it was just beginning.

Lucas reached out, his fingers skimming her bare thigh beneath the blanket. Not to seduce, not to demand, but to anchor.

"I won't let him get to you," he said, voice steady. Unshakable. "But you need to trust me, Amelia. Completely."

Her pulse stuttered. Because she already did.

"I do trust you," she murmured.

Lucas's grip on her leg tightened, his jaw clenching like he was holding something back. Something darker.

"Then let me take care of you."

Thirty-Two

Chapter 32

The day had been long, but not unbearable. And for a few fleeting moments, Amelia almost let herself believe things were starting to feel… normal. Or at least, whatever *normal* looked like with a bodyguard trailing her every move and Lucas never more than a breath behind.

Mason had driven them through the city, his eyes always scanning. Rearview mirror, side streets, every passerby a potential threat. He was calm, efficient, unreadable. Just like Lucas had promised.

She'd moved through her errands on autopilot. Grocery store, pharmacy, dry cleaner. Each step calculated, each smile forced. A performance for the world. A mask for her own sanity.

Even with Lucas at her side, his presence like a wall between her and the rest of the world, and Mason keeping watch from the driver's seat.

That feeling still lingered. A gnawing ache in her gut. A whisper in the back of her mind.

The sense that something was coming. Something she couldn't see yet.

It followed her through every doorway, every conversation, every attempt at pretending she was fine.

Because even in the light of day, surrounded by protection, she still felt hunted.

And deep down, she knew…. Ethan wasn't finished yet.

By the time they arrived back at the penthouse, Amelia felt exhausted.

Lucas stepped in first, his instincts razor-sharp as always. Mason followed behind, scanning every corner before nodding in approval. The security team had eyes on the building, and no one unauthorized could have entered. At least, that was the assumption.

But as Amelia stepped inside, her blood ran cold.

A package.

Sitting perfectly in the center of the coffee table. Unmarked. Plain.

Her stomach twisted painfully.

Lucas saw it the exact moment she did. His entire body tensed, and in one swift movement, he pushed her behind him. Mason immediately stepped forward, pulling his gun from his holster as he scanned the apartment.

"How the hell did this get in here?" Lucas's voice was dangerously calm, but Amelia could feel the fury simmering beneath his words.

Mason moved methodically, checking the locks and the windows. Nothing was broken, and there was no sign of forced entry.

"Security logs don't show any breaches," Mason muttered.

"Then someone let him in," Lucas growled. "Or he found a way past them."

The thought made Amelia's skin crawl.

Lucas cautiously picked up the package and unwrapped it.

Amelia's breath hitched when the contents spilled onto the table.

Two bullets.

One for her.

One for Lucas.

And the note.

If I can't have you, no one will.

A sharp gasp slipped from Amelia's lips. Her body locked up, ice flooding her veins. She wanted to run, to scream. To do anything, but all she could do was stare at those two bullets, her heart slamming against her ribs.

Ethan had been inside. He had stood in this very room.

Lucas's fist clenched around the note, the paper crumpling under the force of his grip. His jaw locked so tight it looked like it hurt to speak.

When he finally turned to Amelia, rage still carved into every line of his face.

Mason stepped forward, voice low and grim. "He's getting desperate."

There was a beat of silence.

"That makes him even more fucking dangerous." Lucas's exhale came out sharp like it cost him everything not to punch a hole through the nearest wall. Instead, he reached for her, pulling her tightly against his side.

His voice dropped, low and lethal.

"We're done playing defense."

Amelia's breath caught. Her body was trembling, and she couldn't make it stop.

Her mind raced. Images. Memories. The feel of Ethan's hands. His voice. That *note.*

Lucas's grip tightened as if he could feel her slipping.

"He wants to keep pushing? Wants to fucking play games?" His voice cracked.

"Fine. But I swear to God, Amelia, he's not getting another fucking chance. I'll burn the whole goddamn city down before I let him touch you again."

Amelia looked up at him, eyes wide, chest heaving.

She wasn't just scared. She was *terrified.* Because Ethan was spiraling.

And Lucas? Lucas was ready to go to war.

Amelia's hands trembled as she yanked another handful of clothes from the closet, shoving them into the open suitcase on the bed. She couldn't even feel her fingers anymore, just the blood rushing in her ears. The thunder of her heartbeat drowning out every trace of logic.

Go. Just go.

If she stayed, Lucas would die.

Ethan had made that crystal fucking clear.

The bullets was the final straw.

This wasn't just fear anymore. This was war.

And Lucas was in the line of fire.

Tears blurred her vision as she fumbled with the zipper, chest tightening with every jagged breath.

Every piece of her screamed *don't do this.*

But this….this was what love looked like now.

Run before he bleeds for you.

She was halfway to the door when she heard it.

"Don't."

One word and it froze her in place.

Her spine went rigid. Her breath caught mid-air.

She turned slowly.

Lucas stood in the doorway. His jaw was clenched, his fists shaking at his sides. Every inch of his body radiated fury, the kind that could level cities.

But when he stepped toward her, his touch was soft.

His hand curled around her wrist like she might break beneath the weight of his anger.

"Don't do this," he said, voice quiet and cracked around the edges. "Don't walk away from me."

Her lips trembled. She couldn't speak.

His gaze dropped to the suitcase. His shoulders shook once and when he looked at her again, there was something hollow in his eyes.

"I don't need protection from you, Amelia. I need *you*."

And that broke her because loving him was killing her.

And leaving him might kill her, too.

"Lucas,"

"No." His voice was firm, commanding. "You're not leaving."

Tears spilled over her lashes. "I have to. Ethan, he's not going to stop. He'll kill you, Lucas. I can't….I won't let that happen."

Lucas exhaled sharply, his hand moving to cup her face. His warm and steady touch grounded her in a way nothing else could. "You think running is going to stop him? You think leaving me behind is the answer?" His thumb brushed away her tears. "You're mine, Amelia. I'm not letting you go."

Her chest ached at his words. "But if something happens to you,"

"Then we'll fight together." His other hand slid to the back of her neck, pulling her closer. "I love you, Amelia. I'm not losing you. And you sure as hell aren't going through this alone."

A sob broke free as she gripped the front of his shirt, her body trembling against his. She had been so sure leaving was the only way, but Lucas…his strength, his love. Made her realize something.

She didn't have to run. Not anymore.

"I love you too," she whispered, her voice breaking.

Lucas pressed his forehead against hers, his breath warm against her lips. "Then stay. We face this together."

Hours ago, her mind had been made up. Run, disappear, sacrifice whatever this was before Ethan took it from her with blood and fire.

But then Lucas had held her. Convinced her to stayed.

Now, the steam clung to the bathroom mirror, curling along the edges like a breath that refused to fade. Her skin was still damp from the shower, hair dripping down her back as she sat on the edge of the tub, wrapped in one of Lucas's towels.

She stared at the floor.

Not thinking, just feeling. She had expected fear. Regret. But what surprised her most… was the calm. Not peace. Not exactly. But something close.

The kind that comes after making a choice you *know* will cost you something, but loving him meant choosing him again and again. Even when it hurt. Even if it killed her.

That's when she heard it. Lucas's voice, smooth and certain, cutting through the quiet like a thread pulling her back to him.

"Get dressed. I want to see you in something elegant," he murmured. "Something that makes every man in that restaurant jealous that they can't touch you." His thumb brushed over her collarbone, slow, deliberate. "But that they'll know, just by looking. That you belong to someone."

Amelia stood in front of the mirror, smoothing down the fabric of her dress. It was deep red silk, hugging her curves, and the neckline was daring but not obvious.

It felt… different.

Like a statement. Like she was claiming her place at Lucas's side.

Her stomach flipped at the thought.

She turned as Lucas stepped into the room. He had changed into a tailored black suit, the crisp white shirt unbuttoned just enough to make her throat dry.

His gaze swept over her slowly, and for a moment, he didn't say anything.

Then, "Good girl."

Her entire body clenched.

He walked toward her, stopping just inches away. His fingers traced the delicate strap of her dress, the exposed skin along her shoulder.

"No jacket," he murmured. "I want them to see."

Her breath stuttered. "See what?"

Lucas's fingers curled around her neck, tilting her chin up until she looked directly into his eyes.

"That you're mine."

And just like that, she was ready to follow him anywhere.

After a quick drive to the restaurant, they were seated at a quiet corner table, the world outside fading beneath candlelight and polished crystal.

Amelia stared into the glass of wine before her, swirling it absentmindedly. She could still feel Ethan's eyes on her, even though he wasn't there.

Lucas, watched her quietly. His eyes tracing the tension in her shoulders, the way her fingers clenched around the stem of her glass.

"You've been quiet," Lucas said, his voice low but steady, the kind of calm that always seemed to draw her in. He leaned forward slightly, eyes narrowing with concern as he studied her. "You know, you don't have to pretend everything's okay."

Amelia looked up. She forced a smile.

"I'm fine," she lied, though the tremor in her voice gave her away.

Lucas' lips pressed into a tight line. "I don't believe you."

The waiter arrived with their food, momentarily cutting off the conversation. Lucas didn't let the interruption distract him. Once the server had left, he pushed his plate aside.

"You don't have to carry this alone, Amelia."

She glanced down at her plate, barely touching the delicate food. It all seemed so... trivial compared to the gnawing anxiety that had settled in her gut. "I know," she murmured.

There was a long silence. "I don't want to talk about it," she finally said, meeting his gaze with a mixture of gratitude and sorrow. "I just... I don't want to think about him right now. Not here. Not with you."

Lucas nodded, the understanding between them palpable. "Then let's talk about something else. Something you enjoy."

She paused, grateful for the change of subject. Even though the weight of her thoughts was never far behind. But for now, she allowed herself the small comfort of his presence.

"Okay," she said quietly, taking a deep breath. "Tell me about your most ridiculous date ever." Her attempt at humor didn't reach its full potential, but Lucas smiled, leaning closer.

"Well, there was that one where I took a girl to a movie, but it turned out to be a documentary about bees. She was… not amused."

Amelia snorted softly, shaking her head. It was a fragile laugh, but it was a start.

"Bee movie, huh?" she said, raising an eyebrow. "Sounds like a terrible choice for romance."

"I was young," he said with a smirk, his eyes never leaving hers. "She didn't think so either. She said I had no idea how to treat a woman."

"Harsh," she teased, feeling the weight of her situation slip, if only momentarily.

"Yeah, but now I know exactly how to treat a woman." His voice dropped a notch, and it was as if the world around them stilled for a moment. The light flickered in his eyes, dark with something that bordered on dangerous, but not in a way that unsettled her. It was a protective kind of heat, that made her feel safe.

"You do, don't you?" Amelia's voice was soft and playful, but something in her tone invited him closer.

Lucas' smile remained, but it softened, and he sat back, letting the easy banter linger between them. For now, it was enough. Just the two of them, in this quiet corner of the world, without reminders of Ethan or the dark things chasing her.

"I do," he said, and for a second, he looked at her as if he could keep all the shadows at bay just by being near.

The warmth of his presence and the ease of the conversation were just what she needed tonight. She didn't know what tomorrow would bring or the next day, but with Lucas sitting across from her tonight, she could pretend, just for a little while at least. That everything would be okay.

Thirty-Three

Chapter 33

Amelia sat at the vanity, the silk robe slipping off one shoulder, revealing her skin still warm from the shower. Before her, the vanity shimmered with beautiful things.

Makeup brushes lined in perfect rows. Jewelry that sparkled too brightly under the lights. A pair of heels that looked more like weapons than shoes.

Pieces of armor. And tonight, she wasn't sure she had the strength to wear them.

"You don't have to go if it doesn't feel right," he said softly, breaking the silence.

Amelia met his gaze in the mirror. "And hide forever?" she asked, her voice low but steady. "He's already taken enough from me. I won't let him take this, too."

Lucas crossed the room in two strides, placing his hands on her shoulders. His touch grounded her, as it always did. "Then you walk in there tonight like you own the damn place," he murmured, pressing a kiss to her temple. "Because you do. You're with me."

Amelia nodded, swallowing down the nerves that bubbled in her throat.

"Let's make him see he hasn't broken you," Lucas said, brushing a strand of hair behind her ear. "And let the whole city see who you belong to."

The gala was elegant, with glittering chandeliers, champagne towers, and the quiet hum of power in every conversation.

Amelia stood at Lucas's side, a vision in deep red silk, her fingers curled lightly around the stem of a champagne flute. To anyone watching, she looked calm. Poised. Untouchable.

But inside? Inside, she was suffocating.

Because he was here.

Ethan.

She had felt it before seeing him, the ice-cold prickle at the back of her neck, the phantom brush of a gaze too familiar to ignore.

And then, there he was. Standing across the ballroom, dressed in a perfectly tailored tuxedo, a champagne flute in his hand. And a knowing, viciously amused smile curving at the corner of his mouth.

Her blood turned to ice.

Lucas felt her stiffen before she even spoke. His hand, warm and grounding, pressed against the small of her back. Protective. Claiming.

He didn't have to ask. He already knew.

"Where?" he murmured.

She didn't have to point. Ethan wanted to be seen.

Lucas's gaze locked onto him instantly. His entire body went still. Dangerous.

Ethan raised his glass in a slow, mocking toast. And winked.

Lucas moved before she could stop him.

Amelia barely had time to set down her glass before Lucas stalked across the ballroom. The crowd parted instinctively, sensing the oncoming storm.

"Lucas!" she called but he didn't slow. Didn't hesitate.

By the time she reached them, Lucas had grabbed Ethan by the front of his tux, shoving him back against one of the grand marble columns with a force that made the crystal chandeliers tremble.

Gasps rippled through the ballroom.

Ethan? He laughed.

"Ah, there he is," Ethan drawled, voice smug, lazy like he had been waiting for this.

Lucas's jaw was tight, his grip ironclad, fingers digging into expensive silk." You shouldn't be here."

Ethan's smile sharpened. "You don't get to decide where I go." His gaze flickered past Lucas and to her. His smile widened. "Neither does she."

Amelia's stomach twisted.

Lucas slammed him harder against the column. "Look at her again, and I break your fucking face."

The threat was quiet. Lethal.

Ethan's eyes darkened, but he didn't lose the smirk. "Do it."

Lucas's muscles tensed, a split-second from delivering precisely what Ethan was asking for. But Amelia shoved herself between them, pressing her hand against his chest.

"Lucas." Her voice was sharp. Not pleading. Not afraid. Commanding.

His breathing was ragged, his pulse hammering beneath her palm, but he didn't move.

Didn't step back.

Ethan exhaled dramatically, adjusting his cuffs. "Amelia, you should be thanking me. If I hadn't shown up, how else would you know your new protector here has such a violent streak?" He clicked his tongue. "Not so different from me, is he?"

Lucas lunged.

Amelia grabbed his arm just in time.

"Lucas, don't. Not here. Not like this."

His chest heaved beneath her touch, but he held still. His fingers flexing at his sides like he was seconds from shattering.

Ethan's smirk returned, his gaze flicking lazily between them. "That's right, darling. Keep your guard dog on a leash."

Amelia snapped.

Before she even realized she had moved, her hand slapped across his face. The sharp crack cutting through the stunned silence of the ballroom.

Ethan's head snapped to the side. His jaw clenched, his smirk vanishing for the first time that night.

When he turned back to her, his eyes burned with something dark. Something possessive. Something dangerous.

Lucas stepped in front of her immediately, his body a shield, a silent promise.

Ethan smiled.

"I'll see you soon, sweetheart."

And then, he walked away.

Just like that. Like he hadn't just torn her world open all over again.

The second he was gone, Lucas turned, his hands cupping

her face, his gaze scanning her like he needed to ensure she was still whole.

"You okay?" he asked, but the way his hands trembled against her cheeks said he already knew the answer.

Amelia exhaled, her pulse still hammering. "No."

Lucas's grip tightened, his eyes flashing. "We're leaving."

She didn't argue.

Because she knew, this wasn't over.

Not by a long shot.

Thirty-Four

Chapter 34

Amelia's fingers tightened around the strap of her purse, nails digging into the leather as she walked beside Lucas, their steps slow against the pavement. The city murmured around them. Distant horns, soft laughter from a restaurant patio, the occasional gust of wind tugging at the hem of her dress.

And then her phone rang.

A sharp vibration in her hand.

No contact name. Just a number. Unfamiliar.

But her stomach *dropped.* Her fingers went numb as she answered, lifting the phone to her ear like it might bite her.

There was a pause just long enough to make her breath catch.

Then his voice spilled through the line.

"Amelia."

Just her name. But it sounded like a noose tightening.

"You think you can run from me?" he hissed. "You think

you can *hit* me?!"

Her legs nearly gave out. She stopped walking, frozen in place as the blood drained from her face.

"Ethan…" Her voice trembled. "Please. Just leave me alone."

A pause then unhinged laughter.

"You don't get to *ask* me for anything."

His tone curdled, turning cruel. "You *belong* to me, Amelia. I'll make sure of it."

Click.

Silence.

Her hands trembled. She lowered the phone slowly, like it had become something toxic.

And suddenly, the street felt too open. The shadows too deep. The night too loud.

She couldn't breathe. Because Ethan wasn't just watching. He was *waiting*.

"Lucas…" she whispered, her voice trembling, eyes wide with terror. She didn't want to show him how badly Ethan had shaken her, but it was impossible to hide the fear now that it was real again.

Lucas stopped walking, his gaze instantly hardening as he noticed the pallor on her face. "What did he say?" he demanded, his voice low but dangerous. He stepped closer, putting a hand on her arm, the warmth of it grounding her even as her mind spun.

"He… he said he'd find me. That I……" She choked on the words, her throat tightening, but Lucas was already taking action.

Without a second thought, he pulled her toward the car. His protective instinct flared like a firestorm. "Get in," he ordered, his voice no longer gentle but commanding. There was no time to waste, no room for hesitation. He guided her swiftly to the passenger seat, his hands steady as he buckled her in.

"Lucas, I'm scared," she whispered, her voice cracking under the weight of her fear.

"I know. Just stay with me. I'll keep you safe." His words were sharp, but there was an undercurrent of tenderness beneath the steel. He slammed the door shut and was in the driver's seat moments later, the engine roaring as they sped off into the night.

Amelia pressed her hands to the seat, staring out the window, her mind racing. She had been foolish to think a night like this could be normal. She could still hear Ethan's voice in her head, taunting her and threatening her, always one step ahead.

Lucas's eyes darted between the road and the rearview mirror, his jaw clenched.

"He's following us," he muttered under his breath, the edge of panic creeping into his tone.

Amelia glanced back, her heart pounding as she saw headlights in the distance, growing closer. "No... no, it can't be him. He wouldn't..."

But the car behind them wasn't letting up, and it didn't take long for Lucas to realize it wasn't just a coincidence.

"Hold on," he barked, swerving into another lane. The car behind them mirrored his move.

Amelia's breath hitched. "He's... he's following us."

The car was gaining on them, moving faster, too fast.

Lucas's face tightened, his hands gripping the steering wheel. "Get ready, Amelia. He's not gonna get away with this."

He floored the accelerator, the car roaring as it sped down

the road, but the pursuing vehicle wasn't giving up. It was getting closer.

"Lucas," Her voice cracked.

The words were barely out of her mouth before she heard the tires screech and the sickening thud of metal against metal. A sudden impact slammed into their side, jolting the car violently. Amelia screamed as the world seemed to tilt on its axis. Lucas cursed as the car swerved uncontrollably, tires screeching as he fought to maintain control.

The car behind them didn't stop. It nudged them again, harder this time, pushing the car toward the edge of the road. The pavement blurred past them in a dizzying rush.

"Lucas, no!" Amelia cried out, gripping the door for dear life.

He didn't answer, his focus fixed on the road as he yanked the wheel hard to the right. The tires screamed as they veered off the pavement, the car flying across the shoulder.

There was a flash of headlights and another screech of tires. Then, with a sickening thud, their car slammed into the guardrail, the metal scraping and tearing against the car's side. The impact sent them both into a violent spin.

The world went black.

When Amelia's eyes fluttered open, she was disoriented, her body aching. The seat belt dug into her chest, and she could taste blood in her mouth. Her head throbbed. Panic rose in her throat as she forced her body to move.

"Lucas?" she gasped, her voice weak.

Through the haze, she saw him. Slumped over the wheel, blood trickling from a gash on his forehead. His breathing was shallow but steady.

She reached for him, her heart pounding in her chest. Hands

trembling as she touched his arm. "Lucas… please, wake up."

His eyes slowly cracked open, blinking as he processed where he was.

"I'm… fine," he rasped. "But you need to get out of here, now."

She could barely think, fear clouding her mind.

The car behind them had stopped, and figures were emerging. The sound of boots crunching against gravel. They weren't alone anymore.

"Come on, Amelia," Lucas said, his voice now firm despite the blood dripping down his face. "We need to move. Now."

Amelia's heart pounded as she glanced toward the rearview mirror. Ethan's men. She didn't know how many there were, but the danger was real. Lucas was still groggy, but his instincts were sharp.

"Amelia," he whispered, his voice low but urgent, as he reached for the door handle with a trembling hand. "Listen to me. You need to get out. Now. I'll hold them off."

Fear gnawed at her insides, but she couldn't leave him like this, battered and bleeding, . To face Ethan's wrath alone. Her breath came in shallow gasps as her hands scrambled to unbuckle her seat belt, her mind racing through a thousand possible escape plans. None of them feeling real.

The shadows were getting closer.

She threw open the passenger door, ignoring the searing pain in her side as she stumbled out of the car, her legs shaky. "No, Lucas. You're coming with me."

But before she could take another step, he was at her side, one arm around her waist, holding her upright. He was barely standing but wasn't about to let her go, not like this.

His eyes were focused. "Get to the trees. Now."

There was no time for arguing. She could hear boots getting closer, the unmistakable crunch of gravel underfoot. Ethan's men were almost there.

They staggered toward the woods on the road's edge. Lucas limping heavily as he guided her forward. Every step felt like an eternity, the world closing in on them. The only thing that mattered was putting distance between themselves and those men.

Amelia glanced behind them one more time, her breath catching in her throat as one of Ethan's men appeared from the wreckage of the car, his gun raised. "Stop right there!" the man shouted.

Lucas didn't slow down.

"Run," he hissed, his grip tightening on her.

Her heart leaped into her throat as they pushed forward. The thud of boots in pursuit growing louder. Her muscles burned. The fear driving her legs faster. The shadows from the trees swallowing them as they ventured deeper into the woods.

Just as she thought they might be safe, a bullet whizzed past her, too close. It struck a tree, splintering the bark. Her breath froze in her chest.

"Lucas!" she cried, her voice frantic.

"Keep moving!" he barked, but his steps were getting slower. The blood loss and the injury to his head beginning to catch up with him.

Amelia pulled him with all the strength she had, even as her own body screamed for rest. She couldn't leave him. She wouldn't.

She glanced around, trying to think and find something, anything that could help them. The woods felt endless. The footsteps were getting closer but Lucas slowed down, each movement less controlled.

"Lucas, stay with me, please," she whispered, her voice cracking.

"I'm here," he said, his voice faint, but his eyes never wavered from her. "I'm right here. We… we just need to,"

A shout rang out from behind them. Then another, and the sound of the men scattering. They were closer now, closer than ever. Lucas pulled her into a small hollow under the thick roots of an old oak tree.

"Stay down," he ordered, his voice hoarse. "Don't make a sound."

Amelia nodded, biting her lip as she pressed herself against him. The chill of the night air seeping into her skin. She could hear her pulse in her ears, as she watched Lucas struggle to stay conscious.

The woods were dark but not dark enough to hide them completely. She could hear the men moving, their voices rising above the rustling of the trees. "Spread out! They're close! Get the girl."

Her stomach churned at the words. *Get the girl.*

The forest felt like a prison and every breath was a dangerous gamble. She pressed her ear against Lucas's chest. Feeling the uneven thump of his heart, but it was slowing. His strength was fading, and if they didn't act quickly…

Amelia's eyes darted around, searching for any way out. Then, she spotted it. Just beyond the trees, a faint flicker of light. A house. It was a long shot, but it might be their only chance.

She took a deep breath, forcing the words past her trembling lips. "There's a house… It's just up the road. If we can make it…"

Lucas shook his head, his voice barely above a whisper. "You… need to go. They're after you, not me. You're…."

"No," she snapped cutting him off. Her eyes wild with panic. "I'm not leaving you. We're going together."

He was too weak, but something in his gaze told her he understood. He was giving her the choice, even if it meant risking everything.

"Okay," he breathed, his voice strained. "We go together."

Without another word, she helped him to his feet. Her body trembling with the effort. They moved again, painfully slow. The sounds of pursuit growing more urgent. She had no idea if they would make it. No idea how far the house was or if anyone would be there to help.

But she couldn't stop now. Not when Lucas was by her side. Not when Ethan's madness was so close.

They staggered forward, their steps uneven. More instinct than direction. Every inch of ground beneath their feet felt like a battlefield

The air reeked of sweat, blood, and panic.

Amelia clung to the only thing that mattered now….*survival.* Not for herself. For *them.* For *him.*

They didn't look back. They couldn't. Behind them, the sound of boots pounding against earth grew louder. Twigs snapped like bones under heavy feet. The men were gaining.

"Keep moving," Lucas rasped. His voice was frayed. Like it had been scraped raw from pain. But still, he pushed forward, dragging one foot in front of the other, his arm still locked around her waist.

His grip had changed. Looser. Slipping. His fingers no

longer holding her. They were *clinging* to her. She could feel the tremble in his body, the way he leaned heavier with each step. His strength, once unshakable, now flickered like a dying flame.

But he wouldn't stop and neither would she. Because if they stopped now… It was over.

She tightened her grip on him, blinking back the panic rising in her throat. They had to keep going.

His face was pale, blood still dripping from the gash on his forehead, staining his shirt, but his eyes remained focused on her.

Amelia's own body was screaming in protest, her legs aching with each step. She had to get him to safety. She had to get them both to that house, and she didn't know if either of them had enough strength left to outrun what was chasing them.

"Almost there," she whispered, though it was more for herself than him.

The light from the house up ahead flickered again like a distant beacon.

Then, just as she thought they might make it, a shout rang out from behind them. Loud and clear. "They're here! I see them!"

The blood drained from her face.

Lucas staggered, leaning heavily against her as his knees buckled.

"Go!" he gritted through clenched teeth, his voice a raw whisper. "You have to go. Now."

"No!" Her heart slammed against her rib cage as she half-lifted him, trying to keep him steady. "I'm not leaving here without you."

He met her eyes, his expression softening briefly, but there was something dangerous in how his gaze darkened.

"You think you can outrun them with me dragging you down?"

She could feel the pulse of panic rising in her throat, but she refused to let go. They had come too far. She couldn't lose him now.

Then, suddenly, there was a rustle from the brush behind them. A figure stepped into the clearing. Tall, broad and menacing. The first of Ethan's men had caught up.

Amelia froze, her heart stalling in her chest. The man held a knife, the blade gleaming in the dim light. His eyes were wide with madness, fueled by Ethan's commands and a twisted smile stretched across his face.

"Where are you going, sweetheart?" the man sneered, stepping closer. "You can't escape. Not with him."

Her blood turned to ice as she shoved Lucas behind her instinctively. Though her body trembled with the sudden wave of terror.

"Get behind me," she breathed to him.

Lucas was too weak to fight, his breath shallow as he swayed, but he gave her a slight, grim nod. He wasn't about to let her face this alone, no matter how much it hurt.

"Get out of the way, little girl," the man growled, taking another step forward.

"Lucas," Amelia whispered, her mind racing. Looking for anything…. anything that could save them.

Before she could react, Lucas did what she never expected. With a force she didn't think he still had, he shoved her aside. Grabbing a jagged rock with one hand and with a growl of determination, he lunged at the man.

The knife sliced through the air, but Lucas was faster, the

rock slamming into the man's skull with a sickening crack. The man staggered back, his hand flying to his head, his eyes wide in shock.

Amelia watched frozen, as Lucas stood before her, panting heavily. Blood soaked through his clothes but he was still fighting and still protecting her.

"Run," he rasped, his voice strained with the effort. "I'll hold them off."

Her mind screamed at her to move, to escape while she still could. But she couldn't tear herself away from him. Not now.

The man staggered, blood dripping from his head as he glared at Lucas, eyes burning with fury.

"You're dead, you bastard," he spat, but before he could reach for his knife again, two more figures emerged from the shadows. More of Ethan's men, surrounding them in a half-circle.

Amelia's throat closed. There was no way out. No more time. She was frozen. Panic swelling in her chest. But just as she thought the end was near, there was a sudden shout from the direction of the house. A voice, familiar and strong. Cutting through the dark like a blade.

"Hello, Amelia".

Amelia turned, her breath caught in her throat as she saw the figure emerging from the woods. The light from the house illuminated him, casting long shadows across his shoulders.

Ethan.

His eyes were dark, burning with hatred, but there was something else in his gaze. Something colder. Calculating.

"No!" she gasped, her voice trembling.

Ethan's smile twisted, dark and cold.

"Did you think you could run from me, Amelia?" he taunted,

stepping toward them slowly as though savoring their fear. "I told you I'd find you."

But Lucas wasn't backing down. Bloodied, bruised, and barely standing. He glared at Ethan through clenched teeth.

"If you think I'm going to let you touch her..." Lucas's voice was barely above a growl, his strength and defiance still burning despite the blood loss. "You're wrong."

Ethan's grin widened. "You think you can stop me, Lucas? You don't know who you're dealing with."

The tension crackled in the air like a storm about to break, and at that moment, Amelia knew this was no longer just about her escape. This was a fight for survival

Ethan's eyes never left Lucas. Cold and calculating as he advanced toward them.

Lucas staggered slightly, his hand gripping the jagged rock tighter as though it was the only thing keeping him standing. His gaze was locked on Ethan.

"You won't win this," Lucas rasped, his voice barely audible but full of venom. "Not tonight."

Ethan's smile widened, a twisted satisfaction playing across his face. "I already have," he sneered. "You should've stayed out of this, Lucas. You're too weak. And now... you're about to be a memory."

Before Lucas could react, Ethan lunged.. He knocked Lucas to the ground in a single motion, a sickening thud echoing through the quiet woods.

Amelia screamed, her breath coming out in ragged gasps as Lucas collapsed. His body went limp, blood staining the earth beneath him. The sight of him lying there....helpless and vulnerable shattered her.

"No!" Amelia cried, her legs shaking as she stepped forward.

She reached for Lucas, desperate to wake him but Ethan's hand shot out. Gripping her by the arm.

"You really think you have a chance?" Ethan's voice was low and cruel, his fingers digging into her skin. "You can't save him. You never could."

Her entire world, was now nothing more than a nightmare. "Please… leave him alone," she pleaded, her voice trembling as tears filled her eyes. "He didn't do anything to you."

Amelia's body burned with adrenaline, her muscles screaming as she lunged.

She twisted in Ethan's grip, her nails slicing across his cheek, deep enough to draw blood. His head snapped to the side at the impact, a red gash blooming against his skin. For a fraction of a second, she felt something viciously satisfying. She hurt him.

And then he laughed. A deep, throaty chuckle that slithered down her spine like ice. He straightened, wiping the blood from his cheek with the back of his hand. His tongue flicking out to taste the crimson on his lips.

"God, I missed this."

A sick grin stretched across his face. His eyes, dark and hungry locked onto hers.

But Amelia didn't stop. She couldn't. She twisted again, bringing up her knee hard. She felt it connect with his stomach and heard the sharp exhale from his lips. But his grip on her didn't break. If anything, it tightened.

"Feisty as ever," he mused, his voice annoyingly calm despite the pain she knew he had to be feeling.

She jerked her arm back. This time hard enough that his grip loosened for one brief, glorious second. This was her chance.

She wrenched free, staggering backward, nearly tripping over the uneven forest floor. *Run.* Every cell in her body screamed the command. *Run.*

And she did. She turned and bolted, her feet pounding against the dirt. Her lungs burning. The woods were thick, the trees looming but she didn't care. She had to escape. Lucas needed her. She needed to survive.

She could hear Ethan behind her. His footsteps barely more than a whisper against the ground like he was toying with her.

"You think I haven't done this before, sweetheart?"

Amelia didn't answer. Didn't look back.

Branches whipped against her skin, slicing her arms and her legs. The house and the flickering light in the distance was so close.

Then a root. It caught her foot, twisting her ankle at an unnatural angle. Pain shot up her leg like fire and suddenly, she was falling. A choked cry escaped her lips as she hit the earth hard, her palms scraping against rocks and dirt. *No. No, no, no,*

She tried to push up tried to crawl, but before she could move, a heavy weight slammed into her back, knocking the air from her lungs.

A strong hand fisted in her hair, yanking her head back.

"Almost," Ethan purred in her ear. His breath warm against her skin. "You almost made it."

She thrashed, kicking and clawing. His grip didn't budge. And then his knife was at her throat. The cold press of steel sent a violent shudder through her body. She froze.

Ethan exhaled, almost as if he was savoring her stillness. "There it is," he murmured. "That sweet little moment when you realize you're not getting away."

Tears burned behind her eyes but she refused to let them fall.

"I hate you," she spat, her voice raw, shaking.

Ethan chuckled, his fingers stroking along the side of her neck. Dangerously close to her pulse.

"No, baby. You don't." His lips brushed against her ear. "You hate that you still excite me."

The knife dragged slowly, teasingly, down to her collarbone. Not cutting, just reminding her it could.

"Let's go home," he whispered.

And with that, he hauled her up as if she weighed nothing. And negan to drag her toward the waiting van.

Her scream tore through the trees like a final prayer. But the woods stayed silent. No one came.

Chapter 35

The van lurched over the uneven road. Its tires crunching against loose gravel.

Inside, it was dark. Too dark. Amelia sat curled against the cold metal wall, her knees drawn to her chest. Her arms wrapped tight around herself but no amount of pressure could hold her together.

Her body shook not just from the chill in the air, but from something deeper.

Terror chewed at the edges of her sanity, a slow, relentless gnawing that made it hard to breathe. Her skin felt too tight. Her heartbeat too loud. Every jolt of the van made her flinch.

Ethan had her.

The thought looped through her head like a cruel mantra. He'd won.

She had screamed until her voice cracked, had kicked and clawed and *fought* like hell but it hadn't been enough. Not this time.

And now?

Now there was only the aftermath The crushing weight of how helpless she was.

She stared down at her hands. Scratched, bloodied and trembling.

Proof that she tried.

But trying didn't matter when no one was there to hear her scream.

Amelia curled in tighter, as if she could fold herself small enough to disappear.

Because right now, hope felt like a luxury she couldn't afford.

And the worst part?

She didn't know if anyone would find her in time.

"You know…." Ethan's voice cut through the quiet like a blade, smooth and mocking, "I really thought you'd be harder to break. But, then again, you never did understand what I needed from you, did you?" He leaned forward, the light from the van's interior casting shadows across his sharp features. "You always thought you could escape me and outrun me. But this… this is where I would always end up with you, Amelia."

She stiffened, her chest tight with the mixture of rage and fear that twisted inside her. She would not let him see how much his words hurt her.

She lifted her chin, looking at him through narrowed eyes despite the trembling in her limbs.

"You're sick," she spat, her voice raw but steady. "You think you can control me? You can't. I'll never be yours, Ethan. I'd rather die first."

His laugh was low, almost admiring. It made her skin crawl.

"Such fire," he murmured, his gaze dropping to her lips as if he could taste the bitterness in her words. "That's what I like about you, Amelia. You're strong. But it's wasted. You see, you don't get a choice in this. Not anymore." He leaned back in his seat. His eyes hardening. "You'll learn to understand that soon enough."

The van jolted as it made a sharp turn, and the sound of tires scraping against gravel grew more muffled as the trees around them thickened. The landscape was unfamiliar, the shadows deep and suffocating as they drove further away from the roads she knew. She had no idea where they were going but it felt like the beginning of the end.

Ethan's voice broke through the silence again, this time quieter.

"You never did understood the game. You played into my hands whenever you ran and tried to fight me off." His fingers traced a small scar on his wrist absently. "You've been mine from the start. You were always mine."

"No," she hissed, her voice filled with a desperate conviction. "I was never yours. I'll never be yours."

The van suddenly slowed, as it pulled into a clearing. Her heart stopped in her chest as she realized they had arrived.

It was a house. Or rather, a compound. A dark, looming structure with high stone walls and iron gates, surrounded by dense woods that swallowed up any trace of light. There were no signs of life. No lights in the windows, no movement but the way the structure loomed in the night made her blood run cold.

A cage. This was a cage.

Ethan reached for the door handle, his lips curling into a satisfied smile as he looked at her.

"We're home," he said softly, almost too calmly.

Without waiting for her to respond, he yanked open the door and stepped out. Motioning for her to follow. She hesitated, her heart hammering as she looked at the walls, The iron gates and the darkness surrounding them. But what choice did she have? She had to get out. She had to find a way out.

She stumbled out of the van, her legs unsteady, feeling the weight of exhaustion and panic settle deeper into her bones. The air was thick and cold, sending shivers down her spine as she was forced to follow Ethan toward the imposing gates.

"You're not going to get away with this, Ethan," she said through gritted teeth, her voice a mixture of defiance and fear. "I'll escape. I will. I'll find a way."

His laugh was soft, almost patronizing.

"You're so sure of yourself, Amelia," he said, glancing over his shoulder at her with an amused look. "But you're forgetting one thing."

"And what's that?" she asked, breathless.

"The moment you walked away from me, the moment you ran… I made you mine. You're already in my world, sweetheart. I've planned everything."

The doors to the compound opened before them with a groan, revealing a dark hallway inside. As they stepped through the threshold, the air grew heavier and more suffocating. The walls were lined with cold stone, and the flickering of dim lights cast long shadows across the hallway.

Ethan led her deeper into the heart of the compound, the sound of their footsteps echoing in the hollow silence. Her mind was racing, but she had no idea where they were headed.

They arrived at a door at the end of the hall, where Ethan stopped and turned to face her. His gaze softened for just a moment as though savoring the moment of victory.

"Here we are," he said, the smile on his lips twisting into something darker. "This is where you'll stay. This is where you'll learn who you belong to."

The door creaked open, revealing a sterile and cold room. There was a bed with white sheets, a chair in the corner, and nothing more.

Amelia felt a sickening pang in her chest, her stomach dropping. This was it. This was where Ethan would keep her. His prisoner. And there was no escaping this time.

He stepped into the room, and she followed unwillingly, but there was no fighting him. The door shut behind them with a final click, sealing her fate.

"I'm going to make you understand, Amelia," he said softly, almost tenderly. "You'll want this. You'll want me and realize it was always meant to be this way."

Amelia's throat tightened, the tears threatening to spill over, but she held them back. She was done begging.

"I will never want you," she whispered, her voice trembling with fear and fury.

His eyes flashed, but they had no anger. Only a cold, terrifying certainty.

"We'll see," he murmured. "We'll see."

Ethan's cold smile never wavered as he turned and began to pace the small room. Every inch of her body screamed to escape, but there was nowhere to go.

The walls of the room seemed to close in on her as he circled her like a predator.

"Sit," he ordered sharply, his voice cold and flat.

Amelia didn't move at first, her body frozen in place as the sheer weight of his presence pressed down on her. She didn't want to obey, didn't want to give him that power over her. But the cold gleam in his eyes told her everything she needed to know. He wouldn't ask twice.

She sat on the edge of the bed, her hands gripping the sheets, nails digging into the fabric as her chest rose and fell with each uneven breath.

Ethan stopped pacing and stood in front of her now. His gaze softened slightly as though he was examining something fragile. He reached out, fingers brushing a strand of hair behind her ear, his touch unnervingly gentle. It sent a shiver through her, a wave of revulsion so strong that it made her stomach lurch.

"You're so beautiful, Amelia," he whispered, his voice almost too soft. "You were always so beautiful. You still are, even now."

She recoiled at the compliment, unable to stop the instinctive pull away from him. Her lips trembled, but she swallowed her fear. "Stop," she muttered, her voice rough with emotion. "I don't want your lies. I don't want any of this."

He chuckled darkly, the sound echoing like thunder in her ears. "Lies? I'm not lying, sweetheart. I'm showing you the truth. You were never free, not really. You were always meant to be mine. You didn't know it yet."

Amelia's heart ached at his words, a hollow ache deep in her chest. He was trying to break her, to make her believe that this.... this nightmare was her fate.

But she wasn't broken. Not yet.

Ethan bent down in front of her, his face inches from hers. His cold breath fanned across her skin, and she could see the darkness in his eyes, the hunger, the twisted affection that seemed to radiate from him.

"You're afraid of me, Amelia," he said, his voice almost a whisper. "I can see it in your eyes. But you'll learn to be afraid of something worse."

Her breath caught in her throat, the hairs on her neck standing on end.

"Worse?" she repeated, her voice barely a whisper. "What could be worse than this?"

His smile twisted into something far darker than anything she had seen before. His hand grabbed her chin, forcing her to look up at him. His grip was firm, almost painful.

"What I do to you now," he said slowly, almost with a sense of delight, "is just the beginning. The physical pain… that will come later. But first, I need to break you. Make you understand just how little control you have. How much you need me."

Before she could react, before she could even fully comprehend his words, he released her chin, standing up, his eyes gleaming with sadistic pleasure.

"You're going to hate me for a while, Amelia. And that's okay. But eventually, you'll see. You'll see what I'm doing is for your own good."

Her heart pounded against her ribs, her entire body trembling as a wave of nausea swept over her. She hated him. She despised him. But she couldn't afford to show him weakness.

He turned away from her, moving to a small table near the bed, his back to her. Amelia's mind raced, the panic building as she watched him. *What was he going to do next?*

Ethan returned, something small glinting in his palm. A glass of water in the other.

He didn't speak as he crouched in front of her. Then he held out his hand two white pills resting in his palm like they meant nothing.

"Take them," he said softly, his voice smooth and sickeningly calm. Like a lullaby with a knife hidden underneath.

Amelia's heart slammed against her ribs. Her breath caught as she stared at the pills, her body going rigid with dread.

"What are they?" she whispered, her voice cracking.

Ethan didn't blink.

"What are you going to do to me?"

He smiled a sick smile.

"Why do you always assume the worst?" he murmured, gently pressing the glass into her trembling hands. "Just take them, sweetheart. You'll feel so much better."

She didn't move. Because everything inside her screamed that if she swallowed what he gave her she'd never come back the same.

The glass trembled in her hands as she stared at the pills in his palm like they were poison.

Ethan's eyes darkened. The patience drained from his expression in a slow, terrifying shift. His fingers closed around the pills, and his voice dropped lower.

"Don't make me do it for you."

Amelia shook her head, backing away until her spine hit the wall. "No…..no, Ethan, I'm not…"

His hand shot out. Fast. Brutal.

She barely had time to gasp before his fingers dug into her jaw, forcing it open. The pills were shoved past her lips, his other hand slamming the glass of water against her mouth.

"Swallow," he growled.

She struggled, choked. Water spilling down her chin as her body fought to reject it. Her hands clawed at his wrist, nails scraping against his skin but he didn't even flinch.

"Swallow it, Amelia."

She gagged, coughed, tried to spit but his grip only tightened until her vision blurred and the fight left her body.

When she finally choked it down, he released her. Shoving her back against the wall like she was nothing.

She collapsed to the floor, coughing, gasping, tears running hot and fast down her cheeks. Her mouth tasted like metal. Her chest heaved, lungs burning.

He stood over her, calm again. Smiling.

"See?" he said softly, brushing a damp strand of hair from her face like a lover would.

"That wasn't so hard."

But Amelia wasn't listening.

The pills were already hitting her system.

The room tilted. Her limbs grew heavy. Her thoughts turned sluggish.

And the last thing she saw was Ethan crouching beside her again, brushing his thumb over her cheek.

"Sleep tight, sweetheart."

Then......darkness.

Thirty-Six

Chapter 36

Amelia drifted toward consciousness like a body dragged through deep water.

Her head pounded each pulse behind her eyes a drumbeat of pain. Her limbs were dead weight. Her mouth tasted like metal and bile, her tongue thick and dry as sandpaper.

She tried to swallow. Tried to breathe. But something was *wrong*. Very wrong.

Then it hit her. She had been drugged.

Panic exploded in her chest. She tried to sit up, to roll over, to scream….but her body didn't obey.

Her wrists were bound. Her ankles too. Spread wide. Tied tight.

She was exposed. Vulnerable. Caged in her own skin.

A strangled sound tore from her throat. Her heart slammed against her ribs, breath coming in short, ragged gasps as she fought against the restraints, raw terror slicing through the fog still clouding her mind.

A slow clap echoed in the silence.

"Look who's finally awake."

Ethan's voice. Mocking. Cruel.

He stepped into the dim light, his face half-shadowed, his smile twisted with satisfaction. His eyes swept over her with the cold calculation of a predator that knew its prey couldn't run.

"Sleep well, sweetheart?" he asked, crouching beside her.

"Go to hell," Amelia rasped.

He tsked softly, brushing a lock of hair from her cheek. She turned her face away, bile rising in her throat.

"You always had that fight in you," he said, his voice a sickening mix of amusement and obsession. "That's why I liked you. Still do."

He stood, pacing the small, windowless room with maddening calm. "You thought you could escape me. You thought Lucas could protect you." His tone shifted. "He touched what belonged to me. That was a mistake."

Amelia's hands balled into fists. Her voice cracked with emotion. "I'm not yours. I never was."

His smile vanished. A beat of silence.

Then he was on her.

His hand gripped her jaw, forcing her to look up. "You'll learn," he hissed. "I will unmake you. Piece by piece."

Terror surged in her throat. She pulled at the ropes until her skin burned.

"No one's coming for you," he whispered against her ear. "Not Lucas. Not the cops. It's just you and me now. The way it was always meant to be."

She shook her head, refusing the reality he was trying to

press down on her. But it was already happening. The walls were closing in. Her world shrinking down to the flicker of the light overhead… and the sound of her own breathing.

"You won't win," she said, her voice trembling.

Ethan tilted his head. "But haven't I already?"

He removed his jacket slowly, deliberately, his movements calculated and calm.

"I'm going to take back what's mine," he said.

Too soft.

Amelia froze.

She knew.

The air changed. The moment fractured like glass, sharp edges slicing through her sanity.

And then….darkness. The light flickered out, plunging the room into blackness.

Her scream never made it past her lips. Time broke apart. Her mind splintered, drifting somewhere cold and far away. Where sound didn't exist and nothing could reach her. Her body felt distant. Disconnected. Like it didn't belong to her anymore.

She was aware of every second. And none of them. Everything blurred and sharpened all at once.

There was no fight left. Nowhere for it to go. And when silence finally returned. When the light buzzed back to life and he stood over her, straightening his clothes like nothing had happened. She didn't move. She lay still. Hollow. The weight of what had been done pressing down on her.

He leaned over, his fingers brushing along her arm.

She flinched.

He smiled. "I'll come back when you've had time to think," he murmured, voice sickeningly calm. Then he turned and walked away, leaving her in the wake of the ruin he'd made of her."Eventually, you'll see. We were always meant to end up here."

The door clicked shut behind him.

Only then did Amelia let the tears fall, silent and hot. Her body trembled. Her wrists bled.

But she wasn't broken.

Not yet.

She curled onto her side and let the stillness, surround her. She repeated a single name like a prayer.

Lucas.

Thirty-Seven

Chapter 37

A dull, throbbing ache pulsed behind Lucas's eyes, radiating through his skull with every sluggish heartbeat. The world around him was muffled, like sound underwater, disconnected, unreal.

Beep. Beep. Beep.

The steady rhythm echoed in his ears, each pulse a cold reminder of where he was.

Hospital.

The antiseptic sting of bleach and sterilized linens filled his nose. His eyelids fluttered, heavy, reluctant. Bright white light pierced through the haze, and for a moment, the world blurred. Shapes and movement smeared together in a dreamlike fog.

His vision began to clear. Fluorescent ceiling panels. White walls. A nurse, speaking in hushed tones to a man at the door. Machines humming.

And then…It hit him.

Amelia.

His heart stuttered. Adrenaline surged. He jerked upright and pain exploded through his chest. Like being stabbed from the inside.

He gasped, teeth clenched, the force of it stealing the air from his lungs.

The forest.

Ethan.

The fight.

Amelia screaming.

Where the hell was she?

"Easy, son."

A firm hand on his shoulder.

Lucas turned his head, wincing as his vision swam again. A police officer stood beside the bed, thick-set, weathered, his expression grim.

"You took one hell of a beating."

Lucas didn't care.

He didn't *feel* the pain anymore not over the panic rising in his chest like fire.

"Where is she?" His voice came out raw. Cracked. "Where's Amelia?"

The officer hesitated, jaw tightening. Just for a second.

And that second said *everything*.

"You were found unconscious on a dirt road just off the main highway. A jogger spotted you early this morning. You had a head wound, fractured ribs, and signs of struggle." He paused, observing Lucas. "Can you tell us what happened?"

Lucas exhaled shakily, trying to steady his racing thoughts.

"We were ambushed," he rasped, jaw tightening. "Ethan. He

had men with him." His heart pounded against his battered ribs. "They took Amelia."

The detective scribbled something on his notepad. "Do you know where he might have taken her?"

Lucas's fingers dug into the hospital sheets. "No," he admitted, frustration searing through him. "But I swear to God, I will find her."

The officer gave him a steady look. "We'll do everything we can. But we need more details. Tell us everything you remember."

Lucas clenched his fists, his breathing ragged as he tried to force his memories into clear, coherent words for the detectives. Every detail felt like a knife twisting in his gut. Because every second that passed, Amelia was still out there, still with him.

"We were out to dinner," he started, his voice rough. "It was supposed to be a normal night. Amelia had been tense all day, but I wanted to distract her and take her mind off everything. We laughed, we talked..." His throat tightened. "For a little while, it felt like things were okay."

The detective nodded, jotting down notes. "And then?"

Lucas exhaled sharply, his jaw tightening. "We were heading back to the car when her phone rang. It was him, Ethan." His fingers twitched, rage boiling beneath his skin.

"What did he say?"

Lucas swallowed hard. *"Did you really think I'd let you keep her?"*

The detective's expression darkened. "That's when you knew he was close?"

Lucas gave a sharp nod. "I didn't want to scare Amelia, but I could see the panic in her eyes. I told her we needed to leave and got in the car. I was trying to keep it together, act like it was just another threat, but then..." He let out a slow, pained breath. "Then I saw the car."

"The one that ran you off the road?"

Lucas's grip on the bed sheet tightened. "Yeah. A black SUV. It stayed behind us, keeping pace no matter which turns I took. I knew we were being followed." He clenched his jaw. "I tried to lose them, but they were faster. Smarter. They cut us off, forced us off the road."

He could still hear Amelia's gasp and feel the impact of the car jolting off the pavement, crashing into the tree line.

"What happened next?" the officer pressed.

Lucas's expression darkened, his muscles tensing. "I grabbed Amelia's hand and told her to run. We got out of the car and into the woods but didn't get far. Ethan's men were already there. It was an ambush."

The detective leaned forward. "How many men?"

"Four, maybe five. " Lucas's teeth clenched. "Ethan didn't even bother looking at anyone else. He only had eyes for her."

He inhaled sharply, forcing himself to push past the sickening feeling in his chest. "Amelia was terrified, but she fought. I tried to get to her, but Ethan punched me. I fell to the ground."

The detective's pen paused over the notepad. "And she went."

Lucas nodded, his throat tight. "She didn't have a choice." He exhaled his voice barely above a whisper now. "The last thing I remember was her screaming my name before everything went black."

Silence filled the hospital room.

Then Lucas lifted his head, his eyes burning with fury. "He thinks he's won." His voice was cold, lethal. "But I swear to

God, I will find her. And when I do… I'll end him."

Lucas sat up straighter in the hospital bed, his muscles tense despite the dull ache radiating through his body. His head throbbed, his ribs ached, and every movement sent pain shooting through him, but none of it mattered. The only thing he cared about was Amelia.

The detective across from him finished jotting down notes. "We will put out an alert for Ethan. Our team is sweeping the area where you were found, and we've got officers checking traffic cams. If he's still in the city, we'll find him."

Lucas's jaw tightened. That's not good enough.

Before he could respond, the door swung open, and a doctor stepped in, her expression calm but professional. "Mr. Cross," she said, glancing at the detective before focusing on Lucas. "We need to discuss your injuries."

Lucas barely spared her a glance. "I don't have time for this. Just tell me what I need to know."

The doctor sighed, clearly used to stubborn patients. "You suffered a concussion from the impact to your head, multiple contusions along your ribs, and some deep lacerations on your arms. We've ruled out any major injuries, but you need rest. I want to keep you overnight for observation."

Lucas shook his head immediately. "No. That's not happening."

The doctor continued, unfazed. "We're treating your wounds, and we'll be watching the concussion symptoms. You might experience dizziness, headaches, and disorientation. It's important that……"

Lucas cut her off. "Give me whatever you need to, and let me go." His tone was sharp, his patience thin. "I'm not staying here."

The doctor's lips pressed into a thin line, but before she could argue, the detective interjected. "Look, I get it. You want to find Amelia. But what good is that if you collapse before you get the chance?"

Lucas exhaled sharply, his grip on the sheets tightening. He knew they were right. He hated it, but he knew.

The doctor gave him a pointed look. "I'll get you something for the pain and fluids to keep your strength up. We'll monitor you for a few more hours, and then we can discuss discharge."

Lucas ground his teeth but gave a reluctant nod. "Fine. A few hours."

The doctor nodded and stepped out of the room, leaving Lucas alone with the detective again.

The officer studied him for a moment before speaking. "You and I both know this isn't going to end with just a manhunt. If we don't get ahead of him, she might not have time for us to track him down."

Lucas's eyes darkened. "That's why I'm not sitting around waiting for the cops to find him.." His voice was low, dangerous. "Ethan took what's mine. And I will tear this entire city apart to get her back."

The detective exhaled, rubbing his jaw. "Just don't do anything stupid before we get to him first."

Lucas didn't respond. Because deep down, he knew, if the cops didn't get to Ethan in time, he wouldn't hesitate to do what had to be done.

Lucas sat impatiently on the edge of the hospital bed. His jaw tight as he checked the time. The sterile white walls, the faint scent of antiseptic, and the constant beeping of machines were all grating on his nerves. He had wasted enough time here. Amelia was out there, and every second he spent sitting in this damn room was another second Ethan had the upper hand.

A nurse came in to check his IV, but Lucas yanked the needle out before she could stop him.

"Mr. Cross, you shouldn't,"

"I'm done here," he said flatly, swinging his legs off the bed. His ribs protested the movement. Pain radiating through his side, but he ignored it. Pain meant nothing compared to the hell Amelia was living right now.

The nurse sputtered. "Your doctor hasn't signed off on your discharge,"

"I don't need permission." Lucas stood, steadying himself momentarily before reaching for the clothes folded on the chair. The detective from earlier stepped into the room just as Lucas pulled his shirt over his head.

"You're making a mistake," the officer said, arms crossed.

"No. Sitting here while Amelia suffers is a mistake," Lucas shot back. He slid on his jacket, locking eyes with the detective. "I'm leaving."

The officer sighed but didn't argue. He had seen that look before. There was no talking Lucas out of this. "At least let us update you if we get anything new."

Lucas barely acknowledged him as he strode out of the hospital, phone already in hand.

When Lucas stepped into the penthouse, the air was already buzzing with tension.

His security team stood gathered in the living room, eyes fixed on the large screen glowing with maps, footage loops, and pulsing red markers. The room smelled like coffee and urgency. No one had slept.

Mason stood front and center, arms crossed, jaw tight. The screen behind him was a battlefield of data.

"You look like hell," Mason muttered without looking up.

Lucas didn't respond. Didn't flinch. He shrugged out of his coat and strode straight into the storm.

"Tell me you have something."

Mason clicked the remote in his hand, the screen shifting to a new frame. Grainy black and white security footage, timestamped from the early hours of the morning.

"We've been combing through everything traffic cams, drone sweeps, even gas station CCTV. He's been moving smart," Mason said, voice clipped. "But not smart enough."

Lucas moved closer to the screen, his body tight with barely restrained fury. His eyes locked onto the image. A van. Faint license plate. Glimpses of a figure shoved into the back.

"Where?" Lucas growled.

Mason zoomed in, pointing to a satellite map. "Here. About an hour outside the city. Middle of nowhere."

Lucas stared at the screen, fists clenched at his sides. His breathing deepened not panic. Not fear.

Focus.

"How sure are you?"

"Eighty percent," Mason said. "It's an old compound,high fences, minimal security, but secluded. If I had to guess, he's keeping her there because he thinks no one will find them."

Lucas clenched his fists. Ethan doesn't know who the hell he's dealing with.

"We're already working on satellite imaging and any back road access points," Mason continued. "We can assemble an extraction plan but must move carefully."

Lucas shook his head. "No. We move now."

Mason exhaled. "Lucas, we need to be strategic. If we rush in and he's expecting it, Amelia could get caught in the crossfire."

Lucas's jaw tightened. He knew Mason was right, but patience wasn't an option anymore. He couldn't sit back while Ethan had his hands on her.

"Then we go in smart, but we go in fast," Lucas said, his voice low and dangerous. "Gear up. We leave in an hour."

Mason hesitated for a split second before nodding. "Understood."

Lucas turned away, gripping the edge of the counter to steady himself. His body was still recovering, his head pounding, but none of it mattered. Amelia needed him. And he would burn the whole world down to get her back.

Thirty-Eight

Chapter 38

Ethan loomed over her, his shadow spilling across the floor like a stain. The dim light overhead flickered, casting his face in jagged glimpses. Bloodied knuckles, a wild, unhinged glint in his eyes. The charming mask he once wore had cracked and fallen away.

What remained was the predator.

"You still don't get it, do you?" he muttered, crouching low until they were eye to eye. His fingers clamped around her jaw, digging into the tender space beneath her cheekbones. "You've always been mine, Amelia. From the beginning."

She could smell the sweat, the fury on his breath.

"You're *sick*," she hissed, trying to twist away. "You don't own me."

His hand moved so fast, she barely saw it coming.

Pain burst across her cheek. A hot, stunning crack that snapped her head to the side. Her skin burned. Blood bloomed on her tongue.

She didn't cry. Wouldn't give him that.

"You'll forget him," Ethan snarled, his voice trembling with hate. "Lucas is nothing. Weak. Temporary. *I'm* the one who knows you. The only one who's ever truly seen who you are."

Amelia turned back to him slowly, her face bruised.

"I will never forget him," she whispered through clenched teeth.

"And I will never love *you*."

Ethan's expression darkened. With a growl, he dragged her up by the hair, forcing her onto her knees.

"You'll see," he whispered. "You'll beg me to keep you. And when you do, you'll know. This was always how it was meant to be."

She cried out as he shoved her onto the mattress, her body jolting from the impact. He was on her in a second, pinning her wrists. She struggled but his strength over powered hers.

Her world shrank to the sound of his breath, the weight of his presence pressing down on her.

"Stop," she choked out, her voice barely more than a gasp. "Please… don't do this."

But her words didn't reach him.

If anything, they fed something darker.

Then *darkness*.

Time shattered.

She floated somewhere far from her body, eyes fixed on the ceiling as everything around her blurred into silence. Her limbs went numb. Pain flickered at the edges of her awareness, distant and dull.

But the terror? The terror stayed.

When it ended, he stood calm and detached.

He adjusted his shirt like nothing had happened. Like she was nothing.

"You'll learn to love me again," he said, voice cold and final.

He walked to the door.

A soft *click* followed.

And then… silence.

Amelia didn't move.

She couldn't. She lay frozen, her body aching, her mind numb. The air in the small, windowless room felt suffocating. Every breath she took felt shallow, each second stretching into an eternity.

She willed herself not to cry. Not to give Ethan the satisfaction. Not to let the broken pieces inside her shatter completely.

But how much more could she take?

Her wrists ached from his grip. Her skin felt tainted where he had touched her. No matter how much she tried to disconnect, the reality of what had just happened wouldn't fade.

The mattress beneath her felt like a prison. Somewhere outside the locked door, she could hear Ethan moving around, whistling a casual tune as if what he had done meant nothing.

A sickening wave of nausea rolled over her.

She needed to escape. She couldn't stay here. Not with him.

With slow, careful movements, she sat up, every muscle protesting. Her head pounded. She reached for the hem of her torn dress, clutching it around herself like a shield.

She took a deep breath, steadying herself.

Think, Amelia. Think.

Her gaze darted around the room. The door was locked, and the single overhead light flickered dimly. The only furniture was the bed she sat on, a small dresser, and a chair in the corner. There were no windows, and there was no obvious means of escape.

Her pulse hammered.

She had to find a way out before he came back.

She pushed herself to her feet and limped to the dresser. She yanked open drawers. Empty. Until her fingers brushed against something metal.

A small, rusted screwdriver.

It wasn't much, but it was something.

She slipped it into her sleeve just as footsteps approached. The lock clicked.

The door swung open.

Ethan stepped in, smug and slow.

"Miss me already?"

Amelia stood still, trying to control her breath. Every instinct screamed at her to run, to scream, but she met his gaze.

"You're still fighting it," he said, amused. "But you'll see. We were always meant to be."

Her fingers closed around the hidden weapon.

"I will never be yours," she said.

He stepped closer.

She struck.

The screwdriver sliced the air but he caught her wrist with frightening ease. Twisting it hard. The weapon clattered to the floor.

"Really?" he growled, shoving her backward.

She hit the bed, gasping.

"You never learn."

He loomed over her. She trembled, heart racing, mind

spinning.

But she wasn't broken. Not yet.

Even as he overpowered her, even as fear clawed at her throat, she clung to one truth:

Lucas was out there.

And she had to hold on long enough for him to find her.

Thirty-Nine

Chapter 39

The SUV fishtailed to a stop, tires screaming against gravel as a cloud of dust swallowed the headlights.

Lucas didn't wait.

The door flew open, and he was out before the vehicle had fully settled, boots hitting the earth with purpose. His chest heaved, every breath tight, every muscle drawn like a loaded weapon.

His heart was pounding but it wasn't fear.

It was fury. Cold, precise, and seething beneath his skin like a fuse waiting to detonate.

Every hour she spent alone with that monster was a weight Lucas couldn't breathe under. And now….now he was here.

Too late?

Maybe.

But he would burn the world down to bring her home.

He'd failed her once.

He would never let it happen again.

Not this time.

Lucas's grip on the gun was iron, his knuckles tight around the steel.

The compound sprawled out before him like something out of a nightmare. Cold, industrial, and wrong. An old warehouse abandoned by the world but repurposed into a cage.

"We're going in hard," Mason muttered beside him, chambering a round in his rifle.

Lucas nodded once. "No one leaves except Amelia."

His security team had already positioned themselves to cover all angles. They were trained professionals. Men Lucas trusted with his life. Tonight, they had one mission: get Amelia out alive.

Lucas exhaled slowly, then gave the signal.

The night erupted into chaos.

Mason dropped the first guard with a single, silenced shot to the head. Another tried to raise the alarm, but Lucas was faster. Two shots to the chest and the man crumpled like a rag doll. The remaining guards scrambled, some reaching for their weapons, others diving for cover.

Gunfire cracked through the air, sharp and unforgiving.

Lucas moved through the battlefield like a predator, cold and efficient. He ducked behind a crate as bullets whizzed past, then rose and fired. Dropping another guard who had foolishly left himself exposed.

A man lunged at him from the side, a knife flashing in the dim light. Lucas twisted, dodging the blade by inches before slamming the butt of his gun into the attacker's temple. The man staggered, and Lucas seized the moment. Grabbing him by the collar and slamming him face-first into the concrete.

Another guard charged from behind, and Lucas wasn't fast enough this time. A fist caught him in the ribs, knocking the breath from his lungs. Pain flared through his side, but he gritted his teeth and countered, driving his elbow into the man's throat. The guard choked, stumbling back, and Lucas put him down with a brutal kick to the knee, followed by a gunshot to the head.

His heart a relentless drum against his ribs. He reached the rusted warehouse doors and kicked them open.

Lucas moved through the darkened halls of the abandoned compound like a predator stalking its prey. His body ached from his injuries, but the burning need to find Amelia kept him going. Knowing she was in this godforsaken place with that monster, every second that passed felt like an eternity. His fists clenched at the thought of Ethan touching her. Hurting her.

Mason was at his back, moving just as swiftly, his gun drawn. The security team spread out, sweeping the building room by room. The compound was vast. An old industrial warehouse repurposed into Ethan's lair of terror. The air was thick with the stench of mildew, damp concrete, and something darker. Something rotten.

Lucas's pulse pounded as he turned a corner, eyes scanning the dimly lit hallway. His gut twisted with dread. The place felt like a tomb. The overhead lights flickered, some barely functioning, casting eerie shadows against the rusted metal walls.

Then he heard it.

A muffled cry. Faint, barely audible. But it was her.

Lucas's heart slammed against his ribs. He surged forward,

ignoring the pain in his body, following the sound like a bloodhound locked onto a scent. His breath came in short, controlled bursts as he reached a reinforced door at the end of the hall.

He pressed his ear against the cold metal. Amelia's voice. Weak. Trembling.

"Please... don't..."

Rage ignited inside him like a wildfire. Without hesitation, Lucas stepped back and kicked the door with all his strength. The first impact sent a jolt of pain through his bruised ribs, but he didn't care. He kicked again, harder. The metal groaned under the force. The lock straining against its hinges.

Mason joined him, slamming his shoulder into the door until, finally, with a deafening crack, it gave way.

Lucas stormed inside.

His blood ran cold.

Amelia lay crumpled on the bed, her wrists bound. Her face streaked with tears and fresh bruises. Her gown was torn at the shoulder, her skin marred with fingerprints that weren't his.

And Ethan stood above her, his expression twisted with triumph.

"You really don't know when to quit, do you?" Ethan sneered, his grip tightening around the knife in his hand. "I told you, Lucas. She belongs to me."

Lucas saw red.

Without thinking, he launched himself at Ethan. The impact sent them both crashing to the ground. The knife clattered to the floor, spinning out of reach. Lucas wasted no time. He drove his fist into Ethan's face, feeling the crunch of bone beneath his knuckles.

Ethan snarled, spitting blood, and swung wildly. His fist connected with Lucas's injured ribs. Sending a bolt of pain through him, but it only fueled his fury. He grabbed Ethan by the collar and slammed his head against the concrete floor.

"You think you can take her from me?" Lucas growled, his voice a dangerous whisper. "You think you can break her?"

Ethan laughed through bloodied teeth. "She was mine first."

Lucas's rage reached a breaking point. He punched Ethan again. Harder, more brutal until Mason's voice cut through the haze.

"Lucas! We need to get her out of here!"

Lucas turned, his breathing ragged. Amelia stared at him with wide, tear-filled eyes. Her body trembling. The sight of her, fragile and terrified, snapped him back to reality.

He pushed off Ethan, disgust curling in his gut as he watched the bastard groan in pain. He had more fight in him, but Lucas didn't care. Ethan would rot in a prison cell for the rest of his miserable life.

Lucas rushed to Amelia. His hands moving with a gentleness that contradicted the fury he had just unleashed. "I'm here little one." he whispered, his voice thick with emotion. He untied her wrists.

Amelia collapsed into his arms, sobbing into his chest. "Lucas… I thought,"

"Shh, I've got you," he murmured, stroking her hair. "You're safe now. He'll never hurt you again."

He lifted her into his arms as Mason secured Ethan, pressing a gun to his temple while the rest of the security team flooded into the room.

As Lucas carried Amelia out of that hellish place, she clung to him. Her fingers clutching at his shirt as if she were afraid he'd disappear.

But he wasn't going anywhere.

Ethan had stolen too much from her. Too much from both of them.

Lucas was ready to burn the world down before letting Amelia feel afraid again.

The flashing red and blue lights bathed the compound in an eerie glow, overwhelming the scene's chaos. Police officers secured the area and paramedics rushed between injured guards.

But Lucas only had eyes for Amelia.

She trembled in his arms, wrapped in his jacket. Her body was weak. Exhausted. Battered by everything she had endured.

"We need to get you to the hospital," Lucas murmured, gently kissing her forehead.

She shook her head violently. "No hospitals," she whispered. "I just want to go home."

Lucas's grip on her tightened. He wished he could give her that, but the bruises darkening her skin, the cuts, the swelling. She needed medical attention.

"Sweetheart," he said firmly but gently, cupping her face so she would look at him. "I know you don't want to, but you need this. Let me take care of you."

Amelia's bottom lip trembled, but when she saw the unwavering determination in his eyes, she finally nodded. "Okay," she whispered.

Lucas wasted no time. He carried her to the waiting ambulance, ignoring the paramedics' questioning glances as he climbed in beside her.

She was never leaving his sight again.

The fluorescent lights overhead cast a harsh, sterile glow, washing the hospital room in a pale, impersonal haze. Everything smelled of antiseptic. A low hum of machines filled the space, broken only by the distant murmur of voices in the hallway and the rhythmic *beep... beep... beep* of the monitor beside her bed.

Lucas sat in the chair beside her, his hand wrapped around hers with quiet desperation. He hadn't let go since they'd wheeled her in. His thumb brushed slowly across the bruises on her skin.

Amelia lay back against the stiff pillows, every inch of her aching. Her body felt like it didn't belong to her anymore. Each breath sent a ripple of pain through her ribs. The thin hospital gown scratched at her skin, and though she was surrounded by doctors and security, she'd never felt more exposed.

Her gaze drifted to the window. Gray skies, no sun.

A part of her still expected Ethan to appear in the doorway.

Lucas's hand tightened slightly, grounding her.

"You're safe," he said softly, his voice low and rough from exhaustion. "He can't get to you anymore."

She wanted to believe him.

She *needed* to believe him.

But the fear was still there, clinging to the edges of her like a shadow that wouldn't lift.

A nurse approached quietly, her presence soft and practiced. She adjusted the IV bag hanging beside Amelia's bed, checking the line already taped to her arm. "We're giving you fluids and something for the pain," she said gently. "You'll start to feel more comfortable soon. Is there anything else you need?

Water? A warm blanket?"

Amelia hesitated, her voice barely above a whisper. "A blanket would be nice."

The nurse offered a kind smile and slipped out, leaving the room quiet again.

Amelia let out a slow, trembling breath. Her throat felt like sandpaper, raw from days of crying, screaming, pleading. There was an ache deep inside her chest that no medicine could touch.

Lucas reached for the cup on the bedside table, filling it with water from the pitcher. He steadied her with one hand and lifted the cup with the other, holding it to her lips.

"Slow sips, sweetheart," he murmured, voice low and careful. "I don't want you choking."

She managed a small sip before sinking back against the pillows. Her eyes flickered toward the bruises decorating her wrists, the stark contrast against her pale skin making her stomach turn.

Lucas followed her gaze, his expression hardening. "I should've gotten to you sooner," he said, his voice tight with barely restrained anger. "I should've been there."

Amelia reached for his hand, squeezing it weakly. "Lucas… don't," she whispered. "This isn't your fault. You came for me. That's all that matters."

He leaned forward, resting his forehead against hers.

"I'm never letting him near you again," he swore, his voice thick with emotion. "You're safe now."

She wanted to believe that, but the terror Ethan had instilled in her ran deep. Even now, in a secured hospital, she felt like he was watching, waiting.

A soft knock broke the quiet, and the door opened gently.

A doctor stepped in. He was older, with silver hair and a calm presence. He wore his ID badge clipped to his coat.

Amelia's body tensed immediately, her eyes flicking toward him. Even though his demeanor was kind, the presence of another man made her flinch.

Lucas felt it. His grip on her hand didn't falter.

"Good evening, Miss Monroe," the doctor said softly, keeping his tone measured and respectful. "I'm Dr. Reynolds. I'm part of the trauma team here. First I want to say that you're safe now. And I'm so sorry this happened to you."

Amelia gave a small, uncertain nod.

Dr. Reynolds remained by the door, not approaching her bedside. "I've reviewed your scans and exam notes. You've sustained multiple contusions. Bruising around the ribs, wrists, and legs and several superficial lacerations. Fortunately, there are no fractures or internal injuries. That's a good sign."

He paused, letting her absorb that, then continued gently. "We'd like to keep you for the next several hours to monitor for signs of shock or delayed symptoms. I also want to offer a sexual assault nurse examine. She's specially trained to support survivors and perform the necessary medical and forensic exam, if you choose to move forward with that."

Amelia's fingers tightened slightly around Lucas's.

"It's completely your decision," Dr. Reynolds added, his voice low and steady. "You are in control of what happens next. If and when you're ready, we'll explain every step before anything is done. You're not alone in this."

A lump formed in Amelia's throat. The thought of being touched, even by someone trying to help, made her stomach twist.

"And just as important," he continued, "we can connect you with a trauma counselor while you're here, or later. We'll make sure you have access to support when you need it on your terms."

Lucas reached up, brushing a knuckle along the back of her hand.

She nodded again, just once. It was all she could manage.

But it was enough.

The sterile scent of antiseptic hung heavy in the air, clinging to everything. Amelia sat at the edge of the examination table, the paper beneath her crackling with every slight movement. A hospital gown draped over her, but it did little to protect her from the chill or from the overwhelming sense that she no longer quite existed inside her own skin.

Her arms were wrapped tightly around her torso, as if holding herself together was the only thing she had control over.

Dr. Reynolds stood a respectful distance away, his tone calm and professional. "Amelia," he said gently, "you've consented to the forensic exam so we can ensure there are no internal injuries and collect evidence, should you choose to report. I want to reassure you that you're in charge of every step of this process. Nothing will happen without your permission."

She nodded, the motion small and stiff.

"The nurse will explain each part before we begin," he continued. "If you feel overwhelmed or want to stop at any time, just say so. You're not expected to endure anything else not here."

Amelia's gaze dropped to the floor. The words were meant to comfort her, but they felt far away, like echoes in a room she wasn't fully in. Detached. Clinical.

The nurse entered quietly, wearing soft blue scrubs and a badge that read *SANE – Sexual Assault Nurse Examiner*. Her expression was warm but professional, her hands moving with practiced calm as she gathered supplies.

Amelia didn't look up. She stared at the white tile floor, her fingers wrapped tightly around the edge of the gown.

Lucas sat beside the exam table, holding her hand. He hadn't said a word since she nodded to begin, but his grip was steady anchoring her to something that still felt real.

"Amelia," the nurse said gently, kneeling to her level. "My name is Maren. I'm here to walk you through everything. Nothing happens without your consent, okay?"

Amelia nodded faintly.

"We're going to begin with photographs of visible injuries only what you allow. Then we'll examine for internal trauma and collect swabs. You're in control. If you want to stop at any point, you just tell me."

Maren helped Amelia lie back on the table, guiding her through each step with clinical precision and quiet care. But the cold stirrups. The fluorescent lights. The crinkle of gloves… they all turned the room into something unbearable.

Amelia's breathing hitched as the nurse began. Her fingers clamped around Lucas's, nails digging into his skin.

His other hand reached up, brushing hair back from her face.

"I'm right here," he whispered. "Just keep looking at me."

She did.

Tears slid silently down her temples and into her hair. Not from the physical pain. Though there was that too. But from the violation of it all. The humiliation. The brutal necessity of being laid bare like this. Again.

Each swab, each camera flash, each sterile instruction felt like being dissected.

Lucas's hand never left hers.

When it was finally over, the nurse covered her gently with a warm blanket and stepped away to give them privacy.

Amelia turned on her side, curling into herself. Her body shaking uncontrollably. She didn't speak.

Lucas leaned over, wrapping his arms around her as much as the table would allow. "You were so brave," he murmured against her hair. "I'm so fucking sorry you had to do this."

She didn't answer. Just wept.

But she held onto him like he was the only thing keeping her from falling apart completely.

Because right now, he was.

Forty

Chapter 40

The ride back to Lucas's penthouse was cloaked in heavy silence. Amelia curled against Lucas in the backseat of the SUV, her body weary. Her mind still stuck in the nightmare she had barely escaped.

Lucas's arm was wrapped around her protectively, his fingers stroking slow, reassuring circles along her arm. His touch anchoring her to reality. Yet every time she blinked, she saw Ethan's face and heard his voice whispering that she would never be free.

She shuddered.

Lucas felt it instantly. He tilted his head down, pressing a gentle kiss to her temple. "You're safe," he murmured, his voice like gravel and silk all at once. "He can't touch you anymore."

Amelia wanted to believe that. She really did. But Ethan's presence still clung to her like a shadow, lurking just out of sight.

Sitting in the front passenger seat, Mason glanced back at them through the rearview mirror. His sharp, calculating gaze scanning Amelia for any signs of distress. He had been quiet since they'd left the hospital, but his presence was just as unwavering as Lucas's. He wouldn't let anything happen to her.

No one would.

The city lights blurred past as they neared the penthouse. A part of Amelia felt relief knowing she was returning to Lucas's home, which had become a sanctuary in the chaos. But another part of her hesitated. How could she ever feel truly safe again?

When they finally arrived, Lucas didn't wait for the car to stop before opening the door and stepping out fully. He reached back inside, his arms sliding around Amelia effortlessly as he embraced her.

"Lucas," she protested weakly. "I can walk,"

"I know," he interrupted, his voice firm but gentle. "But I need to do this. Let me take care of you."

Her heart clenched, and she nodded, resting her head against his chest.

Mason stepped ahead, entering the penthouse first to check the space. He scanned the room, his hand hovering near his weapon before giving Lucas a sharp nod. "All clear."

Lucas carried her inside, straight to the bedroom, without hesitation.

The second they crossed the threshold, Amelia felt her breath quicken. The familiarity of the space should have comforted her. But instead, her mind played tricks on her, making her feel like Ethan could be watching, waiting, just outside the glass.

Lucas noticed her hesitation instantly. He set her down gently on the edge of the bed and crouched before her, his hands framing her face.

"What is it?" he asked, his eyes searching hers.

Amelia swallowed hard. "I don't know how to stop feeling like he's still out there. Like he'll always be out there."

Lucas's jaw tightened, his hands sliding down to her wrists, his grip grounding. "He won't touch you again. I'll make damn sure of that."

Tears burned at the edges of her vision, but she held them back. "I hate this," she admitted in a shaky whisper. "I hate feeling weak. I hate that he still has this hold on me."

Lucas exhaled slowly, his thumb tracing soothing patterns along the inside of her wrist. "You're not weak, Amelia. You survived him. And you're still here. That makes you stronger than he ever was."

She let out a shaky breath, nodding, but her body still trembled with exhaustion and emotion.

Lucas studied her for a long moment before his expression softened. "Come on, little one. Let's get you cleaned up."

He stood and disappeared into the bathroom. Moments later, she heard water running and the scent of lavender filling the air. When he returned, he reached for the hem of her torn dress, his movements slow and deliberate. He gave her time to pull away if she wanted to.

But she didn't.

She trusted him.

She shivered when the ruined fabric slid from her skin, but not from cold. Lucas's gaze darkened as he took in the bruises marking her body. His fingers grazing the edge of a particularly nasty one on her ribs. His breathing turned ragged, his fists clenching at his sides.

"Lucas…" she whispered, reaching for him.

His hand covered hers instantly, his grip warm, steady. "I hate seeing you hurt."

She swallowed past the lump in her throat. "I know."

Lucas bent down, pressing a lingering kiss against her forehead. Then, without another word, he guided her into the warm bath, sliding in behind her.

The hot water washed over her. Easing the ache in her muscles. Lucas's strong arms wrapped around her from behind, his chest solid against her back. He rested his chin on her shoulder, his breath warm against her skin.

For the first time in days, she felt safe.

They sat there in silence, his fingers lazily trailing up and down her arm. He didn't rush her. Didn't push. He just held her, his presence an unspoken promise.

She tilted her head slightly, her lips grazing his jaw. "Thank you," she whispered.

Lucas turned his head, his lips barely brushing against hers. "For what?"

"For not letting me fall apart."

A slight smirk played on his lips. "Even if you did, I'd be here to catch you."

Her chest tightened with emotion. "I love you."

Lucas's expression softened. He cupped her cheek, tilting her face toward him fully. "Say it again."

"I love you," she repeated, her voice stronger this time.

His thumb brushed against her lower lip, his gaze burning with something more profound than desire,something un-breakable. "I love you too, Amelia. More than I ever thought possible."

A tear slipped down her cheek, but for once, it wasn't from fear or pain.

Lucas kissed her deeply, slow and unhurried as if he was pouring every ounce of his devotion into her. She melted into him, letting his touch drown out the last remnants of Ethan's presence in her mind.

By the time they reached bed, Amelia curled into Lucas's embrace, her head on his chest, listening to the steady rhythm of his heartbeat. His fingers traced soft patterns along her spine, his lips brushing against the top of her head.

"Sleep little one," he murmured. "I've got you."

As her eyelids grew heavy, she knew. Ethan may have stolen pieces of her, of her past. But he would never take her future.

That belonged to her.

And Lucas.

It had been a few weeks since Ethan's reign of terror finally ended. The bruises on Amelia's skin were beginning to fade, but the ones inside her heart lingered like shadows she couldn't quite shake. She was healing, though slowly.

Lucas had barely left her side since bringing her home. He was her rock, holding her through the sleepless nights, grounding her when the nightmares returned, and reminding her in a thousand little ways that she was safe and loved.

Now, as she curled up on the plush couch in the penthouse, a soft blanket draped over her, she stared at the television. The news broadcast filled the room with its usual hum, but tonight, the story on the screen made her pulse spike.

"Breaking news.....Ethan Walker, wanted for multiple charges including kidnapping and assault, was taken into police custody today after an extensive investigation. Authorities report that evidence provided by private security teams was instrumental in leading to his capture. He is currently being held without bail as he awaits trial."

Amelia sucked in a sharp breath. Ethan's face flashed across the screen. A cold emotionless mugshot. Even through the TV, his empty stare sent a ripple of unease down her spine. But then, something shifted inside her. For weeks, she had lived in fear of him, waiting for the next time he would strike, the next moment he would rip away her sense of peace.

But now?

He was in custody.

He was behind bars.

He couldn't touch her anymore.

The weight pressing down on her chest for so long began to lift.

She felt Lucas before she saw him, the warmth of his presence filling the space beside her. His hand found hers, his grip firm and steady, anchoring her in the present.

"It's over," he murmured, his voice low, reassuring. "He'll never hurt you again."

Amelia let out a shaky exhale, turning to face him. "I know," she whispered. And for the first time in what felt like forever, she truly felt it.

Lucas studied her, his eyes searching hers as if making sure she believed the words as much as he did. He reached out, gently tucking a strand of hair behind her ear. His touch was so tender and protective that it made her throat tighten with emotion.

"You don't have to be afraid anymore," he said softly. "You're safe now."

Safe.

The word settled deep in her soul, pushing back the lingering darkness.

She leaned into him, resting her forehead against his shoulder. "I don't know what I would have done without you," she admitted, her voice barely above a whisper.

Lucas exhaled a quiet chuckle, his fingers tracing gentle circles on her back. "You'll never have to find out," he murmured. "Because I'm not going anywhere."

Amelia closed her eyes, letting his warmth wrap around her. He had been her protector, her lifeline, the one person who had stood by her side through it all.

As if sensing the shift in her, Lucas pulled back just enough to tilt her chin up. His gaze locked onto hers, intense and filled with something that made her heart race.

"I love you, Amelia." The words were spoken with certainty, with conviction, as if he had always known it.

Tears welled in her eyes. Not out of sadness, but out of the overwhelming realization that, despite everything, she had found something real. Something safe. Something that could finally be hers.

"I love you too," she whispered, her voice trembling but sure.

A slow smile tugged at Lucas's lips before he kissed her.

When they finally pulled apart, Amelia let out a breathy laugh, wiping at her damp cheeks. "I think I'm finally ready to move forward," she admitted.

Lucas smiled, brushing his thumb across her cheek. "Then let's do it together."

Amelia nestled into Lucas's embrace as the city lights twinkled beyond the floor-to-ceiling windows. She wasn't just surviving anymore.

She was living.

And for the first time in a long time, she allowed herself to believe in a future free from fear.

A future with Lucas by her side.

A future that was entirely, beautifully, hers.

About the Author

About the Author

Chantel Nunn writes stories for the women who've been through hell and still crave love that consumes them. Her words live in the shadows , exploring trauma, trust, obsession, and the kind of dark romance that doesn't ask you to be perfect… just *honest.*

A bookish witch at heart, Chantel blends emotional healing, sensual surrender, and power reclamation into every page she writes. Her heroines are soft but not fragile. Her men? Dangerous, devoted, and just unhinged enough to ruin your standards.

When she's not writing fictional chaos, you'll find her lighting candles, pulling tarot cards, baking in her kitchen like a cozy domestic goddess, or creating bookish magic for her small business. She believes love should feel like safety and fire , and her stories make space for both.

Whispers of Passion is her debut novel , a dark, intimate, healing journey into the arms of a man who doesn't flinch when the past shows up… he *fights it off.*

She writes for the survivors, the soft-hearted, and the ones who still believe in love after the storm.